05223

ANITA

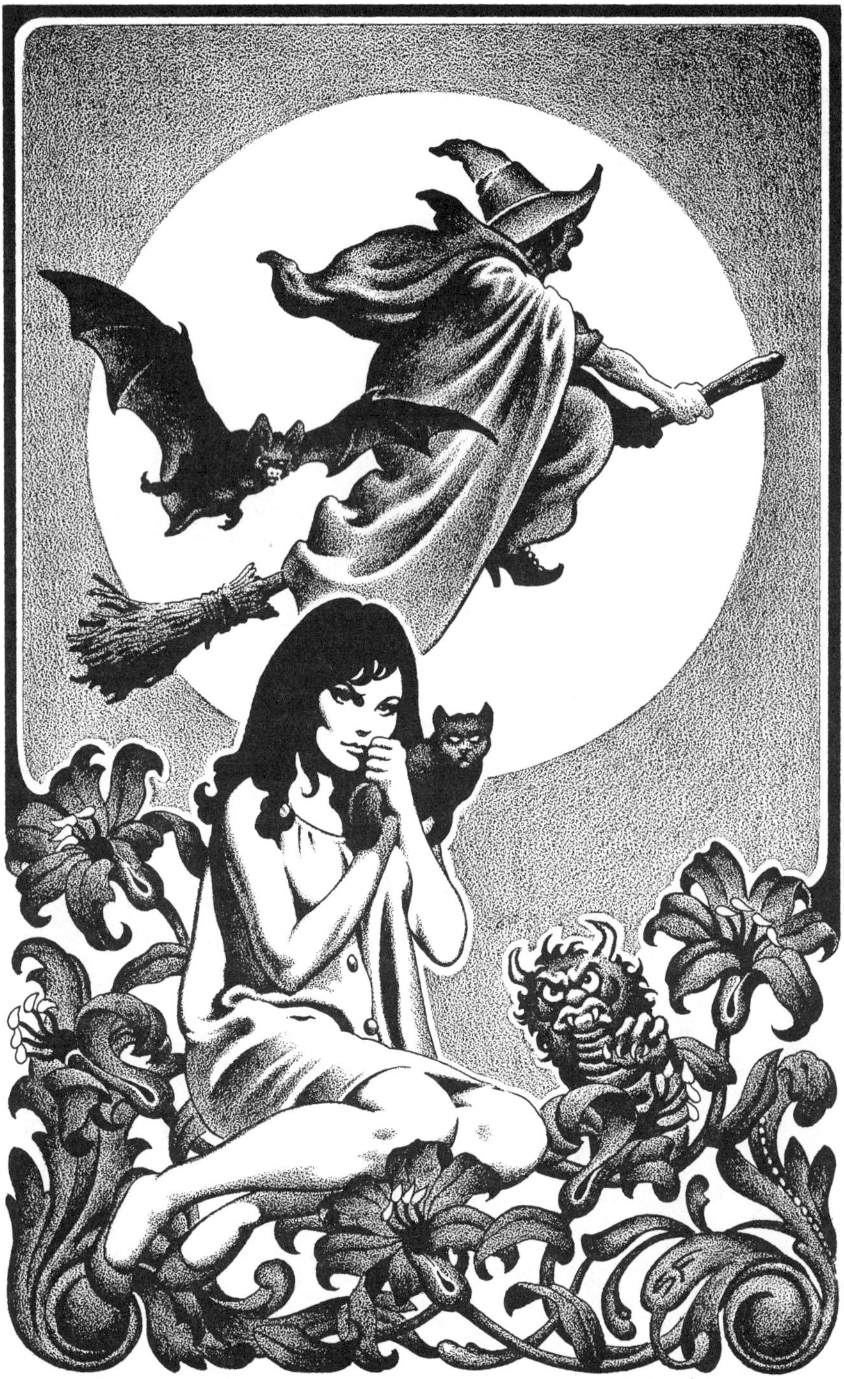

ANITA

by Keith Roberts

illustrated by Stephen E. Fabian

Owlswick Press   Philadelphia

Copyright © 1970, 1986, and 1990
by Keith Roberts
Artwork Copyright © 1990
by Stephen E. Fabian

All rights reserved under International
and Pan-American Copyright Conventions.

Manufactured in the United States of America.
Published by Owlswick Press,
Post Office Box 8243, Philadelphia PA 19101-8243

International Standard Book Number 0-913896-27-6

CONTENTS:

Anita: an Introduction	1
1: The Witch	5
2: Anita	11
3: Outpatient	21
4: The Simple for Love	31
5: The Charm	45
6: The Familiar	59
7: The Jennifer	65
8: The Middle Earth	75
9: The War at Foxhanger	85
10: Idiot's Lantern	95
11: Timothy	107
12: Cousin Ella Mae	119
13: Sandpiper	135
14: Junior Partner	147
15: The Mayday	161
16: The Checkout	179

ANITA: AN INTRODUCTION

THE ANITA STORIES, like a whole lot else, owe their original inspiration to Dorset; to a young girl and her father, running a village pub. It seemed despite the age gap they revolved around each other, twin parts of a whole; they knew each other's foibles, second-guessed every good line. Over all was a certain rural charm; when Mam'selle went to Town it wasn't London, it was Bournemouth. I tried a couple of pieces based on such a duo, but they wouldn't run; too near the knuckle maybe, too close to home. I was on the point of discarding the idea when Granny Thompson, like many another character, came stumping unbidden from the dark. And I knew I had a series.

I've since been told the stories have become classics. Exactly how one achieves that status I've never been too sure; maybe just by sitting around long enough, like the Parthenon. Certainly the pieces, with the odd exception, were written in the middle to late sixties. Working over them for the Owlswick edition raised some powerful memories. Trips to Dorset with long-vanished friends; Kyril Bonfiglioli, my first editor, and his bizarre, rambling home in Oxford; the tall, gaunt warehouse a stone's throw from the Tower of London from which emerged the shortlived *SF Impulse*. I did my own editing stint there, my sole equipment a typer, a pair of kitchen scissors and a rickety lino-topped table. The experience was salutary to say the least.

One hears a lot these days about the sixties. To me they weren't a Golden Age at all; such times lie always in the future, or some dim, heroic past. Essentially, the period was one of change; much that was worthwhile was being swept away, the future was already casting shadows. One famous remark, "You've never had it so good," attached itself indelibly to the British Premier, Macmillan; though in fact he never coined it, merely reflected back a heckler's shout. What struck home far harder was his speech about the Wind of Change. It's blown a few storms since, and not just through Africa. Rereading the Anita stories, I find similar notions underpinning many of them. The smile freezes to a rictus, the laugh turns too easily to a scream. Essentially they are products of their period; a kind of half-intentioned *Zeitgeist*.

Granny having established herself so firmly, the locale was changed to my own once-native heath. Northamptonshire, patient, unspectacular, ravaged by iron ore workings, is maybe the real performer. Certainly I was conscious of recording habits of speech and thought that even then were fast dying out, smothered by the levelling influence of, among other things, the "Idiot's Lantern." Longeared notions, perhaps, for a comedy witchcraft series; but witchcraft is a longeared sort of subject. In the days of the dread Matt Hopkins, the East Midlands of England added their own dark chapter to its annals; Salem wasn't so far away, in time if not in space.

Two main themes infuse the stories. Anita and her Granny, as I've hinted, are really one and the same; two sides of a coin, inseparable. More interesting perhaps is a notion I'd had for years, of a moral code not crudely based on the mores of sex. But a code nonetheless. The joke surfaces at several points. Anita, who has shocked her first friend Ruth by her bluntness in such matters, is appalled in turn to find she doesn't grow her own food. Nor, presumably, can she polish brass. Anita, like her Granny, would use lemon juice and salt. Thus, very easily, are "folksy" reputations established; they're the devil's own job to get rid of later on. Though in the present instance I'm not too worried; I can think of worse books than *Anita* to be remembered by.

Some ten years after their last magazine appearance, the stories finally achieved English hardback. In the main the collection was well received; but the ultimate rave notice came from *19 Magazine,* a British glossy aimed at the late teenager. "Buy it, read it, treasure it," said the girl reviewer firmly. I felt Anita was finally vindicated. A decade before, the outlet hadn't existed; because the intelligent, liberated young woman at which it aimed, living her own life, ordering her own affairs, didn't exist in sufficient numbers as a market target. Now she owns a flat, a car; and while her freewheeling views on life may still shock a little in certain quarters she'll also, if she chooses, sail with Greenpeace, report on seal culls to abort the trade in furs. I'd like to think Anita would do no less.

A year or two later I found myself back in Kettering, my old home town. The centre of the place was gutted, the Odeon, my father's theatre, long since gone. Towering, dark red brick was replaced by concrete; some of the single storey shops had false fronts over them, like the Old West towns Dad showed on his great silver screen. A couple of miles away, the valley where my "Fyne-brook" ran was choked by a pallid new estate; it climbed to the horizon, obliterated the farther slope. Anita's "little houses" had won. What's the saying about never going back?

I was saved from total despair by a fan letter. Like all such things, it came out of the blue; the excellent soul who wrote it professed herself fifty years old, but "still young at heart." She suggested, with some deference, a supermart location; so I sat down and wrote *The Checkout*. I was maybe feeling a little ashamed. I'd realized I hadn't given Anita and her Granny proper credit; there's far more steel in their makeup than I guessed. Towns and lives may well be pulled apart; but the "old team" are still there somewhere, defying "mere 'oomans," scoring their points off each other, casting their high-tech spells. Now, courtesy of Owlswick Press, they'll cast them for a new generation. I hope you enjoy the results.

Keith Roberts
Amesbury, Wiltshire, 1988

KEITH ROBERTS

1: THE WITCH

ANITA PROTESTED FEEBLY. "But I'm sure I'm not ready yet, Gran. I just don't *feel* ready. Can't it wait till next summer?"

The old lady snorted. She was already stirring the big spell-pot, sniffing from time to time at the far from aromatic steam that arose. She said, "Never 'eard nothink *like* it." She added a pinch of black powder to the brew and shook in a few frogs legs from a polythene bag. The fumes intensified. She said, " 'Ere y'are then, sit yer down. I ent got orl night. Bring that there chair uvver." The contents of the pot had begun to solidify; she withdrew a horrible-looking blob on the end of a stick. She said, "Undo the top o' yer dress then. Look smart."

Anita wailed, "Oh, no!" She clapped a hand to her throat. Granny Thompson's eyes gimleted at her. She said, "Git it *orf.* Clean on yisdey, that were. Think I got nothink ter do but wosh for y' all day? Wan' it all done for yer, you young 'uns do. Oh Satan spare us, the gel's all thumbs. Come 'ere, let me." She undid the little fastening at the neck and opened the dress across Anita's shoulders. She said testily, "Well 'old it then, else it'll all a-flop back." She picked up the stick again and advanced. Anita said faintly, "Can't I have gas?"

Granny Thompson said, "Oh, 'old still. The fuss you young 'uns *mek* uvver a little thing." She dabbed the stick on her granddaughter's forehead and throat. Anita yelped. The brew was still decidedly hot. Grandma said, "Fillet of a fenny snake, in the cauldron boil an' bake; eye of noot, an' toe o' frog, wool of bat an' tongue o' dog; adder's fork, an' blindwumm's sting . . . I kent remember ner more. Kent see the book neither, om a-lorst me glasses agin. Anyways 'E wunt bother. Long as yer Made Up, that's the thing. Disgustin', I calls it. Gel o' yore age, an' not even *confirmed.*" She hobbled back to the cauldron elaborating her criticism of the Great Enemy.

"Time was when the Old Man 'ud come regular, jist fer a chat like. But not ner more. Oh, no." She prodded the fire beneath the pot and added a couple of handfuls of powder. The first made the flames leap up magenta, the second sent them bright blue. Anita sat with her eyes closed, rigid in a web of polychrome shadow. " 'Oo does 'E send now then?" asked Granny vindictively. "All these jumped up kids, that's all. Area managers they 'as the cheek ter call thereselves. Never 'eard nothink like it. Enough ter send yer 'Oly. Course I know what 'E's at. Tearin' about doin' all these tomb robbings an' such." She wagged a great black ladle in the general direction of her granddaughter. "Now I dunt mind a bit of old-fashioned sacrilege now an' agin. 'Oo dunt? But it's all fer show reely. Flashy. Like these noo-fangled business notions. It's good solid work that counts, the year round. But that jist dunt git done. Just a few old 'uns like me keepin' things a-gooin'. An' precious little thanks *we* git fer it neither. I dunt serpose you'll be a sight better. Yore tired now, an' you ent even *started.*" She topped up the cauldron with fluid from a big stone jar and its contents promptly went green and started to bubble again. She lifted the ladle and stumped back to her granddaughter. Anita tensed herself, expecting a scalding, but for some reason the liquid felt ice-cold. Granny said rapidly, "Liver o' blasphemin' Joo, gall o' goat an' slips of yoo sliver'd in the moon's eclipse, nose o' Turk an' Tartar's lips —"

Anita said, "Oo, it's running!"

"Will yer keep still? Finger o' birth-strangled babe, ditch-deliver'd by a drab —"

"But I've got all clean things on!"

"They wunt *'urt,* I tell yer."

"But Gran, it's all going *down!*"

Granny said, "Oh . . . 'ere." She put a towel into her victim's hands. "No, dunt wipe it all *orf,* it ent *took* yit! Weer were I? Finger o' ditch-strangled babe, om done that. Summat or other orf a tiger, any'ow. I reckon that's all on 'em. No, dunt git up. I ent finished." She took a cocoa tin from the shelf, removed the lid and dipped her finger inside. The contents were certainly not cocoa. She began to draw cabalistic signs on her granddaughter. Anita screwed up her eyes and nose as if she were being tortured. The old lady said grimly, "Whin I were done, I were done like this *all uvver.* 'Ave summat ter goo on about yer would, if yer were done proper." She stood back to view her handiwork. She said, " 'Spect that'll 'ave to answer." Anita opened large, reproachful eyes. Granny Thompson said, "That stops till yer gits undone ternight. Yer kin wash it orf then; it's fresh sheets."

Anita buttoned her dress gingerly. She said sullenly, "It feels all sticky and beastly. I'm not keeping it on a minute longer than I —"

Her grandmother turned in the act of lifting down the cauldron, and

1: THE WITCH

glittered at her again. She said, "*Wot* were that I thort I 'eard?"

Anita gulped and said, "Nothing, Gran."

"Orlright then. See to it it wadn't. Well then gel, *goo on!*"

Anita said, "G-go where, Gran?"

The old lady propelled her toward the door of the cottage. She said, "*Out*, o' course. Goo on out an' *do* summat. Yer Made Up now. Yer can do anythink. Change summat. Turn summat inter summat else wuss. Try some shapeshiftin'. Yer know y'ent much good at that. Satan, I can turn meself inter more than wot you can an' I'm got me sciatica. Yer a witch now, yer can do *anythink*. Goo on out an' try. Dunt come back 'ere until y'ave. Time you started earnin' yer livin', my gel. I 'ad to afore I were yore age." She opened the old wooden door and shoved Anita outside. She pointed up at the turquoise sky. "Look, it's just a-right. Night's a-comin'. Couldn't be better. An' mind; I want ter feel some magic gooin' on afore mornin', or you'll get it, my gel. Dunt think yer too big . . . an' mind where yer walk. You get them there shoes in a state again, you'll clean 'em. Tired o' runnin' about arter yer." The cottage door closed with an emphatic bang.

Anita stood and pouted for a moment, then she took off the offending shoes and flung them at the door, taking care they fell short. She walked off barefoot through the little copse that surrounded her home, scrinching her toes in the leaf-mould under the trees. She emerged in the meadow beyond, where the cool grass stroked her ankles.

She hardly knew where to begin. She had never visited the outside world; she had never worked a really malicious spell, and apart from her granny she had not seen another human being for years. She did not greatly feel like growing up but somehow before morning she had to be bad, and justify her witchhood into the bargain. She felt very small and afraid. When she had gone a few more yards she sensed an owl in the distance and called him up but he was too busy to bother. He sent back a cryptic message, *Big mouse,* and went off the air. Anita crouched by the brook and washed herself disobediently clean. Then she stood up, took a deep breath and stopped the current. The little stream was deep here and moved fast between tall reed beds. The water foamed most satisfactorily, gleaming in the August dusk. Anita soon tired though. The trick made her giddy and in any case it was nothing new. She had been able to do it when she was six. She persuaded a grass snake to slither a little way with her but he soon turned back, unwilling to get too far from his beloved water. Anita did not really mind. He was not very nice to be with, his thoughts were too long and wriggly. A little farther on she opened a gate for herself from about twenty-five yards, but the effort made her feel quite ill. She had to sit down to recover. She was sure she would never become a really good witch.

The sky was deep blue now, with the first stars showing. The evening was warm and very still. Anita lay back and opened her mind to everything. The countryside was alive with rustlings and squeakings, pouncings and little sharp hunting-thoughts as the night creatures went about their affairs. Anita heard these things with her ears as well as her sixth, seventh, and eighth senses. Her ears swivelled slightly from time to time. They were wide and pointed, and until recently had had delicate hairtufts on their tips; but these days you can do wonderful things with skin creams.

Above her, very high in the night, she heard the clatter of a dragonfly, the scrape and clang as something bundled into the jointed cage of his legs. She warned the dragonfly he was out too late but the insect, who was not very coherent, sent back something vague about killing and sped on. Nearer at hand a weasel scuttered along the hedge bottom, quick and dangerous as a brown flame. He paused to glare at Anita and she shuddered at what he was thinking. She levitated a stone and tried to drop it on him but as usual she was not quick enough. The malevolence faded into the distance, leaving behind one last horrible thought. *If only I were bigger* . . . Anita shivered, then pricked her ears again.

It took a few moments for her to recognize the callsign, for it was very distant. When she did she answered joyfully. It was a bat, the noctule who lived in the church over the hill. She waited until he came zigging across the moon to her, then got up and walked on with the little animal circling above her head. She talked to him as she went. He always intrigued her. His mischievous little mind was full of strange thoughts about glow-worms and bells, and spires so old God had forgotten them. They crossed several fields together, then Anita saw lights in the distance. They were white, yellow and red and they moved very rapidly. She wondered what they could be. She had never been as far from home as this in her life. She moved on toward them, tensed up and ready to bolt but very curious as well. It was only when she got quite close she realized she had come to the road.

The bat became suddenly alarmed and turned away. Anita called him but he would not answer. When his sonar had vanished in the distance she felt very lonely again and almost turned back herself, but the curiosity was still there. She crept to the gate by the road and stood looking over it for a long time, dodging back into the shadow of the hedge as each car glared at her with the bright eyes of its headlights. Then she became bold. After all, she was not an ordinary country girl; she was a witch. She tossed her head, climbed the gate and stepped down onto the road. It was like a soft black river. The macadam still held the heat of the day and felt warm and comfortable to her feet. She began to walk along it, turning to stare at each car as it swooped toward her.

She got back to the cottage in the still, chill-dark time just before dawn. The dew was lying heavily on the grass and Anita swished slowly along feeling that she was made of electricity from head to toes. She picked up her shoes from the step and carried them inside with her. Granny Thompson was still up, dozing by the fireplace. When Anita closed the door she woke with a jerk. She said sharply, "Where yer bin, gel? Where yer *bin?*"

Anita smiled dreamily and sat down with some care. She was thinking about that big Aston-Martin. The warmth and coziness of it and the smell of leather and tobacco and petrol and summer dust. She was still trying to decide whether she had really liked its young driver or not. She said, "I've been out, Gran. I've been doing some magic."

The old lady rose in wrath. She said, "Thet you 'ev *not,* my gel. Thet you 'ev not done at all. Not one bit did I feel, noweer about. Look at yer. Orter be ashamed, y'ad straight. Ter see all the trouble I took mekkin' you up. Yer washed all the magic *orf,* ter start with. Arter what I tole yer, an' all. That's the 'ole trouble wi' you young 'uns. Allus was. You ent got no gratitude an' you ent got no thort . . . 'ere am I, doin' me best for yer, an' all yer kin do is traipse about 'arf the night while I sits 'ere wonderin' if yer've fell into summat an' bin drownded, or what's 'appened to yer . . ."

Anita drew herself up. She said, "It's all right, Gran. I told you, I did some magic."

"Weer?" asked the old woman fiercely. "An' wot? I dunt know as I b'leeves yer. Ter rights I should 'ave felt it goo orf. Did yer change summat?"

Anita looked far away, and smiled again. She said, "Yes, Gran, I did change something. I turned a perfectly lovely motorcar straight into a side road. . . ."

KEITH ROBERTS

2: ANITA

ANITA COULD ALWAYS TELL when there were humans by the lake because everything went quiet. The breeze still shifted the leaves, the rushes whispered as their tall heads bobbed at the water, but the little tingling voices that spoke to her were silent. She watched the young folk who came to the spot for many weeks but they never saw her. The boy was rather fine. He was a Romany from the camp on the other side of Foxhanger Wood and wore beautiful shirts of lilac and russet. Anita did not know the girl. She was fair and tall and she moved as gracefully as grass bowed by the wind.

One evening the girl was there on her own. Anita, peeping through the leaves, saw her sitting by the edge of the lake dabbling at the water with a stick. Anita sensed sad-feelings and crept toward her. She came so silently that the girl heard nothing. When she turned round Anita was squatting beside her. The girl jumped and put her hand to her throat. She said, "Gosh, you did frighten me. Where on earth did you come from?"

Anita said, "Sorry." She spoke a little awkwardly because she saw so few human beings. She pointed at some distant woods. She said, "I came from over there. You're always here, aren't you? I've seen you."

The girl blushed a little. Anita, studying her candidly, wondered why. The girl said, "How do you know I come here?"

Anita shrugged. "You stop things. That's how I can tell."

"What things?"

"Just things."

The girl started to get up. She said, "I'm sorry. I didn't know I disturbed you. I only came here because it was quiet."

Anita put her hand on her arm. She said, "You needn't go; I don't mind you being here. You are sad, aren't you?"

The girl smiled. She said, "I suppose I am. Where do you live?"

Anita pointed again. "Over there."

"Where's there? What's the name of the place?"

Anita frowned. "I don't know. It's just where I live."

"Is it Foxhanger?"

"No!"

The girl said curiously, "You don't know much, do you?"

Anita pouted. She said, "Of course I do. I know about lots of things."

"What?"

Anita considered. "Well, I can make clothes and plant things so they grow. And I know there's a church over there that no one goes to any more and I can show you where the bee-orchids grow and . . . and I know about red motors with boys in them." She finished with a rush.

The girl laughed. The sound tinkled on the water. She said, "You're funny." Anita narrowed her eyes. She was not used to being laughed at. Momentarily she considered doing several nasty things that would make the girl sorry. Then she found the laughter was infectious and began to smile herself. And so a friendship was born. The girl's name was Ruth Draper.

The next time Anita found her alone she asked about the Romany. Ruth said simply, "We're in love." Anita was puzzled. She asked a very basic question and Ruth coloured furiously then got up and walked away. Anita had to run after her to explain. She said, "I'm sorry. I didn't want to upset you. That's what I do when I like boys. I thought that was what you meant."

Ruth looked at her very oddly. She said, "You are the strangest girl, Anita. You aren't like anybody else I've ever met."

Anita stuck out her chest. She said with some pride, "I know. I'm a witch." Then a shadow crossed her face. She said, "Least, I could be if I tried really hard. Gran says it's still sort of dormant. I think I could be a good witch. Gran is terribly clever."

Ruth merely laughed.

Anita told Granny Thompson about her new friend. The old lady snorted. She was trying with the aid of an ancient pair of glasses to fill in her weekly football coupon. She only did the pools for kicks as she could have levitated a thousand smackers from a bank as easily as she floated the coupon to the village postbox. She said, "Ent wuth the bother, these 'oomans. Lets yer down evry time. Satan, I could tell yer some tales. Bad as these 'ere teams 'ere. Look at this 'un. Worrum . . . summat or other. Lorst be thirty they did last week, an' I'd got 'em fer a banker. I dunt reckon yer kin esspect nothink else orf these Orstralyerns."

Anita said, "I don't care. She's nice. She's in love with a Romany."

Granny Thompson whooped. "Dunt you git yer 'ead full o' stuff like that, else I knows wun what's a-gooin' ter knock it out agin, smartish.

2: ANITA

Yore got enough ter do, my gel, keeping yerself up ter the mark. Call yerself a witch? Soured four churns o' milk last week, an' then lorst 'art an' turned it orl back orlright agin. Shent stick up fer yer ner more when that young area chap comes a-pokin 'is nose, that I shent. 'Ave the Old Man down on yer neckit you will, afore yer done. Then you'll know summat." She dabbed in a line of crosses and said, " 'Ere, tek this fer a walk. Gettin' sorft you are, sittin' 'round 'ere moonin' about love an' such. Never 'eard the like."

But the advice came a little late. Anita already loved Ruth; she had never had a friend before.

She saw her every night now, even when the Romany came. Strangely enough Jem did not mind her company. Anita had a trick of being there and yet not being there, so the lovers could talk and laugh as if they were really alone. Anita learned a lot from them. She already knew about Jem, and snaring rabbits and making clothes pegs and how to light a fire in the wind and the best way to polish brass. These were things she had in common with his folk. Ruth's life was a mystery to her. She lived in a new development two miles away across the fields. Here there were bungalows and little houses that thrust out in lines across the grass like the arms of a stubby dark-pink octopus. One night Ruth persuaded Anita to walk back with her so she could see her home. When the houses came into sight Anita stopped and refused to go any farther. She said, "They aren't like mine. They're just not proper places to live. Where do you grow food?"

Ruth laughed. "We don't grow anything. We just buy it. Or at least Mummy does. There's a van that comes round on Tuesdays. We put a lot of things in the refrigerator. They keep for ages like that." Anita winced. She thought she had never heard anything so sinful.

From Ruth she learned a new vocabulary and a new way of thinking. She found out the cost of putting up a garage, and how Ruth's father wouldn't have the walls rendered because it was too expensive although the man next door had complained then written to the council because the bricks were unsightly and the council had said there was nothing they could do because it was a private estate. And what Mr. Daniels across the road had said to Ruth's father because when there was a drought and the people had come round asking everyone not to use too much water Mr. Daniels had turned his hose on the garden that same night and Ruth's father had told him off about it and how Mr. Draper had paid him back for what he said because the laundryman always used to leave the Daniels' laundry in the Drapers' shed and Mr. Draper had put the bundle out in the rain so it got all wet before anyone knew it was there. And how bad it was when the tube went in the telly because it was only a week outside the guarantee but the shop wouldn't even meet them halfway. And what happens to fibre-board ceilings when storage tanks burst and what the Drapers had said to the gas people because the central heating cost more than it ought. As she

[13]

listened Anita's frown got deeper and deeper. Several times she mentioned what she had learned to her Granny but the old lady's reply was always the same.

" 'Oomans. Ent wuth a candle."

One night Anita asked Jem and Ruth about love again. To her surprise Ruth burst into tears and Jem looked very angry. It seemed he could not go to Ruth's house because he was a Romany and therefore beneath her station. Nor could Ruth see him except unofficially. When she came to the lake she was supposed to be visiting a friend from the office. Anita sat with her mouth open. She had never heard anything so extraordinary. She said, "But when I want a boy I just —" She stopped, remembering Ruth's sensitivity. She said, "Well, I don't think about things like that. That's horrid."

Jem nodded. "That's the way on it though, miss."

Anita frowned. She said, "Can't you run away or something? You know, just go off? You could come home with me but Gran doesn't like humans. She might do something nasty."

Ruth shook her head. "It wouldn't work. You see I'm Under Age. It would just get us all into trouble."

The next night Jem did not come and Ruth cried again. Anita put her arms round her and felt most peculiar as a result. She was not supposed to be sorry for humans, only hinder and impede them. At this rate she would not go to Hell at all but to the Other Place. Mimicking her Granny, she said, " 'Ere, 'old 'ard. I kent stand orl this sniftin'." It made Ruth laugh and she began to talk again. But it was all about unhappy things; how her father had told her the Romanies were no good because they had lice and even if Jem's folk got a house on the council estate she still could not see him because he was only a Gippo and would never do an honest day's work, and how would she like looking after a dozen kids while he was down in the pub swigging his money away and anyhow he was sure to beat her. She told Anita how her parents wanted her to go out with someone on the estate because he was more Her Class but Ruth didn't like him because all he could talk about was his father's company and it was not a nice company anyway it was a little firm that dealt in electro-plating.

Ruth sat up and wiped her face. She said, "I don't know what to do, Anita. I thought this thing with Jem would go off but it's getting worse. Things like this aren't supposed to last but I must be different or something because it keeps getting worse and worse all the time." She looked at the lake, the ripples moving far out on the surface in the fading light. She said, "There's only . . . well, the water; and I mean . . . well, it wouldn't matter any more then would it? Not afterwards?"

Anita was shocked. There are two ways to be evil, knowingly and unknowingly. The latter is worse because it gives you such a time afterwards. There's Limbo and it goes on for centuries. Anita knew a lot about such things from the texts her Granny kept all neatly printed

2: ANITA

on the outside covers of Bibles. She could see that Ruth did not believe her. After her friend had gone Anita crept to where she could see the little houses and glared at them. She was beginning to hate the people who lived there. She had never hated before because she had never loved. The feelings had come together like the two sides of a coin.

Ruth was a sensitive creature and the clapboard jungle was destroying her. As the evenings grew shorter Jem came less and less often and she knew he was losing interest in her. It was not his fault, you could not expect him to come creeping up to the lake night after night when he could go with some other girl and have a good time and not be afraid to show his face. There were times when Anita did not come either; even she seemed to have deserted her. This was not strictly true. Anita was always there watching from the undergrowth just along the bank but when she sensed the pain waves she kept away, as an animal will from something it doesn't understand. Anita was hurt too, because her life had begun to centre on the girl by the lake. She had no idea what she would do if she had to be on her own again and did not try to imagine. Her anger against the little houses and the whole half-understood cult of suburbanism was like a steady flame.

One night when Ruth could stand her solitude no longer she went to the Romany camp. It was deserted; there were not even markers to show others the way the people had gone. Jem had taught her to read such things and she would have seen them had they been there. She went home, not really knowing how or why. Her father saw her face and laughed. He said, "What's this then, just found out the Gippos have done a bunk? I could have told you that a week ago, my girl. The police cleared 'em off the common. Damn good thing too; now perhaps you'll believe me when I tell you they aren't any good."

Ruth stood staring, feeling how complicated everything was. She said, "I think I hate you."

Something went *biff* across her ear and her hair flew up and her head started to ring. Her father said, "And that's for going there after I'd warned you off. Now go to bed. And don't let me hear any more from you. We've always tried to bring you up right my girl, and here you've been acting like a tuppenny little trollop. I know you've been seeing him again. . . ."

But it was all so sordid and horrible. Unbearable. Ruth was through the door and away before her father could stop her. He shouted after her down the path but she did not hear the words because she was panting with her running.

At the end of the lane she slowed down. She thought how queer it was that when you knew you were really going to die you were not afraid any more. She headed for the lake. When she reached it she did not stop for any great last thoughts but walked steadily into the water. She was surprised at the depth of the mud. The lake was quite dangerous. She sank to her knees almost at once and then to her thighs. Her skirt floated out in a circle, pushing aside the leaves and scum that floated on the surface. Old branches snagged at her and she stumbled, still instinctively trying to keep her balance. The water was icy and knifed at her as it rose above her waist but she only noticed it in a detached fashion. Soon she was half-swimming, kicking awkwardly to push herself into the deep places at the centre. She felt sorry for her parents, for Jem, for Anita and herself but she would have to do it now; to go back muddy to her neat home would be worse than not going back at all. Soon her clothes became heavy with water and began to pull at her like hands urging her toward the mud of the lake bottom. She relaxed, feeling herself drawn down to the dead leaves that waited there, and apart from the first few moments it was not too bad at all.

Walking toward the lake Anita felt the quietness that meant Ruth was ahead of her. As she neared the water there was a little surge of fear from the animals there, then silence again, then a great uproar. Scores of messages piped at her as if her mind was a radio set tuned to all wavelengths at once. There was the shriek that a weasel always made when something died and a softer thought from an owl who had seen a strange thing. There were quick sounds from beetles and night birds and all manner of creatures, even spiders and worms, and a panic-thought from a fish about hair and clothes waving in the water of the lake. Anita started to run, knowing she was too late.

She stood on the edge of the dull grey water clenching her hands and feeling drums roll inside her head. Then everything went red and started to flash and when she could see the lake again there was a furrow in the water like that made by a plough in a field and Ruth was walking up it toward her. She came jerkily, swinging her arms and legs like a puppet and with her eyes staring straight ahead. Anita felt the little bit of her mind that was still alive saying *Had to, had to,* then even that was gone and there was nothing. Bright tear tracks shone on Anita's face and she could hardly see as she wiped the mud and weed from Ruth. She said, "Why did you have to, Ruth? Why did you have to?" There was no answer. Ruth stood there stiffly and Anita finally realized she was dead.

She sat on the bank for a long time with her head down and when she looked up again her face was quite different. She stood and pointed at the middle of the water and there was a crash and something like a bolt of lightning. Steam rose in a column and the animal-thoughts piping all round were shocked into silence. Anita moved Ruth's hands and feet one by one to make sure she had control, then capered away from the lake with Ruth jerking stiffly along behind. As Anita ran she shouted. "Come on, Ruth. Come on, little soldier. Pick 'em up; one-two, one-two. That's the style. Chin up and swing those arms. We don't care about the little houses, do we? We don't care!" She sang and Ruth

2: ANITA

joined in, bubblingly because of the water in her lungs. She called, "Dance, Ruth. You wanted to be a dancer, didn't you? Now's your chance. Dance away, little dancer. Let's see those pretty legs!" And Ruth turned stiffly, swirling the material of her dress and filling the night lane with the smell of ponds.

It was late before they reached Ruth's home because Anita had turned in great circles through the fields, flushing the coverts ahead of her and sending foxes and badgers and roosting birds squealing away in fear. Her dress was torn and Ruth's legs were ragged where the brambles had scraped the flesh that could no longer bleed. Nearly all the lights of the little houses were out and the cars stood in the drives, patient humps waiting for the morning. Anita squealed to the sky. "Come on, 'oomans, up yer gits. Jump about!" She took Ruth's cold hand and skipped in a mad imitation of gaiety. "See wot om brought yer!"

She stopped by the hedge that bordered the lane and glared with eyes that were phosphorescent with rage; then she summoned all her power and sent the zombie running awkwardly across the road and through the first gate to fumble and beat at the door. Then the next and the next. "You tell them," choked Anita. "Tell them who sent you. Tell them what I am. Say I'll come in the night. I'll be the thing that jumps in the river when all the fish have gone. The bush on the common that isn't there in the morning. The bird that screeches when the owls are in their holes. The branch that bumps the roof when they've cut down all the trees. Tell them I'll kill them all!" And Ruth went bang-bang-banging along the doors while inside saucepans danced with pressure-cookers and mincers and dinner-mats and old stacks of women's magazines burst into flames in their cupboards and the tubes of Murphys and rented Cossors imploded and refrigerators vomited their scraggy contents and wept ammonia, while spillholders and plastic roses jumped from their shelves and the hardboard backs burst from cheap wardrobes and shiny city suits leaped in the air and lights and screams came on in every little house. . . .

Granny Thompson shot out of her bed as if propelled by a charge of explosive. "Satan a' mercy," she cried to the darkness. "Wot were that?"

The familiars crowded round the cottage scratching and whimpering and explaining all in different tones. There were foxes and badgers, rats and voles, snakes and little Hodges with their prickles quivering with shock. Granny Thompson began feverishly to invest herself with the various bands, the strappings, the corsetings, the voluminous and mysterious garments suited to her age and dignity. She said, "Orlright, orlright, om a-comin'. 'Old *still*, wunt yer, yer'll 'ave them *panes* in. Dang me if the gel ent gorn orf 'er 'ead." She tottered downstairs grabbing for coat and shoes, for stick and old felt hat. She flung open the kitchen door and bats and moths exploded at her face."I kent 'elp

2: ANITA

'ow you 'oller," said Granny firmly. "I kent be ner *quicker.*" She headed down the path through the wood feeling the air around her crackle with hate and magic. "Served out proper, I am," panted the old lady. " 'Ood a' thought she 'ad it in 'er? Never 'eard sich a carryin' on, sich a squawk an' kerfuffle in orl me born days. Got the 'ole place a-gooin' she 'as." An extra-heavy buffet swung her completely around and she crammed her hat desperately back on her head. "Good Lor' a-daisy!" she gasped. "If ever I should say so." And then to her distant granddaughter, "Tek it steady, yer'll a-*bust* summat. An' I dunt want none o' yer *chelp,* neither! Oo, you little *varmint.* You wait till I gits my 'ands on yer . . ."

Behind Foxhanger there was another copse called Deadman's because once a great huntsman broke his neck there, and it was toward this that Granny Thompson headed. Anita had gone to earth in the little wood. As the old lady panted up the slope to it she breasted waves of hate and violence like a swimmer in a rough sea. Under the shadow of the trees she stopped, gasping. She raised her stick and sent out a thought that was like a great invisible sword. "*Silence!*" roared Granny. "Silence, or I'll bring the legions of *'Ell* down on yer!" Then she picked her way forward, guided by ordinary hearing toward a sound of sobbing.

Anita was curled beneath a bush. She was whimpering and quivering like a dynamo for she had done more to herself than to all the inhabitants of all the little houses. Granny Thompson lifted her chin and scrubbed with nobby fingers at the tears on her face, the twigs and leaves in her hair. " 'Ere now," said the old woman tenderly. "I told yer 'oomans wadn't wuth botherin' uvver. Not wuth a tinker's cuss they ent. Come on gel, yer kent goo on like this. We're gotta get you 'um. Right dance yore led me, I dunt know." She made Anita sit up, then stand, and soon she was able to walk. They got to the cottage an hour later, but the dawn was in the sky before the last of the magic died away.

KEITH ROBERTS

3: OUTPATIENT

IT WAS ONE OF THOSE DAYS that only half happened.

When Doug first woke it was early morning. He knew that because there was a ventilator in the wall of his bedroom through which the sun shone soon after it rose. He lay and watched the little orange penny of light inching along the white-painted door. The doorpanels bore repeating patterns of geometric flowers, bad things to stare at if you were feverish.

When he next became conscious it was eleven o'clock and his mother was coming into the room with a tray. There were biscuits and lemonade and a spoonful of jam with an aspirin crunched up in it. He drank the lemonade, swilling the liquid round in the glass so that the bright bubbles stung his nose. He asked if he could get up but his mother said "no" very firmly and rearranged the pillows and told him he could read if he liked. Doug had not really expected to be allowed out of bed. He knew he wasn't well yet; the lemonade had tasted wrong. He sat propped up with a book on his knees and alternately read and dozed. Dinner was peas and carrots and potatoes mashed with gravy the way he liked them but he was not really hungry. He could hear Carol and Ben in the garden and from time to time he could just see the top of his brother's fair head as he used the orchard swing. It made Doug feel more out of things than ever; he called his mother and asked her please to find *Bevis* for him, and read instead about the making of a raft, and stuffing the chinks of it with moss.

His father was home at six and brought him some tinned fruit and sat on the bed smelling of the open air. Doug lay and listened to the sounds of the family having tea; the clatter of china, scrape of a chair, thick bump of the fridge door once, quick piping of Carol's voice raised in protest at some small impasse. His brother and sister were allowed to look in on him before they went to bed. They stood and stared wide-eyed at Doug as though he were somehow different. That hurt him more than his confinement but there was nothing to be done about it. He let himself doze, half closing his eyes so that the still bright evening appeared to darken. One good thing, they wouldn't put the electric fire on tonight. It was a pleasant little fire with a circular, good-tempered sort of bowl and one small coiled element, but sometimes when he woke in the dark it frightened him. If he stared at it long enough the glow would seem to recede into a void till it looked like a ship burning at sea, terribly alone. He preferred the little pressure lamp that hissed away for hours on the floor like a friendly dragon; only they wouldn't let him have it often because there might be fumes, and they were bad for his chest. He slept at last, hoping he would be allowed up tomorrow. With luck and care it might be a month or even longer before he had another Attack.

He woke in the night. The moon was shining straight into the window and everything was very quiet. Doug lay motionless knowing he was better. After a few minutes something flicked across the moon. He half sat up. That was a bat! Night animals fascinated him. He had never been afraid of them, and one of his chiefest treasures was a book with pictures of every sort of bat and owl and moth there was. Soon he saw another bat, then another and another, then three together. The night seemed to be full of them. Flitter-mice, the book called them; it was an old name. He watched the flittermice for a long time, feeling himself drifting back toward sleep.

He was roused by a tapping. It seemed to come from the window. He opened his eyes and saw a big owl gliding away in the moonlight. Had it touched the glass? That would be an extraordinary thing. . . . Doug could lie quiet no longer. He got out of bed, pushed slippers onto his feet because of the coldness of the linoleum and crossed to the window. He looked out and gasped.

The garden was full of animals. The bushes were rustling and swaying as things chuntered about beneath them and near the house he could see hedgehogs, toads, snakes, all manner of rarities. From time to time they looked up, boot-button eyes shining. They all seemed highly excited. It was a queer sight though not at all alarming. Doug half wondered if he might still be asleep.

He undid the catch and pushed the window open a little way. The night air moved gently on his face. He was tempted to climb outside to find out what was happening but loyalty prevented him; he knew how hurt his parents would be if he did a really sinful thing like that. Even the other children were not allowed out after dark and he had to be extra careful because of his illness. Regretfully he pulled the window shut. There was Pollen in the air at this time of the year and he knew that could be very harmful.

He couldn't make the latch close. He fiddled with it for a while, then his hand slipped and made a noise. Immediately he heard a creak from somewhere inside the bungalow, and a sound like a footstep. He scuttled for the bed, dived in without stopping to remove his slippers and pulled the blankets up round him. It would be terrible to be caught running about at night; after all it was positively inviting an Attack. "Asked for it," his father would say, heavily. "Brought it on himself. *Asked* for it. . . ." The excitement had already made his breath rattle and scrape. He lay still, relaxing in a way he'd had to teach himself. No one came; his breathing settled down and soon he was asleep.

When he sat up again he knew without doubt he was dreaming because there was someone in the room. He could see the moonlight shining on her hair. He felt the bed move slightly under her weight; she turned to look at him and he knew immediately he wasn't going to be afraid of her. He said, "Who are you . . . ?" She put a finger against her lips. The gesture was eloquent even in the near darkness. She whispered, "*Sshh*. . . . You'll wake everyone up." Doug chuckled. That was absurd; you couldn't wake people by talking in a dream. He kept his voice down though. He said again, "Who are you?"

The girl said, "I'm Anita. Who are you?"

"Douglas Carter. How on earth did you get in?"

"Through the window, of course. You took a jolly long time opening it."

Doug looked at the window and sure enough it was ajar. He said, "I shouldn't open it at all really. Mummy always keeps it shut."

"Whatever for, on a lovely night like this?"

"Because of the Pollen." Doug was an expert on his own ailment. "It's an Allergy. There's Pollen, and Dust, and Horsehair, and Feathers. Feathers are worst. They make me have Attacks. You see," he wound up, "I'm an *Asthmatic*. . . ."

Anita said softly, "That's terrible. Were you having one of these Attacks today?"

"No. Well, not a real one. I had one yesterday. I had to stay in bed though. I always do, afterwards."

She nodded. "Yes, I felt you wanting to go outside and run about. That's why I came."

Doug pondered the information and gave up. "How did you get through the window? It isn't very big."

"I can get through anywhere. I can make myself . . . well, quite small."

A thought occurred to him. "Was it you who brought the animals?"

"Yes."

"And made the owl knock the glass so's I'd open it?"

"Yes."

Doug said with great solemnity, "You're a witch then. Only they can

[23]

do that. I thought witches were horrible."

She laughed. It was a soft sound, like wind in trees. "I am, sometimes."

"You won't be like it with me, will you? I shouldn't like that."

"No, I won't be like it with you." She stood up quickly. "You have to sleep now, so you'll be better soon. We can talk again another time."

"I'm better now."

She bent to do something to his pillows. He felt more comfortable at once and very tired. She moved away. She said, "Sleep well, Doug. Nice dreams."

He fought the drowsiness. "Will you come again? When I'm asleep?"

"Yes. But you'll have to leave the window for me. Like putting the fire out for Santa Claus."

Doug said, "Promise?"

She crossed to him again and leaned over the bed. He felt her lips brush his forehead. The touch was cool and soft. She smelled of grass and of being under hedges. She said, "Promise. Now go to sleep or I'll take it back." His eyes were closed before she reached the window.

Doug woke next morning with the dream still in his head. He was sorry it hadn't been real. He even remembered the name of the witch. Anita. It would be nice to talk to her every night, it would almost make up for being ill.

His mother let him get dressed. It had rained in the early morning and the Pollen was Laid; he went outside for a short time, muffled up in a scarf of course, the badge of his invalid status. Just before dinner he remembered the window and rushed into his bedroom. The latch was still undone; he was lucky his mother hadn't seen it. So that part had been true anyway. And there was another thing. The evening before, his father had repaired the drive outside the garage and Doug saw him bending over his work and frowning. "Look at this," he complained. "Can't make it out. Looks as if all the cats in Creation have been across here. Just as if there was nowhere to walk except my new concrete." Doug looked and was exultant. The surface was scuffed and scraped and there were faint pattery footprints all over it, but he knew it hadn't been cats.

He unfastened the window again that night. He hardly expected Anita to come back but it seemed he had scarcely closed his eyes before something woke him. He sat up and she was there just as she had been the night before. She said without preamble, "What's Asthma?"

Doug puzzled. He was not very sure. "It's a sort of catchy thing. It gets in your throat so you can't breathe very well. And like I said, things start it off. You have injections in your arm and they come up in lumps and the lumps are the things that start it, they're your Allergies. And it comes when you get mad as well, or someone upsets you or you have a fight at school. I wish I didn't have it."

Anita nodded sympathetically. "It sounds rotten." She leaned back on

3: OUTPATIENT

the bed, extended one leg and wiggled her foot in the moonlight. Doug gasped. "I say, where on earth are your shoes?"

"What?"

"Shoes. Did you leave them outside?"

She laughed. "I didn't put any on. I often don't."

Doug was awestruck. "Gosh, all that grass. It must be *soaking*, I should have an Attack. . . ."

"Do you have to stay in bed all the time?"

"No, only when I have Attacks. I'm having injections all the time."

Anita made a horrible noise. "When will you be better?"

"I don't know. My Auntie still gets Asthma and she's . . . oh, very old." Doug changed the subject. "I wish I could go about at nights like you do."

"Why?"

Doug was launched on his pet topic. Animals after dark . . . He talked about owls and foxes, badgers and frogs. He was a housebound naturalist; he knew how slugs mated and snails, and what beetles ate and how bats found their way. He told Anita about Richard Jefferies and Fabre of Sérignan. She interrupted from time to time to tell him where pipistrelles lived, and noctules. Did he know there were a lot of foxes in Deadman's Copse? Or about the badgers in Sayer's Wood, or that there were otters in the Fyne-brook now? She stayed a long time; the dawn was in the sky before she left. Doug slept very late. His mother thought he was ill again.

Anita came every night for two weeks. Sometimes she wove strange fantasies for Doug, stories in which fact and magic were so mingled they defied unravelment; but always she brought news of the outside world. The owl had taken a huge rat near the old tithe-barn on Rapley Hill; the otter cubs had caught their first fish and eaten it and been sick; a bat had been frightened by the fall of an ancient church roof, and had left home; a mouse was building a new nest because his old one had got stepped on. Doug wondered how she could possibly know so much. He saw the countryside through her eyes, and his nights became more important than his days.

Then it rained. For hours the spots hammered on the bungalow roof, fled streaming down the window panes. That night Doug tried to open the window and could not. The wood had swollen, jamming the frame tight. He struggled for a long time but the thing defeated him; he had to leave it shut. Anita didn't come.

By first light Doug was gasping and coughing and by midmorning he was delirious. The Doctor arrived, a big young man in a dark coat who always smelled faintly of disinfectants. He sat by Doug and touched him with the burning-cold mouth of his stethoscope, tapping and listening. Then he folded the chrome earpieces, twirled the rubber tubes around them and looked stern. He said, "Well young man, what's caused all this? What's bothering you?"

[25]

Doug choked and his mother answered for him. "I don't know what's upset him I'm sure but it's something, something's brought it on. He was going on this morning, Doctor, all about opening the window because if he didn't Anita couldn't get in. He's worked himself into an Attack over it, that's what he's done."

Doug was appalled. Had he said all that? The Doctor glanced at him keenly. He said, "What's this, Douglas, who's Anita?" Doug could only lick his lips and look feverishly at the window. The Doctor said, "Is there anybody? Does he know someone called Anita?"

His mother shook her head. "I don't think so. I've been trying to think but I don't know anyone. It's something he's made up."

The Doctor said, "Hmph." He got up and went to the window, stood and looked through it at the garden and the woods beyond. Doug's mother said, "It isn't ever open anyway, because of the pollen. We always keep it shut."

The Doctor lifted the catch and gave the window one bang with his great freckled fist. It opened and there was a gust of clean, rained-on morning air. He said, "If he wants it open let him have it open. He can worry himself into more illness than pollen will cause him. The lad's got a lively imagination, haven't you, Doug?"

Doug said weakly, "Yes, Doctor."

The Doctor laughed, and ruffled his hair. Privately he was wondering if the boy had ever come across the legend of the vampire. He knew what Doug was for his books. You could never tell with kids, they had some funny ideas; he was a firm believer in humouring fantasies where they were not positively harmful. Children lived in a dream-world of their own and they had to leave it soon enough . . . He pushed the blankets round Doug's chin and said, "Well, young man, you've got your window open. No more pranks now, understand? Do what your mother tells you, stay there and keep warm. We'll have you up in no time then. All right?"

"Yes, Doctor."

The Doctor picked up his case and walked out of the door. Just before it closed he was saying something about "all that could be done for the present."

After a while Doug heard his car start up and drive away. He lay feeling very grateful, then he slept.

Anita came that night but she didn't speak. Doug tried to sit up and reach out to her but he seemed to have lost the power of movement. A strange thing happened; Anita seemed to become rapidly smaller, as though she were moving back at great speed. It was all confusing. Doug cried out, and a great bird flew away from the house straight and fast as an arrow. Doug fell back panting, and the fever took him again.

He lay all next day and the next, not eating, with the clock for company and the medicine bottles and the quick scurrying clouds. By the third day he was very weak, and turned his face to the wall

3: OUTPATIENT

whenever his father or mother came into the room. They gave him his favourite book, *Night Creatures*, with its green Morocco-grained cover and the gold stamped picture on the spine that showed a bat crossing the moon. He turned the pages listlessly for a time then pushed the thing away. It only served to remind him that Anita didn't want him any more. She had let him down like everything else. Instead he read a little from *Famous Sailing Ships* but that was no good either, it gave him daymares where the great broken carracks of the Armada loomed over him, rolling to make him see their bleeding scuppers. His parents were desperately worried; it was the worst Attack he had ever had.

He woke halfway through the third night. It was still and cool, with a quarter moon slipping among the clouds. Anita was sitting at the foot of the bed, knees drawn up and chin in her hands. She said softly, "Feeling better, Doug?"

He was silent.

"Douglas?"

The little boy said bitterly, "Go away."

"What?"

"Go away. I don't want you. I don't want to talk to you again. Ever."

She said, "Douglas!" She leaned forward and Doug felt her hands like little animals moving on the covers. She said, "I couldn't come the first time, honestly. I tried but the window wouldn't open, I couldn't undo it without a noise. And then I had to do some things for my Granny. I had to go . . . well, to some very odd places. A long way away. I was fetching things to make you better because I knew you were so ill. I wasn't going to tell you yet but there, I have. Don't be angry with me."

"I don't believe you," muttered Doug. "You don't care. Nobody cares. You aren't even real." He began to weep.

Anita sat silent, biting her lip and frowning. Then she said, "You won't understand this but I'm going to tell you because when you're grown you might remember it and then you'll know you weren't just talking to the moonlight and the wind. I used to hate humans, Doug, because they did something awful once and I wanted to punish them all for it. I'm not human because I know what bats think and how the foxes talk. I've got to go away soon and you won't see me again but I don't hate any more and I'm going to make you well first. But you must believe me and do what I say. Are you listening?"

Doug said suspiciously, "What do you want me to do?"

Anita became businesslike. "Right then, leave the window tomorrow night like you always do. I'll come for you and you've got to be ready to go out."

Doug said, "What? Out *there?*"

"Yes. You'll be perfectly all right because you'll be with me. You're going to see my Granny because she's going to help you. You must do what she tells you and not be frightened because she's very fierce but

[27]

she doesn't mean half of it. Okay?"

Doug lay wanting to believe. At length he said grudgingly, "Yes."

"Good. And after that I'm going to show you something special. I'll take you to a Badgers Wedding. Now I've got to go because I've got to get it all ready. It'll be fun; I haven't been to one since I was a little girl."

"Anita, please, what's a Badgers Wedding?"

"No more questions. You'll see tomorrow. Now go to sleep." And she was gone.

Next night Doug was awake when she arrived. The manner of her coming was marvellous but he was getting used to magic. He was up in a moment and struggling into dressing gown and slippers. She said, "Are you ready?"

When he was standing beside her she seemed very big and grown-up. He nodded. "Yes."

"All right then. Come on."

She took his hand and went to the window. She slipped through it quick as an eel, turned and swung him over the sill. Doug was amazed. He'd never realized she was so strong. They sneaked away, turning back at the end of the garden to see how the house was watching them with its dark windows. Then they walked into the trees.

The woods were dense and full of noise, squeakings and rustlings, clicks and chirrings, barks and hoots. There were brambles and snagging branches, bushes under which Doug had to crawl. Anita seemed to know every inch of the path even in the blackness. Doug, puffing a little, asked her a question. "Anita, do you have radar . . . ?" She chuckled briefly. "Yes. . . ." They went through some fields, crossed a road, and there was a brook with stepping stones. Doug wondered if it was the Fyne; he'd lost all real sense of direction.

The cottage stood in a little copse. As they got near Doug saw a light in the window, smoke coming from the chimney. Anita hurried forward and pushed open the old door. She called, "Gran, we're here. . . ."

Doug followed her in and gasped. The whole place was filled with smoke and steam; it smelled appalling. He began to cough almost at once. The vapour was pouring from a cauldron set on an iron trivet above the fire. Bending over the great pot and prodding its contents was an old lady. Her face was lined, her hair grey and scraggy and she had fierce snaky black eyes. On her head was an old felt hat and she was wearing what she would call an "eppon" of floral print. When she looked up Doug drew back. He felt Anita's arm round his shoulders. She said, "Don't be scared, it's all right. Gran, this is Douglas."

The old lady squinted at him. She said uncompromisingly, "Oh, is it? Orlright then, sit 'im down uvver there. An' dunt you start a-fidgetin' and frettin' my lad, it ent ready yit. . . ." Then to Anita, "Did yer bring them mandrake bits?"

"Yes, Gran."

"An' that rat stuff?"

"Yes."

"Gis 'em acrorst them. Look *smart,* I ent got orl night.... Ar, that's it." She opened the packet and sniffed. "That's the stuff orlright, drop o' good jollop that is. Kent be bothered refinin' it meself. Teks hours thinkin' it out of orl them leaves...." She shook the contents into the pot. Doug gulped. He'd seen his father put "that stuff" down in the shed. When rats touched it they died. Anita laughed. "Don't worry, it isn't for eating. It's just for the spell, it's a sort of catalyst."

The old lady said, "Bronchial, ent 'e ... ? Orl them toobs an' such ..."

"The Doctor says he can't be cured."

"Stuff," said Granny Thompson firmly. She held a saucepan over the pot and poured in what looked like batter. There was a rumbling and seething inside, then a frightful cataclysm. Everything was blotted out by vapour. "That's it!" shouted the old lady, invisible in the steam. "It's *come up....* Quick then, ketch 'olt o' this. You'll need a *clorth,* it's *'ot.* ..." Strange lights wavered in the fog; mysterious instructions were shouted and acted upon. "Weer's the digitalis?" roared Granny. "Look lively, gimme them there frogs whotsits...." And again, "Well, you'll *'atter* read it, I kent find them glasses *nowheer.* They was on that shefferneer this mornin', I could swear to it. You must 'ave shifted 'em. ... An' watch that there pot, you'll 'ave it *uvver.* ..."

Douglas sat still, afraid to move. He was quite certain he was going to die. He was prodded and shoved and told to " 'old still" and "give uvver." He had quick impressions of Granny wielding a ladle from which poured orange stuff that shone and twinkled like fire, of Anita, book in hand, intoning something while flamelight leaped pink on her face, reflected sparklingly from her great eyes. He was anointed with liquids that sometimes burned and sometimes ran cold as ice. The pot was placed at his feet, fumes gushed round him. His head was whirling; he looked down into a place of stars, vast and cold. He felt himself falling toward nebulae that spun green and glowing. There was a roaring in his ears; he whooped for breath, one last tremendous catch; then Anita's hands were on his shoulders, she was shouting something to him. The steam vanished and it was all over.

He looked around the room: the old furniture, the clean stone floor, the oil lamp and the embers of the fire, the dresser hung with cups. Anita was laughing. She was on her knees in front of him, shaking him gently. She said, "You're cured, Doug, can't you feel it? I can...."

Doug breathed deeply and for the first time ever the air moved sweetly in his lungs, no longer rasping and hot. He yelled and hugged Anita, then the old lady. She shoved him impatiently and told him to "Git *orf.*" Anita took his hand and they ran out of the cottage to see the Badgers Wedding; and as they moved through the woods they were followed by a host of creatures, scurrying and invisible.

Mrs. Carter missed her son just before dawn. She'd got up because Carol had had a bad dream, and some impulse made her look into Doug's room. The bed was empty, the window wide, the curtains flapping in the breeze. The hue and cry spread as the Carters searched and neighbours joined in the hunt. A police car growled down the lane; torches flashed, paling as the sky began to glow. They found Doug wandering wet through and happy. He was singing a song the like of which they'd never heard, that he called the Badgers Anthem. He was put to bed and the Doctor sent for, but there was no need. He was not ill, nor did his asthma ever come again.

The Doctor tried to make some sense of his story. The first part was easily enough explained; the image of the witches' hut could have come from a score of his books. The rest was more disturbing. He described a ruined church hung from end to end with black drapes that waved in the night wind; moonlight squirting through cracks in the roof; the smell of damp, like old hymn books opened for the first time in years; the creeping, blotchy mildew on the tall pews. There was a congregation, he said, though of whom or what he could never remember; and there was music, thin and mad, that shrilled on the brain. There were candles, black as pitch, burning in sconces, and it was a Badgers Wedding. He even described the dazed little animals jerking up the aisle, very stiff and formal in gowns and morning suits; the train of bridesmaids, the little dark minister poring over his book. The Doctor shook his head when he had finished, and passed the thing off somehow. As for the cure, well, asthma was a strange illness that plagued the nerves of the sufferer as well as his tissues; and he'd always kept an open mind on faith healing.

Doug remembered for a time, before it was all swamped in the great business of being normal. He wanted to thank Anita again but that was impossible. It's useless to talk to the moonlight and the wind; they have a trick of never listening.

4: THE SIMPLE FOR LOVE

ANITA POSED MAGNIFICENTLY before the mirror in panties and hair-ribbon. She was uncertain about the hair-ribbon; she put her head first on one side then on the other while the ribbon shuffled about tying itself into obedient bows here and there, constricting the waves of her hair and letting them slacken again. Anita pouted. The ribbon wouldn't do, it was red. The night was warm; she must wear no hot colours or she would feel sweaty. She was colour sensitive; she would have liked a bow of electric blue but that would jazz her mind, start thoughts as bright and irresponsible as lightning, and that would never do. The ribbon swept from her hair and riffled away into a corner of the bedroom. She pulled at her lip with her teeth, sat down, put her chin in her hands and regarded her reflection worriedly.

Anita had ribbons of all types, sizes and colours; they were a passion with her. The whole collection sprawled over her dressing table; there were ribbons of red and ribbons of blue, ribbons of yellow, green, lilac, white; ribbons spotted and ribbons plain, gingham checked, sombre, brown and black, vilely fluorescent . . . the mass churned about as her mind probed into them. Yellow and green were useless, she bought the colours but never wore them, they didn't suit her . . . what about white?

A white satiny thing looped forward like a caterpillar, shook itself, flew around her head to burrow ticklingly behind her ears. She made a huge Alice bow with it, then it went the way of the red. White was for chastity, and Anita wanted no omens. Pink was discarded as well; it was too pretty, she'd look like a birthday cake. Once on a time there would have been no problem; she would have bound her hair with dragonflies, made their wings flutter around her head like a tinsel coronet. But that needed a spell, and spells were finished, done, through . . . Anita sighed. Black was mournful, it was the colour of witchrites and death and in any case it would take the heat worse than red; and spots were out of the question . . .

Something caught her eye, and her mind flicked it out of the pile and hung it up for inspection. A pale, ice blue. She tried it on and it was right, there was just the correct measure of coolness. And that solved the dress problem too; she would wear her new one, that sleeveless job in the offbeat coffee colour. Ice blue and brown; she would be like a frosted leaf blowing on the June wind. The dress flapped out of the wardrobe cupboard, hung round her shoulders and wriggled till she slipped her arms into it. She fastened the buttons, shutting herself away for the moment carefully.

She pulled the ribbon undone, by hand this time, and started brushing her hair again. It was hard trying to give up all her powers at once but she was managing very well. Soon she would be a normal girl; it was a wonderful thought.

Shoes . . . No shoes at all, she thought, wriggling. *Just glow-worms on my toes . . .* There were only five glow-worms in the whole of Northamptonshire; she nearly sent for them before she remembered. She decided reluctantly on plain sandals and no messing about. She retied the ribbon, gave her hair a final pat and tuck and opened the bedroom door. She crept downstairs and through the house, trying not to disturb her Granny. A sharp thought tapped her on the back as she was opening the kitchen door. She slipped through quietly, ran hare-quick down the garden path and into the copse. She emerged from the trees no longer a witch, and feeling marvellous.

Out on the main road the little red car was waiting, just as he had said it would be. Anita scurried toward it and bumped down in the seat smelling of elderberry and crushed grass. He smiled at her.

"Hello, Anita."

She tried to say "Hello, Roger" back but the words got stuck somehow. She made a guk-guk noise instead, just like last time. He laughed and drove away and Anita hung onto the dash tingling a little because steel is nearly like iron, feeling the wind bustle her, seeing the gearlever snick forward and back, hearing the tyres whimper on the bends, wanting to go at a million miles an hour and spin right off the earth. The MG purred, making a noise like a great bee. *He drives so well,* thought Anita, *oh he isn't like the people in the little houses, he isn't like anybody else at all, I shall fill right up and explode, vanish in a green puff and a shower of sparks like one of Granny's spells when she hasn't read the book right. I don't know what will happen to me, I want to run and scream and swim and jump and laugh all together . . .*

Roger shouted over the wind and the insect-noise of the engine. "Where do you want to go?"

"Don't know, don't care."

4: THE SIMPLE FOR LOVE

"I know where there's a dance...."

"Oh no please, not a dance." *I can't do your dances yet, I know the dance that sends bees to pollen but there isn't music for it, not music you could hear.* . . . "I don't know," said Anita.

He glanced at her sharply. "You nearly look frightened!"

"I *didn't* . . ."

He laughed again. "Anita, you are a funny girl."

"But I'm trying. I'm trying to change."

He drifted round a bend and let fly at the straight beyond it. The MG declared war; Anita watched the speedo needle playing with the number seventy. The other thing, the dial that moved in funny jerks, was the rev-counter. She was learning fast. "I don't want you to change," said Roger. "Why do you want to do that? You're perfect as you are."

Anita glowed. "Let's go somewhere quiet," she said. "A long way away."

The car leaped forward; the engine sounded angry because there was so much road . . .

The pub was cool and still, set back from a main road that ran straight as an arrow into the distance. The cars passed steadily, *veeee-whooom, veeee-whooom.* The sound was not disturbing; it was a summer-night noise, and just right. Anita sat at a table on the lawn, under a great rustling tree, and felt thoughts probing at her. She tried to shut them out but they were insistent, like little ASDIC pulses. *Who . . . PING . . . who . . . PING . . . who . . . PING . . .*

"What do you want to drink, Anita?"

"I . . . don't know. Choose something."

"Lemonade?"

"No!"

"Shandy then . . . okay?"

WHO . . . PING . . . WHO . . . PING . . .

She had to send her callsign; there were improbable things in the hedgerows, there could easily have been a mobbing. After all, she had crossed a county boundary without a proper clearance . . . The questions and pipings faded, leaving one insistent voice.

THERE y'are, yer young VARMINT!

Gran, please, not now . . .

Come 'um this MINUTE!

Gran, I can't. . . . I'm in LOVE. . . .

Airy profanity. Anita shut her mind. Far off, a summer storm rumbled over Foxhanger. There was no rain, but the thunder was audible for miles.

"Please, Anita," said Roger, half laughing and half worried. *"What do you want to drink?"*

"A beer," said Anita a little desperately. "A big one . . ." He stared at her and she lifted her nose a trifle, regarding a distant view.

[33]

The pint arrived; she buried her nose in the froth and drank lustily. Hardly ladylike, but she was past caring. Roger gave her a cigarette. She had been smoking for two weeks now and had disposed of a whole ten. They did unmentionable things to her queer complex of senses, but that was all to the good. Roger shook his head. He said again, "You are a funny girl."

"Why?"

"You just are."

"Tell me."

"What about?"

"About how I'm funny."

He laughed. He was tall and almost gaunt with straight dark hair; he had a soft, velvety sort of voice and his hands were bony and strong and smelled of nicotine and carbolic soap. He cupped one over the other now on the table, looking down and watching the smoke drift away from his cigarette. He said, "I don't know how you're funny. That's why you're funny. . . . I like it, Anita. But half the time you just don't seem to be *there*. . . . Oh I didn't mean that, you know what I mean. . . . What do you go dreamy about? Come on, penny for your thoughts. Right now."

"No."

"Twopence then."

Perhaps I should have worn a little choker ribbon instead, they say they're very fetching . . . "No," said Anita. "I want a golden guinea."

"You shall have one. Promise."

Anita laughed. "It wouldn't be worth it. I wasn't thinking at all."

Something prodded at her mind and she acknowledged irritably. *You are cleared for area G-6,* said the Northamptonshire Controller frostily. *Huntingdonshire, and Cambridgeshire as far as Ely. And don't do this again or I shall have to report it downstairs. . . . Please state your destination and E.T.A.*

Efficiency, always efficiency . . . The Dark One was making a fetish of modern business methods. Anita snapped, *I'm going back to Foxhanger. I'm taking a boy.*

There was unholy laughter. *Good Hunting* from the Controller, and a babble of monstrous suggestions from the lesser fry. Anita's mind sent out a series of red flashes, confusing all wavelengths; when they died away the Huntingdonshire folk let her be.

Roger put out his hand and placed it over hers. He said, "There, I told you. You keep drifting away. You did it then, while I was talking to you."

"I didn't!"

"You did. I bet you don't know a thing I said."

"I do too, it was about giving me a golden guinea."

"Well that just proves it, that was ages ago. I said I wanted to talk to you rather seriously."

4: THE SIMPLE FOR LOVE

Anita gulped. Five miles from Foxhanger was a hayrick; she'd spent the whole of last night lying in bed and tousling its surface into softness. Baled hay was uncomfortable but this would be soft as a mattress. We'll do circles, she thought, going a little crazy. Round and round, wheeee . . . "Roger," she said, "can we talk l-later, please? And can we go now?"

"Of course," he said. He was frowning and grinning at the same time. "Of course. . . ."

"Then come on . . . *wheeeee* . . ."

The stack showed in the twilight, a dark shape with the moon rising behind it. Anita relaxed as well as she could in a bucket seat, feeling dreamy. Roger touched her hair thoughtfully, starting shivers down her back. "Why did you want to stop just here, what's so special about here?"

"Hmmmm . . . nothing . . . Tell me about your house in London again."

"I've told you a dozen times already."

"Again. Please. . . ."

He lit a cigarette, offered her the packet belatedly. She shook her head without opening her eyes. It was a mistake, but he didn't spot it. "It's in Hampstead," he said. "It's a very nice place. It's quite open; there's a little High Street with trees, it's just like a country town. You hardly know you're in London. And the house is . . . well, it's quite large, and it has a drive, and there are garages. Inside, it's nearly all white. . . ."

"Your parents won't like me."

"Of course they will."

Anita's heart fluttered. "They won't. They can't. Roger, I'm not supposed to tell a soul but . . . you see, I'm a witch. It's terribly difficult."

He was very firm. "Now don't be silly, please. We've been into all this before, we've got to be serious now. The first thing we've got to do is sort out about this Granny of yours. If I could just come along and meet her . . ."

Anita's eyes opened wide. *"No. . . ."*

He shrugged a little helplessly; then he tried another tack. "Is she your legal guardian?"

"Who?"

"Your Granny of course."

"I don't know," said Anita, totally confused. "I suppose she must be."

He played with her hair, twirling a little coil of it around his finger. "Anita, I'm afraid this is rather personal but . . . how old are you?"

"A million and three."

"Anita, *please* . . ."

"But I am, honestly. . . ."

He sighed. "I wish you'd try to be serious."

[35]

She was watching him steadily. Her eyes seemed to be glowing. "All right," she said. "I'll tell. I'm two minutes old. I was born when the car stopped."

He seemed to be searching for the right thing to say. "Anita, I wish you'd try because it's very important. You see I love you rather a lot and —"

She shot upright, galvanized. *"What?"*

He looked miserable. "I'm sorry, I shouldn't have said that. It just sort of slipped out. Don't be angry."

Anita scrambled out of the car, her long legs suddenly as ungainly as those of a grasshopper. She bolted down the road, shedding a shoe on the way. Roger jumped up. "Anita, come back . . . Don't be scared . . . Oh, Lord . . ."

She piped at him from a hundred yards away. "You never even said it before. I love you too. . . ."

"Anita . . ."

"Come and catch me . . . !"

The haycock was a little plateau with a horizon of stars. Anita wriggled luxuriously and the autumn leaf began to come apart. Buttons slid magically undone, she lost her hair-ribbon and her other shoe. Her heart was thudding violently and things round her seemed to be spinning in giddy vertical planes. *"Roger . . ."*

He was trying to stand but the surface of the hay was not sympathetic. "Anita, *what are you doing . . .*"

"It's all right, we're in love . . ."

"Anita, he said, floundering. "You must be mad . . ."

"MMMMM . . ."

He shouted at her. *"Do your dress up!"* He caught her bare shoulders and shook her. "Look at yourself!" he said. *"What do you think you're doing?"* He shoved her away from him and Anita rolled across the stack thinking lightning had struck at the very least. He slid down awkwardly to the field and his voice floated back to her, distant and cold. "Tidy yourself this minute," he said. "And then come down. It's very late, I'm going to take you home."

Anita lay on her face, still feeling the fiery teasing of the straw, a thoroughly shattered witch. The sobs came soft at first then louder, shaking her stupid body in the silly undone dress. Her tears ran into the hay, trickling together as though they would reach the bottom of the stack.

Anita faced Granny across the kitchen table. The old lady stood stock-still, eyes screwed up, as she tried to take in what her granddaughter had said. At length she said faintly, " 'Ave you gorn completely orf yer 'ead? Well, 'ave yer?"

Anita's jaw quivered. "No Gran, I haven't. This is awful, I feel absolutely awful but I . . . mean what I say. I'm going away."

4: THE SIMPLE FOR LOVE

"Weer?" asked Granny Thompson, still dazed. "Weer, gel? Weer yer *gooin'?*"

Anita took the plunge. "L-London. You see, Gran, there's this boy. R-Roger Morrison. And I'm in love with him, and I can't do anything about it, and there's no use trying. An' he . . . he won't do anything until I go away. He wants me to stay in his house in Hampstead. . . ."

"Ter see the time om *took,*" Granny broke in, muttering and shaking her head dolefully. "Orl the years om brought yer up . . . I never thort I'd see nothink like *this,* straight I din't . . ."

Anita's lips began to tremble. "It's no good, Gran," she said. "Not a scrap. If you go on like that I know I shall start to cry, but it won't make any difference. I shall still go, it's j-just one of those things . . . I'm going to Hampstead and I'm going to get a job, and that's that. And I'm going to be married. Properly married, in Church . . ."

Granny Thompson's mood changed abruptly. "Married?" she screeched. *"Married?* An' to *'ooman* . . ." Her voice began to take on some of the quality of a circular saw ripping into steel plate. "I never 'eard nothink like it, not in orl me born *days* . . . Gel, yer a *witch,* kent yer *see* that? Yer got power uvver the beasts o' the field an' the win's o' the air, yer kin call the lightnin' down inter the cup o' yer 'and . . . Yer got senses piled atop o' the senses o' mortals, yer soul's bought an' paid fer down under this twenty year, an' yer talkin' about *marriage* . . ."

"And I'm giving it all up!" screeched Anita, beating her Granny down by sheer volume. "An' I'm going to be *baptized,* an' married in *Church* . . . I'm goin' to be like Roger, a *Catholic* . . ."

Queer lights flared, fumes rolled around the room. Ceiling and walls quivered and a noise like millstones began, shaking the cottage. Anita was deafened and blinded; when she could see again her Granny was leaning over the table quite still, her spellstick pointed unwaveringly between Anita's eyes. On the old lady's shoulder a familiar crouched, back spiky with hatred, yellow eyes swimming. Anita began to tremble as though there were an engine inside her, running raggedly. Her teeth started to chatter; she lowered her head and slowly clenched her hands.

"By 'Im Wot's Down Under," said Granny Thompson slowly, hissing the words between her teeth. "I never thort I'd see the day. The *langwidge* . . . an' under my roof an' orl. I never thort it'd come ter *this.* . . ."

Anita's voice was very wobbly; it almost refused to come at all. "You'll have to d-do away with me then, Gran," she said. "I'm sorry, but I can't change. Spell me to a cinder, it doesn't matter now." She stayed with her head down, shaking.

Granny Thompson champed her lips, took a breath, let it out again, paused and seemed momentarily to swell. The familiar crouched slowly; its eye pupils contracted to tiny dots, its ears flattened and it began to purr. For a whole minute that was the only sound in the room; then

Granny lifted the animal from her shoulder and set it on the ground. She crossed to her chair, using the stick to walk with, and sat down. After a time the long wooden creak of the rockers sounded. Anita opened her eyes and looked up slowly. A streak of sweat ran down her face and she wiped at it automatically with the back of her hand. Then her eyes brimmed. "Gran," she said. "Oh, Gran . . ."

"I dunt want none o' that neither," said the old lady firmly. "*Waterworks*. Dunt 'elp nothink ner nobody. When are yer gooin', gel?"

"Gran, I . . ."

"There's a sootcase somewheer about," said Granny. "Yer kin 'ave that. Yer'd better goo in yer noo things, yer old 'uns wunt 'urt fer bein' scumbled."

Anita spread her hands on the table helplessly and stared at them.

"Yer'll 'ave ter give the lot up o' course," said Granny Thompson sternly. "Ent no good 'arf doin' it. I shall atter report it, so's we kin get yer signed orf the books. I dunt esspect there'll be no trouble . . ."

A large tear splashed onto Anita's wrist.

"Times ent wot they were," said the old lady. She was sitting half turned from Anita; her profile looked pinched and thin. "I dunt say as 'ow I altergether blames yer," she said. "Times is shiftin'. Too fast fer us old 'uns . . . We'll just atter git on as best we can, same as we allus 'as. I dare say 'e's a nice enough young bloke, I'd 'a' done the same meself mebbe, fifty year or more back. I shall 'atter write a note though, jist in case any o' them up there wants ter know. An' 'oo kin tell, mebbe yer'll be comin' back now an' then jist visitin' like . . ."

Anita broke, and fled from the room.

A bat called her up at 4:00 A.M., as he was passing the cottage on his way to his home in the bole of an ancient tree. An angry thought burst at him through the thatch; a split second before it reached him it relented, spun a bubble that twitched him half a mile off course and a hundred yards above his normal ceiling. He floated down puzzled, reoriented himself on the tall trees of Deadman's Copse, just growing out of the night.

Anita walked slowly toward the main road. She was wearing a new dress, very white and clean, and a little jacket. It was early evening again, and there had been rain; the wetness in the grass made the fields look rough and grey. Droplets flew like pearls, splashing her ankles; her suitcase bumped her knee. Twenty yards off something scurried along a hedge bottom but she ignored it. There was a wall around her mind through which no thoughts could penetrate; above her a swooping bird braked and spun away, puzzled by the blankness.

Anita was thinking about her home. About the red tile floors and limewashed walls, the thumpings and night chirpings and scratchings she had always heard in the thatch. The old beams and the deep windowsills with their scatter cushions and well worn paint. The

4: THE SIMPLE FOR LOVE

warmth and coziness of the kitchen hearth, the tall cupboards full of ancient spells and mysteries. They were things she could never take with her; she'd had to leave them all behind as she'd left her ribbons and her dresses and her boxes full of toys and curios, the little fossils so old she could put them to her ear and hear all the years inside singing like a kettle . . .

Somewhere a ripple ran across the grass. Something chattered, something drummed, something sat up and scrubbed its ear. The grass waved, complicating itself with private patterns. The green stems chafed a message. "Anita's going away . . . *going away* . . ."

She had wanted to fill her case with stupid things, with corn dollies and old mouse nests and ammonite shells and long bright ribbons and pressed flowers and spellbooks and old leaves and pieces of ironstone for drawing ginger pictures on the ground; but Granny Thompson had made her be sensible and there were woollies and undies and a spare dress and her comb and brush and a strong pair of shoes and some money, and a letter in the old lady's improbable handwriting that said she was over twenty-one, and a free agent.

The noise increased, the rustlings and quiverings, the thumpings like little drums beating strange rhythms through the grass. To others it might have been the wind but to Anita it was a song, a crying, something black and strange . . .

There was the road, and a bus stop. A big green United Counties omnibus, quivering and noisy and hot. Anita climbed onto it and the anthem stopped, blown away by diesel fumes. The bus ground off, and soon home was nothing but a memory and a dream.

The train compartment smelled of dust and old sticky sweet wrappers. The seats were upholstered in faded reddish cloth and there were spotty narrow pictures of castles and lakes in Scotland and a little map with all the stations of the region printed on it and a mirror with the letters *BR* engraved in its centre. Anita sat waiting for the train to start. She was sure she would feel the jerk, but there was nothing; the carriage glided away so smoothly the platform was slipping past before she realized. Roger smiled at her reassuringly. "Don't look so worried," he said. "Everything's all right."

Anita smiled back, conscious of the station buildings and sidings falling away behind and the fields coming into sight. Roger offered her a cigarette but she shook her head. He said, "It's a good fast train, we'll be in Saint Pancras before dark . . . Anita?"

"Yes?"

"*Are* you all right?"

Anita nodded, suddenly feeling a glow. It was done, the old way was broken. She was going to Hampstead, to see the open spaces and the tall houses and the High Street that was like a little country town. She was going to meet Roger's parents and start everything new and there was going to be no more magic . . .

Roger was still talking. She tried hard to follow. "I'm sorry we couldn't drive up; the motor broke a half-shaft and had to go into a garage. Got to come down again later in the week and fetch her, awful bore . . . I showed Sis your picture; she thinks you're smashing . . . I've never seen that dress before, is it new? . . . Mother would have fetched us but she doesn't like driving the Jag, and Father's abroad till the end of the month . . ."

Anita?

Far away, tiny with distance, a hare was pounding along keeping pace with the train. A thought pinged up to the carriage; the glass of the window was so thick the message barely came through.

Tell Anita the weasel's run over. He was crossing a road and a car came, it broke his back . . .

Anita doesn't want to know . . .

The train was swaying now as it picked up speed. Anita could imagine what it looked like, long and tall, racing in the late sunlight. She was able to see it from outside, through eyes set very close to the ground.

"*Anita!*"

She blinked, and smiled again a little desperately. "Trains p-pick up water don't they, from sort of troughs in between the rails? They have a sort of scoop . . . I was looking at a train book last night and there was one doing it . . ."

Roger came and sat with her, putting his arm round her shoulders. "Anita, you're just like a child sometimes . . . Anyway, this is a diesel. Only steam trains pick up water." He paused; then, "You were dreaming again, weren't you?"

"No, I . . . yes . . . Roger, I'm trying so hard . . ."

"Don't. It doesn't matter, it's all right . . . Anita, what do you dream?"

"I mustn't tell, I've got to forget . . ."

"It doesn't matter now that you know they're only dreams. Tell me about them. Telling helps, it's the best thing to do."

One of those little knolls must be Foxhanger. Far away, blue with distance . . . Anita used a flash of one of her abnormal senses and the scene through the window altered. Strange eddies were visible, and lines of force. Foxhanger winked like a jewel. She turned away, playing with a button on the boy's coat. "I can fly in the air . . . did you know that, Roger?"

"Go on. I think you have pretty dreams."

Suddenly it was wonderful just to be talking about it. Talking made things seem nearer for a little while longer. "I can fly," said Anita "and I can change into things. I can be a hare or a fox, or a badger . . . And I know how it feels when dragonflies mate, it's wonderful, you go soaring up in the air till there's nothing round you but blueness and sunlight . . . And I can be a bat and squeak like a bat and fly up and

4: THE SIMPLE FOR LOVE

try and hear the echoes bouncing off the moon . . . An' I've been to the moon, everything's stiff and black and white and the stars are huge and the sky's like velvet and there isn't any air . . . And there's drifts of dust you could sink right into, and cracks and rifts everywhere and nothing growing. Nothing there at all except little scampery things in the shadows and you never see them, you just hear them calling . . . An' I know what it's like to . . . be a fish, how the current feels pushing against your nose and how the weed touches your back . . . And how the sun looks on the top of the water, the ripples are all gold and swimming fast's like driving under trees . . . I know about everything, I can go into crayfish burrows to feed them, I can hunt with the foxes . . . An' I know about weasels, they're terrible. If they catch you when you're small . . ." She stopped and bit her lip. "It's all finished with though, Roger, I mustn't think about it. Granny said it was best. She was t-terribly kind . . ."

He looked worried now. "They're dreams, Anita. You have fantastic dreams."

"No. They're *real*. . . ."

He looked at her searchingly. "You still believe it, don't you?"

"They're real, Roger. I wish they weren't."

He took her hands. "Look," he said. "Look, when we get to London there won't be any need for you to find a job or anything silly like that. You won't even have to get a flat or a place to stay because you'll be at my house. You can stay there as long as you like, it's quiet and nobody will bother you. You'll probably see the priest from time to time, he's a nice old man and he's very interested in you, I've told him all about you. But he won't worry you till you're ready. Now the dreams will go away, you'll see. And if they don't . . . well, there's a friend of Father's. He's a sort of doctor, he'll just come and talk to you and find out all about it and after that there won't be anything else to frighten you. You'll be all right, promise . . ."

Anita's eyes began to open slowly. They grew wider and wider till they looked like bright, shocked marbles. She said, *"What* did you say?"

Roger patted her hand. "Please don't *worry*. I shouldn't have said anything about that perhaps, not just yet. But it'll be all right. I love you, and everyone else will. . . ."

Anita said, "You mean a *psychiatrist!*"

He smiled gently. "Don't think about it any more. Not now. If you need help, we'll help you. We'll all be your friends. . . ."

Anita's hand went to her face and everything, the train, the countryside, time itself, seemed to stand quite still. Anita screamed.

If she'd screamed with her voice, it wouldn't have been too bad. . . .

The sun had gone and night was pushing grey fingers overhead but the rim of the sky was still bright turquoise. Along the horizon was the dark line of the railway embankment. Anita stared back at it one last time then climbed the stile to the road, lifting her left leg awkwardly. The suitcase in her hand felt as if it were stuffed with lead; it seemed she'd carried it half a century. She used her seventh sense fleetingly, just long enough to locate Foxhanger. She detected a whirling world; there were owls and foxes, little scuttling things in the grass, beetles and birds by the score. Queries piped at her and she closed her mind again. She wasn't ready for them all yet; there would be a welcoming, and she didn't feel she could cope. She limped on down the lane, using her human shape as a penance.

The woods were black silhouettes against the flaring afterglow when she met a farm boy. He came walking slowly toward her, whistling to himself. He stopped when he got close, and scratched his head uncertainly. He said, "Evenin', miss. . . ."

Anita felt suddenly dead tired, "Hello," she said, "who are you?" Then before she could stop herself, "I'm lost. And I've got a t-terrible way to go. . . ."

He crossed the road to her, anxiously. "You all right, miss?"

"Yes," said Anita. "Yes, of course. Don't fuss, please . . ."

"Cor," he said. "What 'ave yer done to yer leg?"

There had been the hot bite of barbed wire as she leaped down the embankment. "I just pulled a communication cord," said Anita. "The train made a terrible fuss . . ."

The boy was bending down; she felt his fingers touching. "That's nasty," he said. "That wants wrappin', miss. Real nasty that is, wants seein' to . . ." Anita held her foot off the ground and whimpered. "Yes," she said. "I suppose it does."

The boy found a clean hankie from somewhere and tied it round her knee. The Northamptonshire Controller began to roar for information and Anita referred him tiredly to her Granny. "Come on miss," said the boy. "I'll help yer, give us yer case . . ."

She leaned on him and he put his arm round her. He was strong, and he smelled faintly of hay and earth. "I'm Anita," she said. "I jumped off a train . . ."

"Yer'll git in trouble fer that, miss, can't goo on like that. 'Ave the p'lice on yer in no time yer will. 'Ow far are yer gooin'?"

"Home. To Foxhanger."

"Yer wunt walk orl that way. It ent 'arf a step."

"I know. It doesn't matter . . ." Anita started to cry. "Farmer's boy," she said, "it's awful. Nothing will ever be right again. It's all changing, all the old things are going. They want to cut through Deadman's Copse to get the ironstone . . ."

"I know."

"An' they want to build all out to Foxhanger . . ."

"I know."

"An' culvert the Fyne-brook," sobbed Anita, hanging on and limping.

"Yes, miss," he said quietly. "It's all right, I know . . ."

4: THE SIMPLE FOR LOVE

The night was deepening. Anita leaned at a greater and greater angle; her bosom jostled the boy, and he could smell her hair. At the bend by the Hollis Farm her limp became much worse; and by Major Brewer's stackyard her foot refused to go onto the ground any more. The retreat ended at the stacks, practically for the night.

Anita had discovered the simple for love.

KEITH ROBERTS

5: THE CHARM

SOMETHING WENT *chuzz—clunk,* and Anita felt shooting pains almost everywhere at once. She sat down with a thump and when she could look up she saw she was encircled by a thin chain that had apparently dropped from the oak beneath which she had been walking. She reached toward the chain then snatched her hand back hastily. The links lay in the grass looking harmless enough but she could not touch them. She tried to get up but her legs were too wobbly. She felt terrible; she had never been completely surrounded by iron before.

In the middle of the circle the discomfort was slightly less. Anita wriggled to the focus, turning over in her mind the various spells that might ease her condition. A gentleman rose from behind some nearby bushes. He was rubbing his hands with quite unnecessary satisfaction and smiling genially. He approached the chain and nodded politely.

"Good afternoon to you."

Anita regarded him coldly. "Did you do this?"

"I did. Extremely effective, isn't it? I always find it difficult to believe myself." The stranger's voice was deep and offensively jovial.

Anita grimaced, tried to get up again and thought better of it. "What is it? What's happened to me?"

"It's a witch trap," said the gentleman, circling carefully. Anita felt a quick twinge of fear.

"What did you say?"

"You heard me well enough I think."

"Well I'm . . . I'm not a witch. I was just out for a walk. . . ."

"Very well then; step over the chain and carry on."

Anita's fear turned to rage. She hissed like a kettle, rolling her lips back from her teeth, but the gentleman did not seem unduly depressed. "I can detect witches," he said. "Made a study of them." He reached into a haversack he was carrying and brought out a small instrument. "See?"

"What's . . . what's that?"

"Something I made. It works rather well. Small enough to fit into the pocket if necessary; it'll pick up a witch from at least a mile. Like a sort of psychic scintillometer. I've been watching you for days, that's why I knew you came this way."

"How does it work?" Anita was playing for time.

"That would be telling . . . Now, I want you to do something for me."

"Open the chain then, and we'll talk."

The gentleman laughed. He had a nice laugh, deep and booming. As a matter of fact he was rather nice altogether; he had blue eyes and dimples, he was bearded and blond and very large without being fat. But this was a crisis . . .

"*Open the chain!*"

"No," said the gentleman composedly. "Not until we've reached an agreement."

"But it's *hurting* . . ."

"I expect it is. Witches can't stand iron. I want you to help me before I let you out. Well at least, I want your promise. Witches' honour of course, so you can't recant."

Anita was beginning to feel hot behind the ears with fury. This man knew too much to live. The curse was almost complete but she held it back, applying the finishing touches. The things it would do to him were almost beyond belief. . . . Anita said, "I'll promise anything within reason as long as I can get out of this thing . . ."

"Ah, that's better. Now, this is the proposition. After I've let you out I want you to come over to —"

"*Yahh!*"

Anita half rose, crouching on her haunches, and her eyes went mad and burned blue like lightning. One hand shot out like a claw and sparks crackled toward her persecutor. "May you —"

There was a flash and a roar. The rebound knocked Anita flat. She sat up feeling more dazed than ever. The gentleman was sitting facing her across the chain. He was quite composed but his face was paler than before. His lips were set in a line and there was a red anger-spot on each cheekbone. He said, "You shouldn't have done that. It was deceitful; I expected better of you. If you want a fight you can have one but I must warn you you're in a very bad position."

Anita put her head in her hands. The gentleman relented a little. "You're very lovely but rather inexperienced. A seasoned witch would never have tried a thing like that across iron . . . please agree quickly and I can let you out. I don't like having to hurt you."

"No . . ."

5: THE CHARM

The gentleman sighed. "Then I'm afraid I shall have to take the offensive. I can't let you go without an oath, it would be far too dangerous . . . I'm Sir John Carpenter by the way. You've probably heard of me."

"Haven't . . ."

In fact she had. He was extremely famous and wrote books about witchcraft. Anita swallowed. She was in worse trouble than she had thought. She tried to work a crafty spell under the chain and had to stop because the ground buzzed so uncomfortably. Sir John got up, stepped back a few paces and consulted a book he had taken from the haversack. He began to intone. The words were only a mumble but Anita knew they were a spell. He finished on a higher note, made a dramatic flourish — sure sign of an amateur — and Anita flinched. She felt something although she was not sure what. Sir John put his hands on his hips. "Well then, I can pass material inside the chain quite readily you see . . . what do you think of that one?"

Anita said cautiously, "You haven't done anything."

He shook his head. "You just keep looking."

She stared. Everything seemed the same. The air was warm, a bird sang overhead, the sun shone brightly . . . She whipped round and screamed. She had no shadow.

"No," said Sir John grimly. "And no reflection either, as you'll find when you get home. Everyone will know you for what you are now."

Anita's heart banged. "But I must have a shadow. Otherwise I can't go anywhere."

"Precisely."

"An' . . . an' a reflection. I can't do my hair any more . . ." She wailed, beginning to realize the difficulties of a half-life.

"I expect you'll make out. The spells aren't reversible of course, except by me . . . they were done over the chain."

"Gran will beat me . . ."

"That's your problem."

Anita's lower lip began to tremble. "I want my shadow. I shall be lonely . . . I loved it, it used to do errands for me . . ."

Sir John folded his arms. "You're not going to get round me like that. I've been deeply upset. You tried to disintegrate me; there was no excuse for that, you weren't being badly hurt at all. I don't know what will mollify me now. Remember, I know witches extremely well. . . ."

"Surely there's *something* I can do. . . ."

Sir John put his chin in his hand and brooded at her. Then his eyes started to twinkle. He leaned over the chain and whispered softly. Anita listened frowning, then her face cleared. "Oh, is *that* all . . . Why ever didn't you say before?"

"There are other things. That will do for a start."

Anita began to smile. It was the first pleasant expression she'd used since the trap had sprung. Sir John was really very sweet . . . She said,

[47]

"Witches' honour" with no hesitation at all. Sir John bowed formally and unsnapped the chain. She fled through the opening gratefully, her shadow dancing at her heels.

Anita lay in bed face down, smouldering a little and listening to the birds. After a time she rolled over lazily. The windows were tall and flanked by brocade curtains. The glazing bars cut the blue of the sky very prettily and outside could be seen the twinkling tops of the trees in the drive. Sir John really had a lovely house. Soon she supposed she would have to get up and go home, but not for a while . . . She began to doze pleasantly.

Sir John called up the stairs. "Come on, get moving. Breakfast's in the morning room. When you come through the hall mind the library, there are Bibles there."

"Mmmmmmm . . ."

"Come on, I want to talk to you. You've only done the first part of what you promised, the rest's more fun."

"Mmm . . . never . . ."

"Oh . . . well hurry up anyway."

Anita felt tired and heavy. Quite unable to move. She fashioned a thought and sent it floating downstairs. It asked coyly, *Hair of the dog?* It finished with a large question mark prettily made out of hearts and interlapping ribbons. Sir John ignored it. He must be busy.

The clock on the mantel did say ten thirty. She would have to move. She got up regretfully, leaned on the dressing table for a yawning fit and began to hunt for her clothes. She found a little dressing gown; it was hip-length and belted like a white furry tunic. She fell in love with it and put it on. In the kitchen she was frightened by a self-ejecting toaster and fled to Sir John for comfort but he merely slapped her and sent her back upstairs to bathe and dress. He was evidently very preoccupied indeed. . . .

Some of the tableware was so nice Anita actually carried it through to the kitchen in her hands. She could levitate anything of course but her cornering was lousy. She went back to the morning room leaving the dishes churning busily as they washed themselves. Sir John showed her an amulet. It was large and wonderfully coloured and it had a thin gold chain. Anita wanted it immediately; it would make a beautiful dally . . . She grabbed for it but Sir John twitched it out of reach. "Steady m'dear, it's very precious. You can look if you hold it carefully."

Anita took it, gripping it by the chain and cupping her other hand round it protectingly. The charm was of ivory, most delicately worked. It was ovoid and made like a little cage. Inside were figures. They seemed to be set with jewels of some sort for they sent out blue glitters in the sunlight. It was hard to see them clearly; Anita tried to make out who they represented and what they were doing but it was impossible to tell, they were too fuzzy and vague. She frowned

5: THE CHARM

and looked at Sir John. "What is it?"

His face fell a little. "I was hoping you'd know. It's a magic amulet of some sort and it came from Tibet. That's all I can tell you about it. I want to find out what it does."

Anita nodded. "I know it's magic, I can feel it . . . but I don't know what it's for. I've never seen one like it. I bet my Granny would know. She's terribly good with this sort of thing."

"You can take it and show her if you promise to bring it back."

"Oh I will . . ."

"And afterwards I want you to help me make it work. I know a few spells but nothing very complex."

"Why do you want it to work?"

"I want to write another book." Sir John waved a hand at a library shelf. "I wrote all these. I write books on magic. Nobody believes them of course but they sell like hot cakes. They're all true although that's beside the point."

Anita nodded. There were many books here as well as in the study. Some of them were very old; she could feel the evil spilling out through their backs. She smiled slowly, holding the amulet. "I think you're very clever. You can do so many things . . ."

Sir John twirled his moustache, far from displeased. "Yes, well . . . we won't go into that now . . . Thing is, will you help me?"

"Oh yes. No, wait a minute . . ." Anita's mind ticked. "You have to give presents you know. It's customary . . . I want some presents first."

"You shall have them, within reason of course. What do you want?"

"Well . . . it's my birthday next week, I want a positively enormous card with hearts on it and you can write something nice inside. You know, something full of double meanings."

Sir John chuckled. "That's easy enough . . . what else?"

"A chunky sweater with a cowl collar and three-quarter sleeves, in a sort of goldy-brown."

"All right, I think I can do that."

"An' a white dress with a circular skirt, permanently pleated, sleeveless and with a scoop neckline — women's size — and —"

"Careful, dark thing. You might kill the golden goose."

"Only one more," said Anita, eyes big.

"Go on then."

Anita's voice was a whisper. "An' . . . an' a fly in amber, to look at the night when it's raining. . . ."

Sir John smiled. He crossed the room to a large writing desk, rummaged in a drawer. He said, "Is this what you mean?" He dropped something into her lap.

Anita gasped and held the little ball to the light. The thing inside winked, his eyes flashing fire. The sparks were ten million years old.

"Oh Sir John, thank you . . ."

Sir John ruffled her hair. "Go on then, don't forget your toothpaste

[49]

in the bathroom . . . You can come back and see me when you've found out what the amulet does. Be careful with it." Anita dithered, then tucked the amber into her bra for safe keeping. She fled, clutching the charm.

"Guz back," said Granny Thompson, prodding the winking jewel with her finger. "Or forrard, whichever soots. Dunt mek no odds in the long run."

"Back where, Gran?"

"In time, o' course . . . Wheer d'yer git it?" Her Granny looked suspicious.

"Off a man."

"*Wot* man?"

Anita could be very annoying. She picked up the dally and began to swing it. Reflections from it danced round the room like little blue searchlight beams. "Just a man."

" 'Oo *were* it? Yer dunt git things like that orf any Tom, Dick, or 'Arry."

Anita raised her nose a trifle. "Very well then, he was called Sir John Carpenter."

Her Granny screwed up her face oddly. "Ho, was 'e? Hoity-toity hen't in it, is it? 'Horf Sir John Carpenter,' she says. An' I needn't arsk *'ow* . . . Comin' yer airs and graces . . . Earned that on yer *back,* didn't yer. . . ."

"Gran, there's no need to be crude . . ."

Granny Thompson snatched the amulet, quick as a snake. "Well, yer kent *keep* it. I'll look after it till yer got more *sense.* . . ."

"But Gran you can't; it's his, it was only lent. I promised to take it back. . . ."

Her Granny softened a little. "Orl right then, dunt git yer 'air orf . . . but I'll tek it down a bit fust, it's too *sharp* as it is, it'll 'ackle too much. . . ." She dropped the charm into a small lead-lined pot she kept on the sideboard. Anita had always thought of it as a tobacco jar. "Yer kin 'ave it come *Toosday,*" said Granny Thompson. "It'll 'ave ter *soak.*"

Anita lay with her head against Sir John's chest and let him stroke her hair. He said, "Anita, what does the amulet do?"

"Mmmm . . . it's a Time Charm. It was put in a prayer wheel in a stream . . . it was there a hundred years and every revolution made it stronger. . . . Tell me about myself again."

"Not now . . . Can you make it work for me?"

"Start at my head," said Anita drowsily, "and work down to my toes . . . and don't forget the dimples on my bottom this time, they're one of my best features."

"Anita, can you make it work?"

"Oh . . . tomorrow. Granny gave me a spell . . . she did something to

5: THE CHARM

it so it would be easier to manage."

"I hope she didn't put it out."

"It's still alive," said Anita. "I can hear it singing . . . Now *tell me*. . . ."

"All right. Well, your hair is like the primal darkness, because that was brown and thick . . . and when the lights come on it, they are the first stars. . . ."

Anita wriggled luxuriously. She could stand this almost indefinitely.

Anita wandered across a field with the charm round her neck. She was leading a seal-point Siamese on a tinkling leash. "I let him come," she explained to Sir John. "He knows about things like this." The Siamese howled, looking at Anita with eyes like bits of deranged sky. She stopped under a spreading oak. "I think here . . . it's as good a place as we'll find."

"Doesn't the place matter?"

"I don't think so. Gran would have said . . . The time's important though, we shall have to start at noon."

"GMT?"

"I suppose so . . . what's the time now?"

"Two minutes to go."

"Gosh, we shall have to hurry." Anita unclipped the collar from the familiar. "Go on, Winijou . . . shoo, it might be dangerous." The animal withdrew to a bush and began inspecting the ground for mouseholes. Anita bit her lip and thought for a moment. Then she took the charm and held it out at arms' length. "Scale-of-dragon-tooth-of-wolf-witches-mummy-maw-and-gulf-of-the-ravin'd-salt-sea-shark . . . That's the catalyst," she explained. She could feel the charm twitching, wanting to be set down. Her palms were sweaty. This was the biggest spell she'd ever handled alone; it was a heavy responsibility. Sir John looked anxious. "I hope we don't get knocked into another probability or something stupid like that."

"We shall be all right. Gran saw to it. Hold hands though . . . just for luck," she explained winningly.

He looked at his watch, twining his free hand in hers. "One minute to go."

"You'll have to help me keep time . . . it's a sort of geometric progression, the speed keeps on going up. I shall want the minutes read off."

"Right then. Forty-five seconds."

"Just time to say I love the woolly," said Anita a little breathlessly. She rubbed her cheek against her shoulder.

"The dress is on its way . . ."

"Shh. Get ready."

Winijou stopped moving and began to growl, his eyes on Anita.

"*Noon* . . ."

Anita started off at the gallop hoping she would remember the intricacies of the language. *Om mane padme hum* figured prominently, reversed of course each time. The charm became so heavy it dragged her wrist down. As the little cage touched the grass it began to spin; the chain whirled out, became a flickering circle of light.

"Gosh, don't put your hand near. It's going like a propeller."

Winijou glared; suddenly there was a mouse in his mouth. The little animal's tail rotated in stiff arcs beside his face.

"One minute . . ."

Anita speeded up, feeling she was going to burst for lack of breath. At two minutes Winijou vanished as if somebody had switched him off, and at three they were surrounded by a wide silver bubble through which they could see the field outside. The charm began to whine. The note rose into ultrasonics and the thing continued to speed up. At four minutes Anita collapsed with a gasp and sat thankfully while air whooped into her lungs. Sir John caught her arm.

"Look!"

Over their heads the tree was shrinking visibly. They watched it change to a sapling, then a twig. It vanished, *plop*. Anita gasped.

The charm was invisible now except as a blur. She could feel the wind from it lifting her hair. Sir John looked at it anxiously. "I hope it doesn't decide to shift; it could do a devil of a lot of damage."

"I think it's all right. It knows what it's doing, it wanted to be set down . . . Gosh look, another tree . . ." The thing must have sprung from dust and levered itself upright but that process was too quick to detect.

They saw it vanish into the ground like a turned-off fountain and there was another and another, like green fireworks against the sky. Day and night were already changing too rapidly to be noticed though the sun was making the appropriate fizzing circle. Anita was glad of that; she had read her Wells.

"Can we slow down at all?"

"I don't know. We might . . ."

The amulet wobbled; the chain dropped down and flicked the grass. A man jerked across the field in front of them. He wore a long hat like an old-fashioned nightcap and he carried a basket from which he was casting grain with quick sweeps of his arm. Around him the old furrows on the hills were alive again, the long strips of growing crops looked like allotments. Anita clapped her hands. "This is terrific . . . where are we?"

"The Middle Ages somewhere. Look, the old three-field system . . . Go on."

The amulet snarled with power. Anita was getting the trick of the thing nicely now. The acceleration startled them both; when they next stopped it was night time. A quick touch on the throttle brought the sun up. . . .

5: THE CHARM

"Oh, *look!*"

The soldiers came tramping across the field, arms swinging together. The Eagles nodded at the head of the column; somewhere a drum was beating. The sun winked on brass and polished leather. Short kilts swung, disclosing burly brown knees; the sandals spurned the grass, the great shields gleamed . . .

"They're *fabulous!*" Anita sprang to the side of the bubble. "Look at that one in front, he's their centurion or something . . . Oh, he's marvellous . . . Yoo-hoo . . ." She began to wave and shout but the soldier marched past stolidly, eyes ahead. The column began to recede in the distance. Anita beat the sides of the bubble till she bruised her fists but her Granny had worked well, the thing was like toughened steel.

The next time they stopped there was nothing. The Romans had gone into the future. They went on again, and again.

Nothing . . .

Nothing . . .

There were men, old and ragged, with long hair and beards that blew in the wind. They had axes and knives and as they walked they glared around them warily like animals. The women trudged after, great bundly things with babies humped on their backs.

"Don't like them." Anita turned her nose up. "The men are all right but women have come a long way."

"Steatopygous," said Sir John.

"I don't care, I still don't like them."

Somewhere a man was fashioning the Venus of Willendorf.

"Go on. . . ."

The ice came. Tumbling and booming, great tongues and rivers of it, miles high. Trees and shrubs and hills sprang upright as it retreated. Then it was a blue blink on the horizon and the roaring stopped. Anita shuddered. "Don't like it . . ."

"You mustn't mind. It'll come again. Go on. . . ."

A temperate land. A placid lake in the distance. Chubby horses with long manes, browsing.

"Go on. A long time this time. . . ."

There was a rank smell like a greenhouse. Trees shooting up high as cathedral arches. Their stems looked pulpy and soft and their branches stuck out like diagrams. There was water everywhere; the bubble seemed to float. Anita brushed the trees away with a burst of speed and there were galumphing noises. Herds of Things crossed the horizon. Something flicked past the sun and there was a pterodactyl with a head like a bright nightmare, diving. It brushed overhead leaving a smell like a roomful of old umbrellas. Something was fighting in the swamp. An animal had been wounded. It was tearing great red carpets of skin from its own back and there were fish-things round it, jaws cracking like gunshots. They hurried on. . . ."

"Well I *like* the Cambrian," said Anita. "It's peaceful." They were under the sea now, the surface twinkling overhead. Trilobites moved slowly like outsize woodlice.

"We ought to go back now. There's so much to see on the way."

"No!"

"It isn't wise . . ."

Anita started the charm again. "I want to see the Prime Creation. I want to see if the Void *was* brown."

"Be careful, Anita. You might see God. . . ."

"Oh!" She strained at the jewel. Then she started to pant. "John, it won't stop!"

"It must do . . ."

"It won't, it's run away with itself . . ."

"Well, try. Try hard . . ."

The humming filled the sphere. Anita fell back, face streaming sweat. "It's no use. It wasn't supposed to do that. . . ."

Sir John put his arm round her. "Don't worry, you couldn't help it. Look, look at the stars."

"They're on all the time . . ."

"No, they've gone again now. Volcanoes . . . we're getting near it."

"Look at the hills . . ." They were leaping up and down, quivering. It was like a picture of a piece of machinery moving almost too fast to see. Everything began to shake. There was fire, for centuries. Then darkness . . .

"It *was* brown." Anita's voice sounded tiny, the only thing in existence. "Look, it's just my colour . . ."

"There's nothing anymore," said Sir John, sitting back. "Just brownness and peace, forever."

The charm sang steadily.

Anita cowered. "There's still God . . . but my Prince hasn't fallen from Heaven. Nobody wants me now . . ."

"There aren't any planets . . ."

The sky cleared and became blue. The sun was back, fizzing round. They stared in amazement. "Where are we?"

"Look." Sir John pointed. There were buildings. They were of no colour; the light seemed to dance on them and shift, as if they were made from butterfly wings. Then fire — flick — buildings — fire — flick — flick

"It was another world," said Sir John, awed. "Before everything . . . There can't have been another world."

The buildings reduced themselves, vanished like bright candles sucked into the ground. There were others but they were whiter and lower. Then more. The charm droned, throwing out golden splashes of light. The cities vanished and a tide of green flowed back. Trees flickered up and down. Anita put her hand to her throat. "It's just like now. I mean, it's just like now used to be . . ."

5: THE CHARM

"But we're trillions of years back. Before there was an Earth."

Anita wailed. "The charm. I can't hold it . . ." The little egg wobbled again; the lace touched the grass; the amulet rolled over, turned in an arc and lay still. Anita put out her hand, hesitated then picked it up. Her voice was like wind in grass. "It's done. Burned out. John, what shall we do . . ."

Above them, the oak became.

Winijou howled. Anita turned startled and the cat was watching her with his impossible eyes. In his mouth the tail of the mouse still flicked, more slowly than before. Sir John got up. He said, "It's all right. It's just your cat."

"But it can't be. It can't be Winijou, we're all those years away from him."

Sir John put his hand under her elbow. "That's Winijou. And just over there's your house. And just over there, mine. Nothing's changed." He began to walk away.

Anita tagged after him, not comprehending. When she caught up with him he was muttering to himself. "So one day we shall find a way. Doomsday. We shall reduce the earth to basic slag, to the igneous rocks. It can't be. Yet it will . . ." He looked at Anita as though seeing her for the first time. He said, "I'm glad you liked your sweater my dear. It looks well on you. Still, almost anything would."

Anita tucked her hand in his arm, craning to see into his face and understand him. The charm hung from her wrist but it was dead and dried, she had forgotten it. "We shall destroy the world," said Sir John, eyes on the ground. "So that there can be another, and another. As there have been in the past."

"But this is the past."

"And the present, and the future. All possible futures." He shook his head. "I can't write this. I don't think I can write anything any more."

Anita walked silently, frowning and scuffing at daisy heads with her shoes.

Winijou watched her go. After a time he stopped growling and laid the wet mouse on the grass. He put his paw on it softly, talons spread. He flensed them into it and watched the life of the little creature flare and go black.

"I *tole* yer," said Granny Thompson. "Tole yer it wadn't wuth the bother. Future an' past, I said to yer, there ent no diff 'rence. It dunt mek no odds."

Anita put her hands to her temples. "I feel as if I've been on a great long bus ride. Gran, are you the same . . . I mean, I am in a different world . . . I mean . . . oh I don't know what I mean. . . ."

Her Granny chuckled grimly. "I'm *allus* the same . . . same as you, same as *'im.*" She wagged a horny thumb at the window and Winijou, crouched outside on the sill, drew his claws excruciatingly across the

5: THE CHARM

glass and licked his mouth slowly.

"But Gran is there a beginning, or an end . . ."

"Or does it all *jine,*" said the old lady wonderingly, her eyes bright with mysteries. "Like a circle . . . nothing in the middle but a gret 'oller 'ole. . . ." She saw the amulet still dangling from Anita's wrist. "Well, yer kin chuck *that* uvver the 'edge any'ow, *that's* served its turn."

Anita lifted the little dead thing curiously, looking at the figures inside. They seemed clearer now. She held it to the window, turned it so the light caught it. She gasped, and flung it away from her. It dropped and rolled back across the floor to her feet. The people, she could see them now, herself in her new cowl-necked sweater and Sir John, tiny and laughing. They were trapped hand in hand in an ivory cage, the bars the colour of a rainy sky.

Anita went to Sir John's house a week later to thank him for the dress but the place was closed up and deserted. She never saw him again. She threw the charm into the Fyne-brook. She had thought it was dead, but the steam filled half a meadow.

KEITH ROBERTS

6: THE FAMILIAR

ANITA'S HEELS SKIDDED and she shot down an earth bank that was like a mud slide. She landed at the bottom with an immense splash, shook herself, spat, and sat up half blinded by rain. Her Granny's *"shower o' shavins"* had developed into a cloudburst. Ahead of Anita the Appearance was still visible, capering along like a silver bubble. She scrambled up and rushed in pursuit.

At first the pouring water had been a huge discomfort but now she was completely soaked she was enjoying it. It was fun, almost like swimming. She took a gate with a huge leap and pounded up across the meadow on the other side. The rain was like a grey curtain blotting out everything but the nearest objects; the hiss and drum of the spots was all there was. Anita would have stopped and done something silly like taking all her clothes off but there was no time. On top of the ridge she stopped and flung her head about, laughing at the water that flew out of her hair. Then she ran on again, still following the bubble.

The thing curved away, trying to reach the cover of a thickly overgrown hedge. Anita sprinted and just managed to head it off. It jinked down the slope toward the Fyne-brook.

"Got you . . ."

Anita launched herself full-length, and missed by inches. The bubble spat with rage and turned uphill again. Anita said something unladylike. She was rapidly running out of breath; she made a final effort and managed to herd the Appearance back down to the side of the brook, where it promptly climbed a tree.

Anita wriggled cautiously along a branch, hoping the bubble would not take it into its head to leap for safety. It didn't; instead it retreated, growling ominously, to the swaying tip of its refuge. Anita paused, glaring, her chest still heaving rapidly. Beneath her the Fyne-brook, already swollen by the deluge, churned along swiftly, its surface a rich yellow-brown. The rain roared into it; except for Anita's hard breathing there was no other sound. She crouched with the spots banging on her shoulders and waited. At least she had the thing now; there was no escape. . . .

The bubble seemed to tense; then it sprang forward in an attempt to run over her back to freedom. Anita grabbed desperately, sensing her last chance slipping away. Her fingers gripped wet fur; she screamed with triumph, there was a crack, a falling sensation, a mighty splash . . .

They reached the bank in a smother of laughter and bad language. Laughter from Anita, bad language from the bubble. Anita struggled out of the brook, by now almost deliriously pleased with the state she was in. "Just *look* at me, I can't *get* any filthier . . . an' you can't get *away*." The thing she was holding growled again, then burst into a series of spitting screams. Anita started to run along the bank, holding the ball of rage as far away from her as she could. "If only I knew which bit I'd got . . . I *think* it's his tail otherwise he'd have had me by now . . . I *hope* it's his tail . . . I'm still all right, it *must* be his tail. . . ." She detoured round a clump of hawthorn, skidded again and sat in another puddle. It really was becoming too funny for words . . . Then across the ford (jumping in between all the stepping-stones) and through the meadow to home. She scurried up the path to the back door of the cottage, calling as she went.

"Gran . . ."

"Gran!"

Mowwooowww . . . pshaaahh . . .

"GRAN!"

The door snapped open; the old lady peered out and her jaw sagged. "You . . . by 'Im Wot's Down Under, wot in 'Ell 'ave yer bin *at* . . ."

"Get a box, Gran, I've got him. . . ."

"*Wot?*" Then, "Lor-a-daisy, it's *'im.* . . ."

"Hurry up and get a box, Gran . . . Please, I'm getting *wet.* . . ."

Granny Thompson gobbled faintly, recovered herself and tottered inside. Anita heard her dragging something heavy from under the stairs. Around her the rain still hissed; she was beginning to dance with impatience.

Granny reappeared lugging a tea-chest. " 'Ere, this'll atter do . . . Tek it *steady* then . . . Wot bit ayya got 'olt on?"

"His tail. . . ."

"Yer'll 'ave ter git 'im further *up* then . . . if 'e touches that box 'e'll scraunch round an' 'ave yer . . ."

Pssssshhhh . . .

"Look out then, Gran . . . get out, you're in the way . . ."

"Om gotta git the *lid* orf, ent I . . ."

6: THE FAMILIAR

"Well hurry up, he'll get me in a minute . . . *Yow,* you little swine . . ." He had "got" her.

"Well 'old 'im further up like I *tole* yer . . . git 'is *neckit* . . ."

"If you're so damn smart you do it . . ."

"Not me," cackled the old lady. "Yore done orl right so far . . ."

"Ow you little . . ."

" *'Old* 'im dunt let 'im git orf *now* . . .'

"Well how do you think I . . . YOWWW . . ."

PSSSTTTZZZ . . .

Clunk.

The lid was down; scrapings and snarls sounded from inside. Anita staggered into the cottage and leaned against a wall gasping. The object of the manœuvre might be invisible but the marks of his displeasure most certainly were not. Anita examined her chewed thumb mournfully; a large spot of blood dropped off and splashed on the floor. She panted. "It was the rain, you could see it bouncing off him. I saw him going across the garden . . ."

"Well git out o' my kitchen, stand there *jawin'* . . . Look at orl that muck . . ."

Anita giggled, lifted the front of her jumper insolently and squeezed it. More water pattered down to join the spreading pool round her feet. "We both fell in the Fyne-brook . . ."

Granny Thompson seized the housebrush. "Out, *out!*"

"But Gran, I've got to change, take all these wet things off . . ."

"Well tek 'em orf in the yard. Ent 'avin yer traipsin' through like *that* . . ."

"Gran, I can't do that!" Anita was propelled back outside, protesting.

"Use the coal 'ole then!" roared her Granny. "Fust time I noo yer were that *pertikler* . . ." An old dress came flying through the door. Anita fielded it just before it fell into the mud.

The two witches sat a little mournfully, regarding the tea-chest that was placed on the table between them. "The 'ole trouble *is,*" said Granny, "we're almus back weer we *started* . . . We're *got* 'im orl right, but we kent let 'im *out* . . ."

"Well we shall have to do something," said Anita, pouting. The tea-chest sneezed. "Oh look there, he's gone and caught cold . . ." She patted the box consolingly. It swore at her. "I don't know why you had to spell him up like that. It wouldn't have been so bad if it had been reversible . . ."

"I done it 'cos of Aggie Everett," snarled Granny. "Om lorst too many familiars orlready on *'er* account . . . Snoopin' an' sniffin' round, she ent ever *satisfied.* 'Er place must be a-bulgin' with 'em, an' orl *Thompson trained.* So I ses ter this one, right me lad I ses, Grade Two fer you then we'll see wot we kent fix *up* for yer. Invisible I ses, so she kent git a look at yer; an' impervious ter radar, so she kent git 'olt on

[61]

yer that way . . . an' non-reversin', so if she *does* git yer she kent change yer *back*. That'll fox 'er, I ses . . ."

"Well you might have tried it out on something else first . . ."

"Didn't think to," confessed the elder Thompson. "Never entered me 'ead . . . As fer 'im turnin' into a *sneak thief*, well oo'd a' thort 'e 'ad it *in 'im* . . ."

"All cats are sneak thieves, it's in their nature. And when he found out he could get away with it . . ."

"It wadn't jist the thievin'," moaned Granny. "It were 'is *pranks* . . . 'Owlin' an' gooin' on an' slummockin' acrorst atween me feet orl the while . . . Nearly *went* four times, yisdey. An' then this mornin', little varmint . . . sittin' atop them brussels. I picks the cullingder orf the sink, Maude, I ses ter meself, they're mortal 'eavy fer brussels . . . an' there 'e must a' bin sittin' atop on 'em. *Whoosh*, 'e come up. Flew straight uvver me 'ead. I spins round o' course, flummoxed . . . brussels evrywheer . . . an' the batter, that went orl of a tip down uvver the lot . . . Om mortal glad you *saw* 'im," said Granny. "I couldn't a' stood much more on it I'll tell yer. . . ."

The box mewed dismally.

Anita leaped up and cooed over it. "Poor ickle thing, he must be *starved* . . . Is 'oo *starved*, den? There . . ." There was an airhole in the tea-chest; she tickled round inside it with her finger, then snatched it back hastily as something lashed against the wood. "I'm going to fetch him some food and milk. Poor little thing, he must be simply *dying* . . ." She stared hard at her Granny and swept into the kitchen like a combination of Florence Nightingale and Saint Francis of Assisi. She came back with a plate and jug in her hands, set them down and started fiddling with the lid of the box. Granny Thompson rose hastily. " 'Ere, wot yer a-*dooin'?*"

"I can't feed him without taking him out. There, mother's coming . . ."

"An' om a-*gooin'*," said Granny, heading for the stairs. "Yer gret sorft 'a'porth . . . Jist yer gi' me time ter git *undone,* an' the snib acrorst the bedroom door, then yer kin do wot yer *like*. . . ."

"Well how am I to feed him, if I don't open the box? And he must want to do his little jobs by now."

"If I know '*im*," foamed Granny, " 'e's *done* 'is little jobs by now. Bein' shut away wouldn't stop the likes of 'im. . . . Gret square-'eaded brute, no sense o' *decency*. I should a' knowed better, orl 'e needed were the *charnst* . . ." She pointed at Anita's hands. One slim thumb was already bulky with bandages; underneath, herbs were working like fury. "Look at that," snarled the old lady. "If yer wants another ter *match,* yer a-gooin' the right way ter *git* it. . . ." Anita hesitated, then sighed. She sat down and began to poke little bits of meat through the blowhole of the box.

The night was far from peaceful. From eleven, when Anita retired, there were periodic concussions and flares of light as spell after spell bounced off the tea-chest. At three the uproar stopped and was succeeded by easily the most appalling stench ever to assault a girl's nostrils. Anita threshed about, winding blankets round her face; her Granny had evidently progressed to the field of organic chemistry. At four the cat started wailing with frustration; at five, Granny Thompson started wailing with frustration. At six Anita gave it all up and went out to swim in Top Canal until breakfast. At seven, when she returned, the chest stood outside the kitchen door, slightly scorched but otherwise unharmed. Its occupant was still very evidently unreversed; from inside it came sounds suggestive of an army of little men destroying a calico factory. Anita put her hand to her forehead, and passed in to breakfast.

Her Granny worked till two in the afternoon, but her heart was no longer in it. Her efforts were feeble to say the least; Anita could have done better with one hand behind her back. She knew it was no good trying though; non-reversing spells are proof against virtually anything.

At two-thirty Granny Thompson decided to make one of her rare trips into town; there were certain medicaments she needed before the battle was recommenced. Anita saw her off gratefully to the bus and began to make her own preparations. She laid out the materials she would need, arranging them in rows by the kitchen sink. Later on she would have little or no time to look for things. . . . She went round the cottage closing all windows and doors and blocking the fireplaces with blankets. Then she hefted the box into the kitchen. She donned a heavy coat, a second pair of jeans, Wellington boots and gardening gloves. She sighed, and started undoing the fastenings of the chest. "I'm sorry about this, Vortigern," she said softly. "But it's for your own good. . . ."

She flung up the lid.

Granny Thompson tramped back across the field at just after four. The sun was bright and she was loaded with shopping. She was looking forward to a mashing of tea and a nice cool sit down; the bus had made her feel very hot and fretful. "Queasy gret things," muttered Granny, transferring the adjective according to her own peculiar custom. "*Queasy,* orl on 'em . . ." The cottage came into sight, small and neat, doors and windows tranquilly ajar. "It's summat not t'ave that there gret cat chargin' orl uvver," she soliloquized. "I'll 'ave 'im wi' these." She patted the bottles whose tops protruded from her basket. Visits to establishments as far removed as chemists and ironmongers had yielded some startling compounds. "Settle 'im down," muttered the old lady. "Directly after tea . . ." She pushed open the gate and hobbled up the path.

Granny Thompson's shriek of fear and horror woke Anita readily enough. She'd been half expecting it anyway. She swung her legs off the settee, where she had been resting to recover from the afternoon's exertions, and trotted into the kitchen. Granny was reeling about dramatically, hand clapped to her forehead. A trail of dropped groceries and smashed bottles led from the garden gate. Anita said, "Gran . . ." and swooped a chair under the old lady just in time. Granny Thompson lay back, breathing stertorously and fanning herself with one thin brown hand. "Salts, gel . . . salts . . ."

"Don't be silly, Gran, you're all right now . . ."

"*Salts!*" bellowed the old lady with startling violence. "*I kin feel meself a-gooin'* . . ." She grabbed the green bottle from Anita, wrenched out the stopper and sniffed shudderingly. "Ar, that's better . . . fer a minute I thort I saw — *aaaahhh!*"

A weird face peered round the doorframe. It was a smouldering pink with the exception of one ear, which was a sharp sky blue. The rest of the creature moved stiffly into sight; it had the shape of an enormous and rather overweight cat, but the colours belonged to nothing living. Sunset hues ran over its body in streaks and blobs; near the rump they blended into an obnoxious violet. The tail twitched slightly; the apparition opened its mouth.

Pshawwww . . . fffffttzzzz . . .

Granny Thompson, who had been staring glassy-eyed, jerked convulsively. Bottle and stopper flew out of her hands; the latter jangled noisily across the floor, the former burst with a considerable report. The thing in the doorway swore again.

"Gran, don't be silly, look what you've done . . . It's all right, it's only Vortigern . . . *Gran* . . ."

The old lady was evincing a desire to climb onto her granddaughter's shoulders. " 'Aunted gel, 'aunted . . . I keep thinkin' I see — *wot* were that?"

"I said it was Vortigern . . . I've done it, Gran, he's visible now, he won't be able to play any more tricks. And you've still got him for a familiar, the way you were going on you'd have blown him up or something . . ."

Granny said, "*Eh?*" She edged forward to the door. Vortigern regarded her with technicoloured disgust. Granny Thompson started to chuckle. "Look at 'im . . . done up a treat, ent 'e . . . served out, 'e is . . . an' Aggie Everett, I kin jist see 'er face . . . I'll send 'im uvver, soon as 'e's bin made up . . . She wunt git uvver it fer months . . ." She subsided on the chair again, this time to cackle.

Vortigern watched her stolidly. It was impossible to tell exactly what expression his eyes held, for they had remained invisible; but it was easy to guess. His tail developed three separate kinks of contempt; he spat once more, turned and stalked off. As he walked he banged his feet down so that they sounded like little soft cushions hitting the ground. All cats stamp when annoyed; but *dyed* cats stamp worst of all.

7: THE JENNIFER

ANITA AND HER GRANNY moved along the beach. Anita was wearing a little white lacy top, hipster pants and no shoes. Granny Thompson was dressed in solemn black. A black dress, long and shapeless, a lumpy black coat, thick stockings and black, insecty shoes. Her old felt hat was as ever jammed slantingly on her head and she carried a large and heavy umbrella. Anita capered, cutting circles round the old lady, spurning up the sand in little plumes as she ran; Granny Thompson tramped stolidly, setting each foot down with suspicion and planting it firmly before taking the next step. Her face was set grimly, her lips compressed into a line and she was a little out of breath.

"Excavators," she pronounced, favouring the cliffs above her with a malevolent glare. "Orter 'ave *excavators* up 'em . . . orl them steps, my legs wunt *tek* it I tell yer. Orl right fer you young uns . . . dancin' round showin' yer belly button," snarled Granny, vindictiveness making her personal. "Never seen nothink *like* it. When I were a gel . . ."

"Oh come on Gran, stop moaning. You're always on . . . It was you that wanted the holiday, whee, isn't it fabulous . . ." Anita accelerated, leaving Granny Thompson in the distance.

The old lady scrambled over a pile of rocks with much of the agility of a mountain goat and plumped down in the shade of the cliffs. "I dunt care 'ow yer goo on," she pronounced to the sand and the rock and anybody who cared to listen, "I ent gooin' no further. Be the death o' me, the gel will. . . ." She subsided, mumbling.

Anita was leaning over something way off down the beach. "Gran, there's crabs. They're marvellous!"

"Come away!"

"No Gran, I'm only looking. There's dozens of them. . . ."

"*Come away,*" blared the old lady, rising in wrath. "Or am I gotta *fetch* yer. . . ."

Anita came slowly, scuffing her feet in a hurt sort of fashion. She dropped down beside Granny Thompson and felt how the sun was like a hot spear on her back, pushing her into the sand. She made a variety of luxurious noises, then she sat up and frowned. "Gran, you're turning into a scold. You've been getting on to me ever since we came away. An' it was your idea too . . ."

"Wadn't."

"It jolly well was. Just because you won the pools . . ."

"Ar, I did it too . . ." The old lady's face began to soften. The subject was still a pet one with her even after six months. "And won nat'ral, that were wot I liked. All worked out, no spells, no rune-casting. It all 'inged on the one team, yer see. 'They're done it afore,' I says to meself, 'And they're on their 'ome ground this time,' I says, 'So there ent no reason why —' "

Anita put her face in her hands. "Please Gran, *not now* . . . just enjoy the scenery."

Her Granny glanced up fleetingly at the huge blue dazzle of the sea. " 'Ell of a lot o' worter," she pronounced grimly. That seemed to sum up her opinion. She went off on another tack. "Orl right fer you ter talk. Gooin' on at yer indeed. Never 'eard nothink like it . . . You're bin orf 'ooks wi' me ever since we started. Jist acause I wouldn't 'ave nothink ter do wi' that *siv* idea. Sailin' down in *sivs,* very thought on it sets me rheumatics a-gooin' . . . 'No my gel,' I ses, 'the train fer me or nothink at orl' . . . an' rightly too. Very idea . . ."

"Well, witches *do* sail in sieves. I've read about it."

"Not in my experience," snapped the old lady. "And I dunt goo much of a bundle on them there old fangled ways neither. They ent 'ygenic . . . I only ever 'alf believed that one anyways. I dunt reckon there's a spell as 'ud 'old, not fer no time any'ow. Wadn't nuthink ter stop *you* tryin'."

"I did try. I got one floating on Top Canal, you know I did."

"Yis, an' come 'um in 'Ell of a stew —"

"It was all right till Aggie's nephew opened the lock . . ."

"Molecular tensions," explained Granny a little more kindly. "You 'adn't put enough *be'ind* the spell. Orl right chantin' uvver summat but if yer wants a spell ter *take* yore gotta work it right *inside.* . . . I expect things got uvver-stressed when yer got in the race. . . ."

"I know I got overstressed. I was nearly drowned."

"Stuff," said the old lady firmly. "Wunt ketch no sympathy orf *me.*"

Anita had been digging her arm into the sand, following a little emission moving along a few inches under the surface. She squeaked with triumph, closed her fingers and yanked. The sand-thoughts, that had been all about food and when the tide was coming back, changed correspondingly into a wail of alarm. Anita sat up and opened her fist.

7: THE JENNIFER

The crab waved its claws, located her thumb, took a quick revenge and hopped away, scuttling toward Granny's feet. The old lady removed herself with startling speed. "Ehhh . . . git it *orf.*"

"No, Gran, he's nice. . . ."

"Creepy," said Granny Thompson, threatening terrible things with her umbrella. "Nasty, creepy . . ."

Anita scooped up the crab and put it out of harm's way under a rock. "Nasty," said the old lady, calming a little. "Crawlies . . ."

Anita settled down again with her head on her arms. Things were not going too well. And she'd worked hard for this afternoon too, spending most of yesterday implanting alternative ideas in the minds of the hundreds of people who would otherwise have packed the beach. The job had seemed endless. As she lay, she detected a car in the distance full of sticky children and red faced men with peeling noses and sandwiches and beach pails and towels and transistor radios. Anita turned it hastily into the next bay. She could just as easily have turned it over a cliff, but the sun on her back had made her benevolent. She began to doze.

The callsigns pinged round the rock, echoing soundlessly in the sky along the hot sand. Anita sat up sharply, pointed ears swiveling. She frowned. There was nothing to see. The VHF continued to sound. Anita put her head on one side. All the codes were new to her. . . . She looked at her Granny. The old lady was huddled in blackness, the umbrella spread above her like an incubus. Her eyes were closed, her mouth slightly ajar. She looked like an old grounded bat at the foot of the cliffs. Anita tested cautiously but she was really asleep. Miss Thompson stood up, flicking sand from herself absentmindedly. Whatever was moving was taking bearings on the headland. And there was a Controller too, though she was not sure where. She'd heard him clear the newcomer through the three mile limit. Anita began to walk along the beach, trying to gauge where the stranger would make a landfall.

The signals moved in until they were muffled by a great slanting headland. Anita was puzzled until she saw the cave mouth. It was well hidden under a sloping rock. She wormed her way through into darkness. It was cool inside and she could hear the great wash of the sea. She switched to sonar. Her mind built up a colourless picture of the things ahead of her. She moved forward until she saw daylight again. It was green and suffused. There was a hidden pool. Light from a rock-arch was striking up through the water. The waves boomed loudly inside the cliff.

The mermaid surfaced almost under Anita's nose and there was mutual panic, a quick fluttering of consternation. Both creatures froze, and for some seconds there was a danger the sea-girl would submerge again and streak away. Anita, mouth open, sent cautious friendship-signals but there was no response. The mermaid lay in the water, rising and falling in the backwash of the waves, and Anita stayed crouched

[67]

on one knee, hands flat on the rock in front of her.

Then she moved to the edge of the water, one limb at a time. She leaned out. The mermaid came toward her across the pool. Their noses touched; they jumped, and their bodies began to quiver all over. Signals raced frantically; two minds found a wavelength mutually agreeable, and locked onto it.

"— beautiful!" Anita bubbled with enthusiasm. "You're absolutely beautiful. Beautiful hair, don't you ever cut it? How do you comb it? Can you make ships sink? How deep can you swim?"

"Who are you?"

"Anita Thompson, from Northamptonshire."

"Where's that?"

"Miles away. There isn't any sea."

"Ugghh! Did you make the beach safe?"

"Yes."

"You've got *legs!*"

"I know. They aren't as nice as your tail."

"I want legs. . . ."

"You can get them. I read a story about it. You have to sell your soul . . . our people would probably take it, and they give good discounts. They'd probably let you keep a bit of it for yourself."

"That wouldn't work. . . ."

"I could fix it," said Anita proudly. "I'm in the Trade. . . ."

"It isn't that, the story's wrong. We don't have souls."

"Oh dear, how awkward. . . ."

The mermaid turned about in the water; her hair slid across Anita's hand as she dabbled. It was yards long and green but it didn't feel slimy. It was soft and fine like silk. The mermaid's flesh was green too, or bluish, it was hard to tell in the half-light. Her body looked translucent and as if there were little lamps set inside. Her arms were long and slender and so supple that all her movements looked like dancing. Anita chortled. "Are there many of you?"

"Quite a lot. Only we never land now because there are always crowds of people."

"I say, you're phosphorescent! Are you always like that?"

"Only for one month in the year." The mermaid rolled in the water, smacking her tail and making gunshot noises, wriggling her shoulders and looping her body. She was as supple and stretchy as a worm.

"Why for only — oh, it's all right, I expect I know. I'm glad I don't go like that," said Anita, "it would be jolly awkward . . ."

The mermaid began to boast. "I've got a new hat of anemone petals. An' a sea-coal necklace. I can fetch dolphins and whistle for storms. My sister mated yesterday and she's gone to live in the Gulf of Guinea. And I've got a cousin in the Caribbean, I'm going there for the winter . . ."

"I can work spells too . . . Where are your gills?"

"Behind my ears. You can't see them till I'm under water, then

7: THE JENNIFER

they're feathery."

"I want to come and see where you live. I say . . ." Anita sat up. "How far down do you go?"

"About a hundred fathoms usually."

"No, I don't mean that. I mean how far down do you go before you change?"

The talk became technical but very interesting.

Granny's thought boomed round the cave. *THERE y'are, yer young varmint . . . Shift yerself, I want ter goo back UP . . .*

Coming, Gran . . .

And change wavelengths, will yer? Piping round up there, squawkin' like a bat, meks me 'ead goo funny . . .

The mermaid was wincing. "Who's that, on the Earth?"

"My Granny. She's cross because she's away from home. She's all right really."

"Will you come to see us?"

"I don't know, I can't just now . . ."

"We've got a great city under the water, you'd love it."

"Granny won't let me . . ."

"The streetlamps are sea-lilies," whispered the mermaid persuasively.

"I'd love to come . . ."

"I'll come back tomorrow, I think I can get you a clearance."

"Do you have Controllers, like we do?"

"We call them Wardens. There's one at Dancing Ledge. I expect you heard him talking me in."

"Are you sure he won't mind about me?"

The mermaid rolled on her back and arched her body so that the water poured off it. "He's nice. He won't mind." Anita started to chuckle. Things weren't so very different in the s—

ANITA!

"I've got to go. See you tomorrow. Please don't forget."

"I'm a Dorset mermaid," said the sea-thing. "I'll be here. Some of us aren't so particular about promises. Don't mix me up with those Scottish creatures." The tail boomed, sending spray flying and making Anita spit like a cat. Then the mermaid was gone.

"Fer the sake of 'Im Wot's Down Under," moaned Granny. "No . . . I kent 'ave you gallivantin' orf everywheer . . . the lock were bad enough, yer nearly got *drownded* in that. An' now yer wants ter goo slummockin' orf under orl that worter. . . ."

"But Gran, the lock, yesterday you said —"

"*Yisdey,*" pronounced Granny Thompson firmly, "were *yisdey*. An' I dunt care *wot* I said anyways. It ent the same, you'd be drownded fer sure, gooin' orf to Americky an' such places . . ."

"I'm not going to America. That's only where her cousin lives."

[69]

"You ent gooin' *nowheer.* Ehhh . . . sea-wotsits." Granny shuddered theatrically. "I dunt 'old with 'em. Creepy crawly nasty things. Like them there crabs, puts shudders up yer ter *look* at 'em, let alone slummocking about with 'em, 'aving 'em crawl orl uvver yer . . ." She shivered again. "Nasty, 'orrible creepies. . . ."

"But Gran, she isn't like that at all. She's fabulous. She's got a wonderful face, sort of thin and sharp like a cat, and her hair's green and it's miles long and down below she's nearly like us but not quite, she's got lovely little —"

"NO!" bellowed the elder Thompson. "Once an' fer orl, *no!* Yer kin goo orf an' *talk,* seein' as yer promised, but that's *orl.* Though I dunt esspect she'll waste 'er time comin' back. Fish . . . nasty, slummocky things, ent no good fer familiars ner nothink. 'Ere today an' gone tomorrer, you orter know that, yore tried with 'em times enough. . . ."

But Anita was already running off along the beach. The signal was coming in; her Granny would have heard it too had she not been so full of her own complaints.

"I can manage gills I think," said Anita. "I suppose I *could* do a tail . . . I won't of course, it wouldn't be polite. I don't know if I can swim deep enough though, it seems an awful long way."

The Jennifer waved her flukes thoughtfully. She was lying on her stomach in the shallow water and Anita could see the big curve where hips became tail. "I'll send the Serpent. You'll need a bridle to hold, he goes terrifically fast. It'll have to be tonight though, he's going away in the morning. He's going to some terrible place in the Pacific, to one of the Deeps. It's a sort of call he gets from time to time. We don't understand him, he's so old."

"Are there many serpents?"

"There's only one," said the mermaid, awed. "There's only been one since the start of the world. He was the first thing ever . . . whatever you do you mustn't be rude to him. He's so old . . ."

"Oh I won't. . . . But I can't get away. Granny says no."

"He'll come to Durdle Door," said the sea-girl. "He'll meet you when you swim out. He'll know you're there, and who you are. He knows everything there is. . . ."

"Mermaid . . ."

The mermaid rolled over and lolloped into deeper water. "I'm going now before your Grandma calls. I nearly lost my detector stage yesterday. Come if you can." She hung onto a rock while the waves washed up and down showing her breasts. "I've got a scarf of Sargasso weed. And a nautilus shell to wear in my hair when I mate . . ." She submerged, and the undertow took her out to sea.

It was evening and the water was like a golden shield. Anita wandered disconsolately along the beach, splashing into the sea and

7: THE JENNIFER

back, head hanging. There was no way to do the thing. Her Granny was adamant, and she was the only person Anita couldn't spell. It would have been courting disaster to try. . . . She would have to go back soon, she could feel irritable thoughts rapping at her mind with horny knuckles. Granny Thompson was getting restless already.

Wait a minute though. Was there a way? Anita stopped in her tracks and stood thinking furiously. It might work . . . it *would* work, she was sure of it. But there was no time to lose, not a second. She ran down to the edge of the water, grabbed a double handful of wet sand, then another. She built them into a mound, started to shape it . . . When the work was halfway through she used a quick spell and after that it was easy because the sandgrains themselves were helping her. She finished the simulacrum, stood back, concentrated; the charm "took" with a pop and the figure sat up jerkily. Its colouring was a little wrong but that was only to be expected; apart from that was as like Anita as a twin. She laughed, and the sand-girl opened her eyes. "Hello," she said dreamily, "I know what you want me to do." She got to her feet and tried to walk. The first steps were very jerky but her balance rapidly improved. Anita clapped her hands and a thought brought seaweed whirling out of the water, shredding it as it came. It fell around the sand-girl making little pants, a lacy top.

"Thank you," said the double softly. "Shall I go along and see to Granny now before she starts shouting?"

"Yes . . . No, wait a sec. Your hair's all mussy, mine's never like that. Here, let me . . ." She worked deftly. "That's more like it. But you'd better take my comb, don't let yourself get untidy. Now stand still a minute, you're not *quite* right. . . ." Anita turned the model sideways-on, backed off and squinted, still frowning. "I *thought* so . . . there!" An adjustment happened under the sun-top. "Now keep your tummy in," said Anita anxiously, "and don't run flatfooted, stay on your toes. . . . All right, off you go."

"Have fun," said the sand-girl. She turned and trotted along the beach. Anita watched herself for a few moments, admiring the way her hips were swinging. For a rush job, it wasn't bad at all. . . . She dusted her hands and walked off in the opposite direction. The first thing was to get to the road.

There was no trouble about the lift. Anita leaned prominently on a bus stop and wagged a slim thumb at the first motor that came along. She didn't even have to throw a spell at it. The car dropped her topside of the Lulworths but she soon found another that was going to the coast. She was at Durdle Door by sunset.

There were still people about but Anita didn't care. She sat by herself, hugging her knees and watching the water. She was suffering the sort of excitement that improves indefinitely with keeping. She could have been picked up three times, by a soldier on furlough from Blandford Camp, by two boys with a cabin cruiser at Weymouth and by a discontented skin diver who'd lost his harpoon, but for once she was deaf and blind. In the afterglow she climbed the clay scree into the bay. It was horseshoe-shaped and surrounded by tall cliffs. The strata turned over until they entered the water vertically; the stone seemed to be pouring into the sea. In front of her was the Door itself, fretted through a vast island rock. Beyond it the sea, alive with diamond winkings, with reflections and flashes and restless lozenges of colour, cobalt and turquoise and aquamarine, all the blues with lovely names. The sea boomed, deep echoes hummed around the cliffs. It might have been the surf in hidden caves but Anita knew there was a blue man under the water, beating great drums.

She undressed when the bay was dark and the rock window framed a colour so intense it made a halo against the stone. Her clothes were forgotten almost before she had dropped them. She walked into the sea, edging around boulders, feeling her toes scrinch in shingle and sand, panting as the water deepened and splashed up her front. Then over a shelving white rock face until the sea slid cool across her shoulders. She swam, kicking softly, guiding herself through the corridor till she felt the movement of the real waves outside. She settled into the tireless rhythm that drives a frog. There were no sea-things that swam like that but the frog-stroke served. When she turned the land was dark behind her and a long way off. She trod water and called softly.

"Serpent . . . Serpent . . ."

Perhaps he was waylaid; maybe some ASDIC finger had prodded him and he'd gone deep to lie under silent routine till the hunt was over. Maybe he'd been too old and wise to listen to the Jennifer. . . . Anita called again, louder this time, conscious of all the black water beneath her.

"*Serpent* . . ."

There was a rumbling that grew to a roar, a burst of phosphorescence that looked a mile long, and he was there. Anita soared and dropped in the great waves that rolled back from him. But he was so big, she'd never dreamed he would be as big as that . . . he was like a reef in the night sea, the swell of his back was curving against the sky and all the length of him was alive with rivulets of turquoise light. . . . His skin was craggy and knobby, wrinkled and rough, his flat head rose towering, his tail stretched away forever. The sea touched him softly, muting itself because he was so old. Anita paddled toward him and the head snaked down till the eyes could see her and those eyes were a yard across, bulging and smooth as black mirrors, and there was everything in them, everything there had ever been in the world. Anita wanted to hug him but he was so huge, so huge. . . .

He nuzzled at her and she saw a harness, the great stems of tangleweed knotted and twisted to make a handgrip behind his head. She took hold, winding the fibres round elbow and wrist. He rumbled and began to move, circling out from the coast. His speed increased;

7: THE JENNIFER

Anita's hair streamed, elbow and shoulder cut swaths in the sea, water flew yards in the air to fall back twinkling into the huger turbulence of his wake. Anita screamed to him and his head dipped, the surface of the sea rushed past her and there was a void, cold and noisy with bubbling. The monster's body canted; pressure rose, like hands squeezing Anita. She chanted mechanically, drowning a little; at a hundred feet she gasped with relief and began to breathe again. Her gills opened, trailing back from her neck like pink chiffon scarves.

The Serpent's body wagged like a metronome, pulses flowing along it seconds apart. Anita sensed the sea bottom dropping away, peaks and hill-ranges flicking beneath, wide curving valleys of grey silt. Then there was no bottom that she could detect. Instead far below was a pulsing, a greenish glow like city lights seen through a coloured fog. It lit the white throat of the Serpent and his long belly. Reflections sparked in the great dish of his eye. The speed was gone; he was sinking slowly and Anita knew from the surface he would already look frog-small, a speck falling into a hugeness of light.

And his voice sounded in her mind like an organ as he began to tell her how the hills were made.

8: THE MIDDLE EARTH

IT WAS STRANGE how Anita knew instantly that the young man was a ghost. He looked solid enough but there was no doubt at all that he wasn't real. Anita was interested; ghosts are not very common. She dropped down beside him on the grass. "Hello," she said cheerfully.

He turned and stared in amazement. "Good Lord," he said. "You can see me. I mean . . . well, you can see me!"

Anita laughed. "Why shouldn't I be able to see you?"

He frowned. "Well, because . . . you know, because of what I am. But you aren't a normal girl, are you?"

"No," said Anita briefly.

There was silence between them for a time. The Fyne-brook chuckled; they were sitting beside it, where an overhanging willow cast a pleasant shade. Weed swayed in the current; a fish darted upstream; beside the bank a patch of whirligig beetles danced like demented pearls. Anita studied the ghost covertly. He was rather nice; he had long dark hair that hung over one eye, he was wearing a doggy sort of sports jacket with a quietly checked shirt and neat tapered slacks. He made her think of moonlight nights and MGs and the smell of tobacco. "I'm Anita," she announced. "Who are you?"

He was very well-spoken and his voice was quiet. He said, "David Fox-Gardiner. Or at least I *used* to be David Fox-Gardiner. I haven't got a name at all of course now. I'm just a sort of clerking error." He looked up and smiled. His eyes were brown and they were full of pain.

Anita hesitated. Ghosts can be very difficult to deal with. She said, "Why are you here? I mean, is there any real reason . . ."

"No." David was staring at the water again. "I'm not haunting the place or anything stupid like that. In fact the place is rather haunting me." He pointed upstream then down. "Do you realize there are fourteen voles in this brook between the bend up there and that big alder tree? Seven holes in this bank, curiously enough, and seven in the other. And two small pike . . . oh, and there's an otter; I didn't think there were any otters near here. And there are about two dozen hedgehogs and thirty-eight bats, nine species of dragonfly, two kingfishers . . ."

"You've been here a long time," said Anita softly.

"Not really. A couple of weeks . . . but there's a lot of time in two weeks, when you're not sort of sleeping or anything."

"Yes. I know."

David pointed to the gable of a house just visible among distant trees. "To be perfectly frank I'm here to be close to that place. It doesn't do any good but at least it's *something*. I mean, it's better than just wandering about. That's totally aimless."

Anita shaded her eyes with her hand. "That's the Dog and Pheasant at Brington. Do you — did you know someone there?"

"Yes. Margaret Davis. Her people keep the pub. Do you know her?"

"I'm not sure. . . . is she sort of tall and blonde and rather nice?"

"Yes. . . ."

"Then I do. She's sweet."

"We were going to be married."

Anita said, "Oh dear. . . . oh, that was bad luck. Would you like to tell me about it?"

The ghost shrugged. "There isn't much to tell. And what there is is rather sordid and very stupid indeed. When we got engaged I wanted to celebrate so I went on the booze with some friends. We all got pretty stinking. It was just one of those things, we didn't mean to have such a terrific jag. And then I tried to drive home. I was coming across the Plain — I used to live in Wiltshire, in Amesbury — and it was a gorgeous sort of night and there was the road stretching out in front and I thought I'd see if I could get the old motor flat out."

Anita nodded. She knew the feeling well. "Was that how you got killed?"

"Yes. Thank God I didn't have anyone with me. I made a fearful mess of old Lottie. . . . that was the car. Rolled her. I died almost instantly." He banged his knee in sudden rage. "Oh what a silly, clottish thing to do. . . ."

"It was very bad luck," said Anita. "Terribly hard. Where are you buried?"

"In the village. I was sorry about my parents. It was rotten seeing how upset they were and not being able to tell them I was all right. Of course I *wasn't* all right. I'm not all right now. I'm about as wrong as a thing can be."

"Is there anything I can do?"

8: THE MIDDLE EARTH

"I shouldn't think so for a minute. Could you exorcise me?"

"NO! And in any case I wouldn't if I could. That's cruel. . . . I should have to call you a sooty spirit from Tartarus and all sorts of stuff like that and . . . well, you're not. . . ."

David smiled. He put his hand out and for a moment it looked as if he was going to lay it over hers, then he changed his mind and drew back. He said, "It's nice to have someone to talk to anyway, even for a few minutes."

"Did you come back all this way because of Margaret?"

"Yes. It took me a little while to find out how to do it. You know, how to move about. I came as soon as I could. In a way I wish I'd never come back at all. Poor Margaret, she cried for days. She isn't really over it yet. I think that's almost the worst part of being dead. Knowing you've hurt so many people, and not being able to do anything about it. The rest's all right I suppose. It's just dull. Like when I was in the army. Having to sit around all day with nothing in particular to do."

Anita changed the subject slightly. "What sort of motor did you have?"

"Austin-Healy three thousand. She was a jolly nice car. She isn't any more though. They've got her in a scrap place in Salisbury. She's written off, they're selling her in bits and pieces. And it wasn't necessary, I went over and had a look at her and her chassis isn't twisted, she's not half as badly damaged as she seems."

"If it would make you feel any better," said Anita, "I'd go down there and buy her. I don't like things being knocked apart either."

"It wouldn't do any good," said David hollowly. "She's nearly stripped already. There isn't very much left of her. When you think of it though, there isn't much left of anything. Not even me."

Anita was watching him narrowly. "You poor thing," she said suddenly. "You still want her, don't you?" She didn't mean the car.

David put his face in his hands.

"This is awful," said Anita. "I've never heard anything like it!" Her whole attention was engaged now. "You've been sitting here watching the fish in the brook and the bats and dragonflies and you can't move away and all the time . . . Oh, that must be awful. . . ." She felt her eyes begin to sting. Humans can usually do something about their circumstances but ghosts suffer huge disadvantages. "I could try and speed up your clearance," said Anita. She knew his papers couldn't have been in order, otherwise he would have been shipped out directly without any time for moping.

"I don't *want* to be cleared," said David. "I don't know what I do want. I want my car but it's all wrecked. I want to be alive again but it isn't possible. Could you put the clock back?"

"Yes, but it wouldn't be a scrap of good. You'd only be killed again when it came forward. . . . You could still go to her you know, if you're really desperate."

David took his hands away. His face looked awful. He said, "I know. But it wouldn't be the thing to do, would it? I mean . . ." He hesitated. "It just wouldn't be cricket, would it . . . ?"

Anita shook her head. She said softly, "A ghost once loved a lady fair . . . Yes, I think I can understand."

"So there isn't an answer," said David a little wildly. "I'll just sit here and count vole-holes and watch the water go by and I suppose everything will come right in the end. Only there isn't an end really, not any more. . . . You'd better run along now, Anita, I'm sure you've got a lot of more interesting things to do. Thank you for speaking to me."

Anita stayed where she was, lost in thought. She said suddenly, "Would I do instead?"

"What?"

"Instead of Margaret . . ."

"You don't know what you're saying!"

Anita pushed off one sandal and dipped her foot in the brook. There was long weed trailing on the surface of the water. She stirred it, enjoying the sensation. She said, "I'm quite good really. Of course if I'm just not your type . . ."

"I wouldn't think of it!"

Anita could be very delicate when she chose. "I know it wouldn't be the same," she said gently. "I just thought it might take your mind off things for a while. I'm sorry."

David swung round. "It isn't that, honestly. I think you're . . . well, rather nice. But don't you see, it wouldn't be fair on you either. You know, the touch of cold dead flesh and all that . . ." He sniffed his jacket sleeve and looked more doleful than ever. "Fusty," he explained with an apologetic smile.

Anita shuddered. "I see what you mean . . . I don't suppose it would really work. We should both be uncomfortable . . . But I must do something, David. I can't just leave you here being . . . rained on, an' blown about by the wind . . . I wouldn't rest, not now I know about you."

"Well, there isn't anything you *can* do."

Anita stood up. "I can try. I'm going to see our Controller."

"He won't help."

"He jolly well will, he's got to. He looks after all the Dark Things in the county, he's bound to be responsible for ghosts." She began to walk away. "Try not to be too lonely," she called. "I'll go and see him as soon as I can. Promise . . ."

"So that's the whole story, Controller," said Anita simply. "An' I came along to you to —"

"*Gee-six,*" said the Controller furiously to the empty air. "I told you area gee-six, you can't cross to Leicestershire . . . No I *won't* clear you.

8: THE MIDDLE EARTH

You know the rules as well as I do, twenty-four hours' notice for a county boundary . . . What? I don't *care* what you think, Ducky, over and *out*. . . ." He muttered to himself. "Old days, old days, it was always better in the old days. That's all I hear, whining about the old days . . . let 'em all Timeshift, see if *I* care. By Golly . . . Cee-kay-nine-four-zero-fifty, you are cleared for Huntingdon, happy landings . . . Come in oh-fife-four . . ."

Anita sighed hopelessly and crossed her legs. She had been talking for nearly half an hour and she had only just got round to telling him what she wanted. The evening air was chaotic with messages, and most of them were passing through this room. Anita's mess of senses detected a roar of silent conversation. She unravelled a strand and followed it.

Four pun, ten? snarled Granny Thompson. *Fer that gret mangy brute o' yourn? Om 'ired better familiars than 'e'll ever be fer thirty bob a week Aggie, an' well you knows it* . . .

The Controller was an odd-looking young man with jet-black, oiled-down hair and angry ginger eyes. His desk took up what little space was left among the amplifiers that lined the room. They covered the walls nearly to head height, their grey facias alive with little red and blue lamps. Anita knew that between the conventional aerials on the roof of the place were other arrays, odd little things like silver chrysanthemums. The signals that poured in from them never would be traced. . . . "Controller," she said, "you just don't understand."

He pushed the 'phones back from his ears and looked at her as if she had just that moment walked in. "Sorry, Ducky," he said, "Not my department. He'll have to do like the rest of 'em. Wait for his clearance."

"But he can't do that . . ."

"*Gee-six,*" roared the Controller in sudden passion. "By the Green, if I have to report you . . ." He swung his feet up on the desk and propped his chair dangerously on its back two legs. "No, by Golly," he said to Anita, "definitely nothing to do with me. I'll send a report down but don't expect — don't *do* that!" Behind him his popsy was watching smokily and chewing a nail. He contrived to reach up and slap her wrist without overbalancing himself. "Trouble with you people," he snarled, "you seem to think we've got time to burn. What you don't appreciate, what nobody appreciates, is *we've* all got businesses to run." He waved his hand at the amplifiers. "Half of this stuff *is* radio mains and it don't look after itself, by Golly it don't. Stop it . . ." Another slap. "Now you just run along, Ducky, I'll get the report off."

Anita thought vindictively that she should have brought Granny Thompson along. The old lady would have settled this character within minutes. . . . She spread her hands. "But that'll take years. And David told me he met somebody who got mislaid in the eighteenth century and he's *still* wandering about . . ."

"If you don't stop," shouted the Controller to his popsy, "I'll tie your hands behind your *back* . . . Kay-nine-oh-seven, your bearing is Green, repeat Green, fife-zero . . . height three-fife-zero, airspeed forty knots, crosswind of . . . three-zero, hold your course and speed . . ." That evidently to a high-flying familiar.

"Please, Controller —"

"Errors," roared the young man. "Mistakes. Mislayings. Errata. Nothing but *errata.*" He opened his hot-brown eyes wide then screwed them up again as if in pain. "As well as running a relay service, as well as pandering to the slightest whim of every bumbling idiot in thirty covens, I have to start progress-chasing every fouled up crossover in the district. Try again, Ducky," he finished offensively. "Uncle is busy. . . ."

Anita had taken two whole hours over her hair and she was wearing a brand new white dress with matching accessories. She'd thought she couldn't lose. She hitched another six inches of leg into view but the Controller merely sneered. "He's lonely," said Anita in a last bid. "And the rain falls on him, and the wind blows through him, and he hasn't got anybody. And he's hopelessly in love . . ."

"I," bellowed the Controller, "am hopelessly in love. Hopelessly in love with peace and quiet . . . I am also lonely, I am also depressed; and odd though it will probably seem, when the rain falls on me I get *soaked* . . ." He slapped the popsy's wrist. "*Will* you stop!"

Anita lost her temper. She stood up violently; his heels were poised on the very edge of the desk and the transmitted shock was disastrous. "Well I shall just have to find somebody who *can* help him," shouted Anita. "Somebody who knows what they're doing. Somebody who isn't a loudmouthed *nit* . . ."

The young man was still getting up, assisted by the popsy. He said dazedly, "You can't say a thing like that. Not to *me* . . . I'm the Northamptonshire Controller . . ."

"Controller?" shrieked Anita in a voice like a buzz-saw hitting a knot. "You couldn't control a sick headache. You couldn't control a riot in a cathouse . . ."

The popsy jumped as if she had been stung, and began to chew furiously.

The Controller looked shattered. The chair had been set to rights; he collapsed into it. "You can't walk in and say that," he moaned. "It just isn't done . . ."

Anita pressed her advantage. "But I *did* walk in, and I *did* say it, and now I'm walking *out* again, and you can report me to just who you like. And don't forget to say what I called you because if you don't *I will* . . ." She reached the door and flung a final insult. "And all I know is, if you're as good at radio mains as you are at your proper job, I'm glad we've got a *transistor* . . ."

"All right," hollered the Controller, beaten. "All right, all right." He saw what the popsy was doing and slapped her wrist. He hauled books

8: THE MIDDLE EARTH

from a shelf. Three vast tomes. He threw them in different directions. One hit Anita in the middle; the impact drove her backwards. "We'll all look," swore the Controller, lilac with rage. "We'll *all* go through the files. We'll find him a mate on the proper energy-level. Then we'll put them *both* through the keyhole (trade term for hyperspace) and that'll be the *end* of it. Then we'll all sit round and invent reasons why I shouldn't be *fired* for exceeding my authority . . ."

Anita began to purr. "Why, Controller," she said sweetly, "I always *knew* you'd help . . ."

The room became busy with turning pages. "How about this one?" asked the popsy, displaying unexpected energy. "Died 1873, age twenty-one . . . still in limbo, some error on her death certificate. A bit before his time but she's got a pretty good figure."

Anita looked at an ancient daguerreotype. "She's very sweet but she wouldn't really be suitable. He loves cars and things like that, it would drive him *crazy* having to explain everything to her."

"Nineteen forty," said the Controller, pushing across a photograph. "Killed in a riding accident. More his type I should think. She's still held up waiting for a cee-thirteen. People down under lost her entire file . . ."

Anita frowned. "I don't really think so . . ." A live girl with buck teeth and pimples might take refuge in simply being homely or a good cook but for a ghost that was out of the question.

"How about this?"

"This" was quite a peach; the picture attached to the filing card showed a blonde girl in a fluffy party dress. The Controller shrugged. "Okay by me . . ." The popsy's hand strayed to her mouth and he smacked her wrist absentmindedly. He was thumbing through a small black pocketbook. He stopped, peered, checked a reference number and swore. "She was cleared yesterday. Shouldn't be in the file . . ."

Anita clicked her fingers in disgust, skimmed through yet more pages. She stopped. Oh, but this was it. This was most decidedly the one. What a beautiful girl . . . she hadn't known there were so many attractive ghosts available. She said, "How long has this one been . . . er . . ."

"About a month. She's still nearly fresh. Devil of a mix-up there, if you'll excuse the irreverence . . ."

"What a shame," cooed Anita, smoothing the photograph. "Look at her little bobbed nose . . . Poor little thing, how did it happen?"

The Controller slapped the 'phones back over his ears. "She died of a fever," he warbled tunelessly, "And no one could save her . . ." The popsy began to chew and Anita knocked her hand away.

"She'll be the very thing. Can you send for her, Controller?"

"Huntingdon Department Nine?" said the Controller, "hold the ether, I have a call for you . . . you don't *send* for ghosts, Ducky, you *drive* 'em where you want them to go. Most of 'em have lost what small wit they

[81]

possessed anyway, read your Homer . . . I'll get her to you if you set up the crossover."

"I will. When do you want it to be?"

"Willco," said the Controller. "Go ahead caller, you're through."

"It'll have to be done properly or we shall have two of them mooning about the Fyne-brook and I don't think I could stand that. She's probably got an Earth-lover as well . . ."

"Fife-four-oh-fife," said the Controller, "you are not, repeat *not*, cleared for landing. Keep in the stack there *please.*"

Anita banged the book. "It's like a *madhouse.*"

"It *is* a madhouse," howled the Controller, incensed beyond all reason. "That's just what it *is*."

"*But when will you send her?* I've got to know for the spell . . ."

"Off peak hours," roared the Controller. "Oh-four-hundred tomorrow. Transfer oh-four-thirty at the outside."

Anita gulped, grabbed for handbag and gloves. "I shall have to run, I've got masses to do . . . Thank you, Controller, thank you very much."

"Don't *thank* me," swore the servant of Hell. "Just don't come *back.*"

"Oh I won't . . . goodbye . . ."

The door slammed behind Anita. Through it floated a last shout. "For *God's* sake girl, don't *chew* . . . remember the Venus de Milo . . ."

Anita pursued a double-decker bus for a hundred yards down the street, put on an appalling burst of speed and caught it as it slowed for a corner. She landed aboard to the delight of its passengers and the fury of its conductor.

The fields by the Fyne-brook were black and wet with dew and mist was floating waist-high, making a setting fit for ghosts and prowling things. Anita crouched over a cauldron hastily improvised from half an oildrum and a blowlamp. She was wearing her spellraising trousers and her heaviest sweater. She shook powders into the pot, and various shriveled odds and ends. There were small rumblings and concussions. Anita's eyes shone in the dark like twin moons; this particular spell had affected her strangely. It was a nasty affair that had to do with all manner of unpleasantness, wormsblood and henbane and gall. And there were mandrakes; Anita had had to plug her ears while she prepared them, they shrieked so as they were being minced . . . "Sing me ye owls nothing but songs of death," she muttered; and again, shivering and quoting all over the place, "Damned spirits all, that in crossways and floods have burial . . ."

Somewhere a car's tyres screamed in agony and Anita knew without looking up that David was there with her. The mist rolled around, making shapes like figures that got halfway solid and then gave up again. "Anita," whispered the ghost, "what are you doing?"

8: THE MIDDLE EARTH

She shuddered, and wiped her hands on her jeans. "Quiet, please. Just wait an' see . . ."

No, no, said the Controller, oddly gentle. *Over here, you silly thing . . .*

It came walking out of the mist. It was prettier than its photograph but very pale . . . David caught his nonexistent breath. "Who . . . who's this? Anita, *what are you doing?*"

"Where am I?" That from the newcomer, dazedly. "It's dark, I can't see . . . is anybody there . . ."

The cauldron fumed; the glow lit the branches of the willow. The Fyne-brook chuckled in blackness. "She's like me," said David, astonished. "Anita . . ."

Zero minus one minute, said the Controller remotely. *Counting now. Fifty-nine, fifty-eight, fifty-seven, fifty-six . . .*

Anita made shooing movements with her hands; she couldn't speak. She listened to the voices in the mist.

"But I didn't think there was anybody else like me anywhere . . . I was so scared, you don't know . . . And then I was sort of pulled, it was like being blown along on a wind . . ."

"Anita did it," said David. "She's terribly sweet. We shall both be all right now. Anita, this is Susan Martin . . ."

"Hello, Anita!"

"Hail and farewell," muttered the witch. She was quivering all over. Suddenly there was tension. A church clock was chiming.

Fife, four, three, two, one, NOW . . .

The last part of the spell "took" with a crash that jarred everything. David shouted; then a huge noise began, a screeching like a thousand klaxons playing at once. There was light, vast and flaring; in it shadows writhed, there were new dimensions. Two Planes touched, grinding and bumping like ships in a storm, like cogs that had never been designed to mesh. Anita pointed into the brilliance. "Quick, David, while it's open. That's your *way through* . . ." She put her hands to her temples. "Quick, please go quickly, I can't stand much of this . . ."

"Anita . . ."

Cast-off, said the Controller, clinically calm. He was doing his job now, and doing it well.

The Parallel Universe began to disengage, grumbling and seething. The ghosts sprinted and scrambled, hair and clothes blowing wild. The light dimmed; voices like morning winds reached Anita. "Thank you . . . Anita, *thank you* . . ."

She began to run in the light of earth-dawn, a grey shadow under a sky bright and raw as cut lead. "Poor David," she shouted hysterically. "Smelling of soil and talking gear-ratios . . . You won't have to count kingfishers any more now . . ." She reached Foxhanger as the farm animals began to stir. "O cocks are crowing on merry middle earth," whimpered Anita, tears shining on her face. She burst into the cottage, ran up to her room and cried herself unconscious. She slept all through the day; nothing Granny Thompson did could rouse her. She was out for nearly twelve hours, but when she finally woke the clamour of the ghost kingdoms had gone from her mind.

9: THE WAR AT FOXHANGER

GRANNY THOMPSON'S temper finally snapped when the jam refused to set. Anita stood by anxiously while the old lady spooned a sample onto a saucer, blew it, fanned it and then inverted it over the table. The jam wobbled, collected itself into a blob and fell off, plunk, onto the cloth. Granny Thompson gave a shout in which frustration and rage were nicely blended.

"Six hours! Nuthink but bile an' bile, an' look at it! It ent even started . . . an' it *wunt*, I can tell yer that, not in a month o' Sundays. Yer kin tek it orf, it ent wuth wastin' 'eat on." She obeyed her own instruction, lifted the iron pot from the range and banged it down sizzling on the hearth. "Spelled," muttered the old woman, casting round for book and glasses. "Spelled, that's wot we are . . . an' I dunt need to arsk 'oo by, neither . . . look at it!" And she whacked the offending jam with a ladle, startling Anita who had leaned over, eyes closed, to sniff the mauve steam of blackberries.

Granny Thompson stirred the mess vigorously. "Ter see the spells om put in, an' orl . . . spells, spells, look, it's thick with 'em, but set . . . set it *wunt*. I'll give 'er spells . . ." She began to leaf through her book, muttering from time to time, licking her horny fingers, eyes gimleting behind her glasses. "Mice in the milk, that ent 'ot enough be 'arf . . ." She cackled. "Toads in the girdle, I reckon I'll 'ave a goo at that . . . no, I kent, we're out of noot's eyes. That's a very pertickler sort o' spell, y'ave to 'ave orl the ingredients right . . . I'll find summat, dunt you worry . . ."

Anita sighed. "Can't we just cook it some more, Gran? It's bound to go eventually."

"I tell yer it *wunt*," said Granny Thompson fiercely. "It's *cussed*, I tell yer . . . dunt yer think I knows a cussed pot when I comes acrorst it?"

"But Gran, if we just tried a bit longer . . ."

"It's that Aggie Everett," snarled Granny, still going through the book. "It's got orl the 'allmarks . . . boils an' buboes, sores an' rashes . . . git me that there big jar o' jollop orf the top shelf in the cupboard, om gooin' ter *start*. . . ."

Anita stretched out her feet in the warmth and put her chin in her hands. A nauseous pot floated obediently into the room to touch down at her Granny's elbow. "An' the frogs legs, an' the cauldron," commanded the old lady.

Anita growled mutinously. "Do your own running about. . . ." Granny Thompson glittered at her and she recanted hastily. She had defied the old lady once and there had been an affair with a hairbrush. Despite all manner of hastily-erected force fields Anita had been unable to prevent it from whacking her into sleeping on her face for a week. . . . There was a clang from the kitchen and a shuffling as the spellpot started to work its way out from under the table. Anita sighed again, pushed back her long hair and watched while Granny Thompson began to work herself into her spellraising mood.

Anita knew Aggie Everett only too well; she was the nearest member of the sisterhood. Her house could be seen from Foxhanger, a pleasant little cottage standing on a rise of ground that overlooked the Fyne-brook. Granny Thompson had tangled with her rival more than once in the past. Events always followed the same pattern. There would be a time of unpleasantnesses, of things catching fire or blowing up or falling over or altering horribly and wriggling away, and the battle would probably end with both witches getting their knuckles rapped from down under for wildcatting. Still that was the way it was; there was no arguing with her Granny in this mood, Anita knew better than to try.

While the witches' powers were more or less evenly matched, their appearances could not have been more different. Granny Thompson was short and square; Aggie Everett was tall, thin and inclined to stoop. Granny Thompson's face was brown as a nut, and seamed with wrinkles; Aggie's complexion was pale and her skin seemed to be stretched like parchment over her sharp bones. Granny Thompson's eyes were snaky black, Aggie's were a rheumy, washed-out blue. Her hair was scraggy and long, her nose twitched with suspicion and distrust and dripped perpetually like a salty stalactite. Aggie's sense of honour was keen; if she had been spellraising, which was not improbable, what had happened would be nothing to what she would do when she felt the first crackle of the Thompsons' resentment.

The old lady lifted the pot onto the fire and added water. A familiar crackling and gurgling began inside. Granny Thompson drew up a chair and sat down with the book still in her lap. "Yisdey were the start," she pronounced, wielding the ladle. "That milk a-gooin' sour.

9: THE WAR AT FOXHANGER

'That's Aggie,' I ses ter meself. 'Aggie, fer a pension. She allus starts orf with a traditional cuss an' then works up.' "

"But the whole truckload went wrong, Gran. The man told me."

"Course it did, wot d'yer use fer *'ead?* She 'ad ter do the lot jist so's she could be sure o' gettin' *us*. I esspect she clapped one on it while it were a-gooin' by . . . an' the wust on it were, it were one o' them noo-fangled non-reversin' jobs. I fretted uvver that bottle," fumed Granny. "Tried ev'ry way I could *think* on but it wadn't no good. I thort I 'ad it —"

"And then it turned green, and blew up —"

"Very like," said the old lady complacently. "It were badly uvver-spelled. An' then it were rats. Now there ent no rats in this 'ouse, I *knows* there ent, an' yit I 'ears 'em scuttlin' orl uvver. 'Arf the night they was on . . . an' the things wot come out the tap this mornin' . . . now that's proof, if yer wants it. . . ."

"Well Gran, it could still have been an accident. Things do come out of taps sometimes, I've read about it."

"They dunt 'ave *golefish* in *reservoyers*," said Granny Thompson with the air of making a point.

"Well I don't care. I thought it was a pretty spell. I've got a bowl of them in my bedroom."

"Well tip 'em out," snarled Granny, "afore she teks thort an' turns 'em into summat wuss, proberly wi' *legs*. I dunt want you screamin' an' jumpin' 'arf the night, om got enough on me plate as it is. . . . Toad that under the cold stone days an' nights 'ath thirty one sweltered venom sleepin' got, boil thou *fust* in the charmèd pot. . . ."

The contents of the cauldron began to heave, showing a little lake of flashing colour. Anita wandered outside. The night was very peaceful. She knew it wouldn't stay that way for long. She sat on the garden fence and brooded. Any moment now. . . .

The first spell zipped out of the window, vaguely visible as a dark blue corrugation in the air. Another followed, and another. Anita counted sullenly. "That's the one about toads in the girdle, she must have found the newt-bits . . . and there's the one that does things to the legs of chairs . . . that's a big one, that must be for rheumatism." ("Twingin' screws" her Granny called it.) Something passed Anita on the way in. The force was opposed by another. The cottage became haloed with blue sparks; there was a brief sensation of tussling and the spell went out with a pop. Anita shook her head. "Gran, you've done it again . . . blocked the dummy . . ." The real curse streaked in under her Granny's guard; there was a crash from within the cottage, and a scream of rage.

"An' that was the one that breaks up the tea service . . . and here comes the one that sets fire to her hat . . ."

Anita's ears swivelled suddenly and began to quiver. There was a calling. Not exactly an audible calling but nonetheless it was there. The sound came from Turnpike Farm. There were new tenants, with a new boy. Anita slid off the gatepost and began to run. She skimmed past a pond, kicking off her shoes as she went. Oh he's not a child and he's not a man, he doesn't know whether I'm his mistress or his mother and neither do I. . . . She leaped a ditch, legs gleaming in the moonlight, pirouetted across a meadow. Oh to be a witch, there was nothing really like it. . . . She sent a thought burrowing into a great sett, in and around and out again, left an indignant badger with a feeling of having been kicked in the rump, snarling and looking round for the enemy. . . . across another field, through a wood . . . Turnpike Farm!

September nights can be chill but the hayrick was warm enough, particularly after they had dug themselves in a little way. Anita made her boy cry first then she took pity on him and helped him with the clasp of her dress and they were just getting to the nice part —

"*Aaaaeeowwww . . .*"

Anita's scream was as unexpected as it was horrible; beneath her, the haycock seemed to convulse. Snakes and toads erupted in a mass, spurting away down the sloping sides like green and brown water. Anita fell off the stack and ran, making a noise like an overworked two-stroke. A field away she stopped, panting, and a little latecomer wriggled between her breasts and popped out of the top of her dress. It took three lengths of the pool by Brington Lock to make her feel even moderately clean. She circled for home, hissing. The fight had taken a personal turn.

The cottage had a distinctly beleaguered look. The fence was down in several places, the garden was strewn with debris and the chimney stack wore its one remaining pot at a rakish angle. Heat radiated out all round; Anita felt her hair crackle and blow back as she ran up the path. Near the door a particularly nasty familiar scuttled past, bearing a small flag and carrying something that was fizzing. It vanished among the trees and Anita heard a bang and an enraged clucking. She was vaguely glad. She had always loathed that creature anyway.

Inside, with the rumble of outgoing spells almost shaking the floor, Anita felt she was really in a battle. Granny Thompson was capering wildly, waving her book and pointing with her great stick. Enemy curses grounding in the garden had accounted for most of the damage but enough had got through to make a fair mess of the inside of the cottage as well. Mats were rucked up and thrown about, furniture leaned drunkenly on rubbery legs, the kitchen was a mess of shattered preserves and the floor was covered with shards, bits of tile, and, unaccountably, with feathers. Something nasty had evidently got in before being disrupted. Anita chittered with rage at the mess and set to work.

The fight went on into the small hours. Anita began to sweat but there was no giving up. She was becoming disturbed by the size of some of the curses. They threatened most thrilling things to her person . . . She shouted to her Granny. "She's in a terrible temper . . . what on

9: THE WAR AT FOXHANGER

earth did you do to her?"

"Didn't do nothink," panted the old lady, using her spellstick like a machine gun. "It were 'er, the varmint . . . took uvver one o' my familiars. That there gret ginger cat, the one wot went orf that night . . . Four months I worked on that, jist got it ter Grade Two — Fetchin' an Carryin' an' Bein' Unlikely — an' she guz an' *filches* it orf me. There it were sittin' in 'er winder bold as brass . . . 'Aggie,' I ses, 'that there cat ent yore property' . . . an' me 'at's down uvver me eyes an' om bouncin' orf down the path afore yer kin say knife . . . an' I wadn't in a mood ter be uncivil neither, not ter start with. 'Aggie,' I ses . . ."

"Gran, look out —"

Whooof . . . cerrrump . . .

"Atomics," panted Granny. "She 'as the nerve . . ."

"Gran, we've got to get out. If one of those hits us . . ."

"I ent never gettin' out!" roared Granny. "I were spellraisin' when Aggie Everett were bein' dandled on 'er mother's knee, I ent runnin' orf from the likes of 'er . . ."

"Gran, there's another one —"

WHOOMPH . . .

"You kin goo," cried the old lady valiantly. "Leave yer pore ole Gran ter cope, she's done it afore . . ."

"Don't be silly . . . in any case, she had me with snakes . . ."

Granny cackled, juggling something on the end of her stick that looked and acted like ball lightning. "Aggie wouldn't do a thing like that . . ."

"Gran! You don't mean —"

"Mucky young cat," roared the elder Thompson. "I knew wot you were at . . . orl of a twitch yer were, I could feel it . . . time an' a place fer everythink. . . ."

Anita's eyes went triangular with fury but she was too busy to take any reprisals even had she dared.

It had to end. Granny's masterpiece, a huge and complex curse that had to do with valency bonds, looped back onto the cottage and had Anita not been prompt with the chicken switch, house, inhabitants and most of Foxhanger would have been reduced to a dust having very odd physical properties. Anita gulped at the narrowness of the escape.

"Gran, come *on*. We can't keep this up . . ."

"I ent *gooin'*. . . ."

"Strategy," pleaded Anita. "Tactics. Present a mobile target . . . we can get up close to her place . . ."

"Sulphur an' smoke an' the noise o' brass," shouted Granny, hugely pleased. "Gel's got 'ead arter orl. . . ."

The two hares jostled each other through the copse and into the meadow beyond, accelerated across a sea of moonlight, ears flat, huge legs drumming. Anita exulted at the whipping changes of the low

9: THE WAR AT FOXHANGER

horizon, the rush of the air, the curve and swell of the grass that invited leaping and running and pounding.

Gran, come on.

Steady up, gel, I ent got your wind. . . .

Rot, you can go a lot faster. Come on, Gran, faster, I want to run till I'm mad . . .

Old 'ard . . .

NO!

Change, shouted Granny suddenly. *Change, fer yer life!*

Gran, I . . . I can't . . .

Jammed! roared the old hare silently. *Aggie, you ole devil* . . . It skidded to a stop and sat up, quivering with strain. It seemed to swell, there was a thud, a flash of blue light . . . Granny Thompson, shoes and stick, long coat and old felt hat, sat up in the field, climbed puffing to her feet. Around her poured a hunt. The dogs ran silently, tongues lolling. Aggie's kennel of familiars, penned under the trees of the far slope, burst into the open, vanished over the brow of the hill ahead.

Anita ran desperately, eyes bolting, white chest-fur glinting. The dogs fanned out in a half circle, heading her away from cover, cutting down her lead as she doubled. On top of the hill Aggie's cottage windows blazed with blue light, shining in the dark like eyes. Granny Thompson moaned. The trap was laid and sprung; it was too late now, they'd lost. From every quarter of the field white flags sprang erect, rippling in the moonlight as their improbable bearers hurried them forward. The Thompson familiars, deployed in the open ground in front of the cottage, converged on the enemy stronghold. The night air became chaotic with messages though nothing was audible.

Aggie, 'old 'ard . . . we give up, fetch 'em orf . . .

I kent . . . an' she's lorst orl 'er magic . . . things 'ave orl gorn rip . . .

Gran, my feet will kick . . . the blood will come out of my nose . . .

There were "no" sounds from the domestic animals, the awful killing-giggle of a weasel as the creature scurried along keeping the hunt in sight.

AGGIE . . .

Keep a-runnin', gel. Come 'ere . . .

The hare turned, racing for the cottage. Jaws clashed behind its neck. It leaped convulsively and there was a well, deep, dark, miles, falling . . .

Mouse, thought Anita, terrified. *Something tiny, soft, no weight . . . please, a mouse . . .*

Strange things happened in the shaft. There was a breathtaking thump, a noise like a pebble landing in moss. Then silence.

Granny Thompson danced on the edge of the hole. "Anita . . . gel, *wheer are yer . . .*"

Faintly, from a long way away. "Gran . . ."

"Are yer orl right?"

"I . . . I think so . . ." Anita tried to sit up on the ledge, and recoiled. "Gran, help . . ."

"Change," boomed the old lady, beside herself with worry. "Shapeshift. Try a bat."

"Gran, I can't . . . please help, there's worms . . ."

Aggie Everett bore down on her old enemy. "I didn't mean no 'arm ter the girl, things went orl of 'eap . . ."

"Chiblings," snarled Granny, wringing her hands. "If anythink 'appens to 'er, I'll 'ave you in *chiblings,* Aggie Everett . . . dunt think I *kent,* neither . . ."

"Gran, there's *worms* . . ."

"I couldn't 'elp it, I tell yer . . ."

"Big ones with collars round them," whimpered Anita, faint in the shaft.

Granny Thompson leaped back to the edge. " 'Old still, gel, om a-comin' . . ."

"Yer kent," protested Aggie, hanging onto her arm. "Yer'll get *kilt,* it's miles deep. One o' yore spells must 'ave blowed the lid orf . . ."

"Our gel's down there . . ."

"Well, look . . ." The two old ladies conferred busily. "Yer kent goo down without shapeshiftin'. An' if yer gits down there *small,* yer kent lift 'er . . ."

"She's lorst orl 'er magic," moaned Granny Thompson. " 'Ad it orl knocked out on 'er, I shouldn't wonder . . ." Deep in the ground Anita started to sob. She was shivering, trying to draw her body into a tiny compass, but she was being touched horribly.

"Besoms," pronounced Aggie. "There ent no other way."

"I kent 'andle 'em."

"Surely you 'ave done."

"Spectakler," snarled Granny. "Dunt 'old with 'em . . . Orl right fer some I esspect. *I* ent never 'ad no call fer that sort o' thing."

Aggie was already dragging a great broom toward the shaft. Firefighting switches, they stack them in the wooded country in Northamptonshire. She poised the thing at the well-lip, stood back and made a pass. The broom became alight with little spots of blue fire. Granny stepped back a pace from the sparkling thing. "Om too *old* fer this sort o' mullockin' . . ."

"Well I kent power it *an'* steer, yer must 'ave read the 'andbook."

"Satan spare us," moaned Granny, straddling the broomstick and gripping with toes that were prehensile with anxiety. "Ent never seen nothink like it in orl me life. . . . Orl right, gel, om a-comin' . . . one way or the other. . . ."

"Are yer ready?"

"I shent get ner readier wi' *waitin'.* . . ."

"Five, four, three, two, one, LIFTOFF . . ."

"All s-systems go . . ." That in a gulpy voice from the shaft. The

9: THE WAR AT FOXHANGER

broom rose with a roar of sparks, hung a moment, then slid into the depths. A nasty aerobatic; the thing was manœuvring on its retros. The jets lit up slimy, dripping brickwork. Granny Thompson peered downward, shielding her eyes with the one hand she could spare.

"Gran, quick, the worms . . . they're awful . . ."

"Noot an' blindwumm do no wrung," bellowed Granny, glad to be of help. Anita squealed with relief. There was movement on the ledge; a wriggling exodus. The broomstick began to spin. "Verniers," shrieked Granny. Then, "Main jets . . . Aggie, *fire main jets*. . . ." The besom hung poised on a level with Anita's shoulders. She climbed on instantly, hugging Granny as hard as she could.

Two old ladies were silhouetted craggily against the moon. "Aggie," said Granny Thompson largely, "yore done a creditable thing. I dunt say as 'ow I *'olds* with yer nor yer ways, an' it were you wot *started* it orl. But om gotta give yer me thanks. It wouldn't be right ter do no less."

Aggie grasped the gnarled hand that was offered her. "Maude," she said solemnly, "Om sorry. Om sorry about the jam an' the rats an' the golefish. Oo, an' the milk . . . an' yer kin 'ave yer cat back tomorrer. Om made 'im up ter Grade One now — Sneakin' an' Prowlin' an' Bein' Above Suspishern." She raised her voice. "Familiars, *dismiss;* I shent need yer no more ternight." She turned back to Granny Thompson. "I wouldn't 'ave 'ad anythink 'appen ter that gel o' yourn fer worlds, Maude, may 'Im Wot's Down Under strike me if I lie. . . ."

Granny whipped round, suddenly startlingly agile. "Anita? Wheer are yer, gel, wheer *are* yer . . ."

A voice trilled from overhead, thin with distance, full of frost and stars. A blue glow moved across the dark quarter of the sky, a wild shape jerked in front of the moon. Granny Thompson raised her stick. "Come *down,* yer little varmint . . . y'ent licensed, y'ent done yer *solo.* . . ."

"Gran, it's wonderful. I'll fly to Mars . . ."

"COME ON DOWN . . ."

"I'll dance on Saturn's rings . . ."

"WILL YER LISTEN WHEN I TELLS YER . . ."

Aggie felt unaccustomed muscles begin to twitch. She started to laugh. "Let 'er *be,* Maude, wadn't you ever young . . ." Her voice floated up to Anita. "Goo an' see Orion . . . spin wi' the Earth, an' see the Southern Cross. . . ."

Granny Thompson was already bumping over the grass in an uneven and long-winded takeoff. Aggie held her sides. "Flaps, Maude, flaps . . ." And then, "Vee-two speed, *rotate* . . ."

"I'll put a girdle round about the Earth in forty minutes!"

"I'll put my knuckles round about your 'ead in forty *seconds.* . . ."

The voices of pursuer and pursued vanished in the tall night.

KEITH ROBERTS

10: IDIOT'S LANTERN

"AN' WOT, MAY I ARSK," said Granny Thompson fiercely, "is *that?*"

Anita interposed herself hastily between her Granny and the men who were carrying in the big shiny box. She sad, "Nothing, Gran . . . Well of course it is, actually. It's a sort of . . . thing I've bought. You'll like it when its working, honestly —"

"Workin'?" snarled the old lady, trying ineffectually to get round her granddaughter. "Wot might it *do* then, when it's *workin'* . . ."

"It's a television set, Gran, don't interfere."

"Television?" The elder Thompson whooped and grabbed for her stick. "Well yer kin jist television it straight orf *out* agin ter start with. Television . . . never 'eard the like. Bad enough with orl this 'lectric shootin' about orl uvver the place without that gret 'ulkin' thing set there blarin' an' mouthin' orl hours. . . . An' wot's 'e doin'?" Her gimlet gaze had caught the pair of feet ascending the ladder propped by the kitchen window. She was through the back door in a flash, apron flying in the speed of her passage. Somewhere en route her felt hat became attached to her head at a belligerent angle. Anita panted after her. "Gran, be reasonable! You can't —"

"Come down orf my *chimbley,*" roared Granny Thompson in a voice that lifted a flock of pigeons two fields away. "Or by 'Im Wot's Down Under, I'll *smite* yer —"

"*Gran!*"

"Come orf. . . ." And Granny raised her stick, pointing it like a rifle at the surprised engineer above her. Anita saw the spell coming and whipped the weapon out of the old lady's hand just in time. She simpered and called up. "Er . . . carry on, please. We were just

[95]

wondering whether . . . whether the stack was strong enough."

"Safe as Gibraltar, ducks. Take two o' these, it would. All right, Fred, let's 'ave it. . . . ." And the aerial began to sway up the side of the house like a large and threatening insect.

Anita towed her Granny back to the kitchen by main force and shoved her down in a chair. She said firmly, "We're having a telly, Gran, and that's all there is to it. Winter's coming and we don't want another time like we had last year. Snow up to the roof and neither of us able to go outside for weeks. You know how difficult you got. Like a . . . a bear with a sore head."

"I didn't git like *nothink,*" snarled the old lady. "It were you, yer young rapscallion. Fidgetin' an' frettin' orl uvver, tryin' out stuff wot you 'adn't got no right tamperin' with. You needn't 'ave done that thing on the cat, ter start with. Best familiar we ever 'ad an' *woomph, splat, scrorch,* that were *that.* . . . It teks time ter mek 'em up as good as that one were, whether you knows it or whether you *dunt.* Dunt jist pick 'em orf the trees yer know, they 'as ter be *trained.* . . . An' then that thing wi' the wood bloke. Turnin' 'is lorry wheels square jist acause yer didn't like 'im callin' yer missis. 'Aughty young cat. 'Ad the p'lice round 'ere that time didn't we, wantin' ter know 'oo'd bin muckin' about. If I 'adn't took thort an' turned everythink back orl right agin while they was pokin' an' pryin' they'd be 'ere *still.* An' orl this *'lectric.* Done ter suit you that were, though 'Im Wot's Down Under knows I dunt 'old with it. . . . Stuff runnin' an' fidgetin' orl about under the floors an' ev'rywheer, it ent *nat'ral.* I never did 'old with it an' I wunt *now.* . . . ."

The house began to resound with knocks and bangs, the whirring of drills and loud and incomprehensible shouts to "try 'er again" and "fire it a bit more, Fred."

"Look at wot 'appened yisdey," foamed Granny. "When I were a-tryin' ter do the floors. Orl I did were turn that there vac thing on an' *whoosh,* sparks an' stuff ev'rywheer. . . . ."

Anita was being very patient. "I've told you before Gran, you mustn't plug it in to the light. It isn't safe."

"No, no more ent none on it. *Whoosh* it went, like one o' them firecrackers. I felt the bits 'it me 'at. . . . Jist a lucky charnst I were wearin' it," moaned Granny, who generally wore the shapeless headgear morning, noon and night. "Might 'a singed me ears orf, it might. An now this thing —"

One of the workmen poked his head round the door. He said, " 'Fraid you're not getting a very good picture, miss. You're a fringe area, see?"

Granny peered at him. "Does that mean we kent 'ev it?"

"Oh no, there's a picture all right. It's just a bit faint, that's all."

Anita squealed with delight. "Oo Gran, it's on. Come an' see . . . ." The old lady stumped after her. Anita knelt in front of the screen, cooing at the flickery picture. Figures showed dimly through a haze of spots. Granny bent, glasses rammed firmly on the end of her nose. She let out a most fearsome shout. "Out! Out with it! Look at that, gels wi' *legs*. ... I ent 'avin' none o' that, not in this 'ouse...."

"Oh Gran, don't be so silly. It's only a ballet programme for schools...."

The men were already edging toward the door. One of them said hurriedly, "We might try a fringe set if this one ain't too good. Give it a try, we'll be back tomorrer...."

Granny Thompson raised her stick. "Not if I 'as anythink ter do with it you wunt. Fact is, you wunt even *leave*...." But the van had already started up and driven away.

The television had its trial run that evening. There was a certain tenseness in the air. Anita sat entranced, blue reflections dancing on her solemn face. The old lady sewed in the far corner of the room, back obstinately turned. Only occasionally did she look up from her work to glare at the offence over the rims of her glasses. In time the periods of sewing became less, the periods of screenwatching longer. Anita's ears twitched joyfully, detecting each tiny rasp as the material was laid in her Granny's lap. At nine an ice show came on. Anita had never seen anything like it. She watched dazzled as the tiny figures swooped about, graceful and remote as birds. After a time there was a *clump* next to her as Granny Thompson banged down her chair. Anita glanced sideways and raised an insolent eyebrow. "Dunt give me non o' yer *chelp* neither," snarled the old lady. "I s'pose if we gotta *ev* it, we might as well *wotch* it...." She settled down to viewing. As the programme went on Granny's face got nearer and nearer to the screen, her hooked nose and chin, that always threatened to meet, seemed to draw closer than ever in concentration. After half an hour she pronounced her verdict. "Skates," she said firmly. "I'm almos' prepared ter swear them there gels is on *skates*...."

The future of the set was assured.

Winter came, not so bitter as the previous year but hard enough. The television was a great boon. The fringe set duly arrived and night after night while the wind howled outside and the snow drove like bitter needles through the trees of the copse Anita and her Granny sated themselves with the little moving picture. Anita adored the dancing and the music, Shakespeare plays when available, current affairs programmes, travelogues and nature talks. Granny watched most things avidly but her greatest delight was the quiz. She saw every one that was screened and if the other side offered something better that was just too bad. Many evenings the witches sat in silence, lips compressed, while in front of them the channel switch clicked backward and forward as their wills contested possession of the set. In the end Anita gave up. It was something to humour her Granny at all, and the telly had certainly done that.

With the better weather Anita began to tire, but Granny Thompson remained a devout viewer. If Anita was out, walking in the woods with something improbable, she was sure to be regaled with a full description of the quizzes she had missed as soon as she got back. "There were this ole gel," her Granny would say, cackling at the memory. "An' that there bloke, that wot's-is-name, wavin' orl that there money, an' she didn't know wot ter do. A pitcher, 'er face were. You jist orter 'ave seen it. . . ." And so on, seemingly forever.

Anita soon discovered another drawback. The cottage was isolated, their television the only one for miles around. The emissions from the set played havoc with her radar system, her sonar and all the rest of her mess of senses. The programmes got mixed and snarled up with the thoughtstreams of animals so that Anita could neither track nor talk to anything. The weasel took her favourite family of mice, she didn't hear him hating till it was far too late; three owls left the district in disgust, rats got to the moorhen eggs, every single thing went wrong. One night she followed a hunting fox for hours; he was close to his kill, and Anita was beaming in on him fast, when flick — *Uppen it, y'ole fool,* roared Granny, distant in her mind. *Yer bound to git* summat, *the booby's gorn.* . . . Anita spun round, retuning desperately, but it was too late; the fox had "gorn" as well, and with him a month-old hare. Anita foamed, biting her lips and crooking her hands, and for a few moments it would have been very bad for anyone who got too close. Then she steadied down and went back home, giving up for yet another night. It was obvious something was going to have to be done.

For once the old lady played right into her hands. The elder Thompson broached the critical subject the next day, sitting scraping early carrots in front of the ever-flickering eye of the Idiot's Lantern. "Yer know I bin thinkin'," she said carelessly. "These 'ere ole gels on the quizzes. I dunt reckon 'arf on 'em knows wot they're at. I reckon I could jist about do as good as wot they do. Mebbe better."

Anita nodded tiredly. "You'll have to go on one of the programmes then, Gran, and show them all up."

Granny Thompson nodded, laid down the bowl and began searching in the capacious pocket of her apron. She said, "Om a-gooin' to. Om orlready rit." She held up a large and impressive-looking envelope.

Anita felt a sudden little gleam of hope. There was no doubt her Granny was what society normally terms a "character," but once or twice in the past she'd seen the results of people taking her over-lightly. She said silkily, "What a good idea, Gran. I'll post it for you."

Granny Thompson snatched the letter away. "Young varmint. You'll a-do summat to it, I kin see it in yer face. I'll tek it meself. That way I shall know it gits there."

Anita held her hand out. "Witches' honour, Gran. I'll post it."

Her Granny still looked suspicious. "By 'Im Wot's Down Under?"

"Yes."

The old lady snorted but she relinquished the letter. "I still says yore up ter summat, my gel. . . ."

10: IDIOT'S LANTERN

Anita was too wise to disagree. "Yes, Gran, I am. But I will post it for you."

She took the letter to the village by hand, resisting the temptation to levitate it even the last few yards or so. She too wanted to be quite sure it arrived. She had slipped in with her Granny's quaint prose a recent picture of herself that she considered showed several of the best aspects of her personality; before resealing the envelope she did several mysterious things that would ensure its being well received. The last of the rites was a breathing inside the flap, the tiniest touch of her lips to the stiff paper. Then away the whole thing went, as loaded and deadly as a little white bomb.

The answer came within a week. Granny Thompson was appalled; it took her two changes of glasses and three lens polishings to resolve the message. Then she came plunging out to the kitchen to her granddaughter. "Look at this 'ere, gel," she said breathlessly. "We're a-gotta goo *up!*"

Anita nodded, hands busy with dishes and suds. "Well that's what you wanted, isn't it, Gran?"

"I ent so sure," gloomed the old lady. "Ent never bin ter Lunnon, not in orl me days . . ."

"So what?" asked Anita scornfully, who hadn't been to London either. "All the more fun."

Granny shook her head. "Well I dunt know. Orl them folk . . . I dunt know as 'ow I fancies it. . . ."

Anita had seen a chance of liberation, and she wasn't letting it slip. "Granny," she said viciously, "don't tell me you're *afraid!* What, and you a witch?" She dropped into the vernacular. "I thort yer could do *anythink.* . . ."

WHUP!

That was the dishcloth across her ear. Anita ducked the backhand, the most dangerous swipe in the old lady's repertoire, fielded a pot that rose somewhat startlingly at her head and rushed out the door giggling. Something else passed her as she ran between the first trees. The object resolved itself into the head of the yardbrush. It missed her, hung uncertainly in the air then returned the way it had come. That was boomerang levitation, a trick Anita was still trying to teach herself. When it became apparent the barrage had finished she headed off through the wood, hearing her Granny's cries of "Young *varmint* . . ." fading in the distance. The first thing to do was to find out about trains.

That was easy although it cost Titchford Halt a timetable. The stationmaster was never able to figure out the sudden gust of wind that sent the book hopping through the window and winging away like a big clumsy moth. He chased the fleeing railway property a moderate distance before returning, scratching his head and grumbling to himself. It was probably just as well he gave up; Anita was excited, and her moods could change very quickly at the best of times. A similar sortie against the local paper shop yielded a map of London, and that was that. Things were all set.

The trip was arranged for the following week. As it turned out, Anita had no difficulty finding where to go; she sensed the studio quite easily by all the radiations coming from it. There was a little trouble in the tube station when Granny caught her heel in one of the steps of what she was pleased to call a "hexcavator" and almost took a dire revenge on the machine; Anita dragged her away hoping her threats to reverse it or turn all its treads flat were merely boasting. At the studio they had to wait what seemed an interminable length of time before they were interviewed. Anita viewed the compère of the coming programme with some distaste. It seemed to her he was probing their characters, searching for the little mannerisms he could bring out with humorous and telling effect later on. She had no doubt that they would be selected to appear; she was wearing her newest dress and her long hair was beautifully brushed, they couldn't miss. When she was asked what subject they would like to answer questions on she said, "Folklore," very firmly. That should cause the ruction if all else failed.

It was evening before they were due to perform, and by then the studio looked very different. An audience had arrived and there were cameras everywhere and cables, microphones on great long booms. Strange machinery clacked and hummed, coloured lights winked, everything was bustle and confusion. Men rushed about with sheafs of papers or stood and gave incomprehensible orders about grams and sound cues and veloscillators. By the time the show actually got under way, with blasts of organ music and much clapping from the audience, Granny's nerves had reached a fine pitch of tension. Anita could feel ideas churning in the old lady's mind. The iron was decidedly hot.

Their turn came at last and they walked out onto the stage. Banks of lights revolved to stare at them; the compère met them, nearly unrecognizable in his makeup, patted and touched till he had steered them into exactly the right position. Behind him a camera loomed like a Thing from Mars, the red light in its forehead glowing like an angry caste-mark. Anita gulped and her own composure began to sag a little. The quizmaster introduced them as "Mrs. and Miss Thompson, from Northamptonshire," and asked for "a big hand" for some obscure reason. Applause pattered like gunfire and Granny looked startled. She muttered to Anita, "We ent done nothink yit. . . ."

The machines caught the words and flung them out on the air. The audience roared delightedly and Granny Thompson's lips set in a thin line. Anita began exultantly planning the best escape route. Everything was working out just as she'd thought it would. It was one thing to watch this show from an easy chair at home but quite another to be up on stage helping provide the kicks. That wasn't quite so damn funny. . . .

The compère beamed. "But you will do something, Mrs. Thompson, you will. We're all quite sure of that. Now, this really most delightful girl, would you step forward a little please, my dear, that's it, let all the folks have a good view. Now this is your granddaughter you tell me, Mrs. Thompson, that is correct is it not?"

Granny turned from glaring at a camera that was very obviously examining Anita's cleavage. She opened her mouth, considered, then closed it again like a rat trap. She said frostily, "No, has a matter hof fact . . . she *ent*. She 'eppens ter be the daughter hof a third cousin. Hon me mother's side . . ."

"But you have brought her up?"

"Yis . . ."

"And very charmingly too if I may say, yes very charmingly. . . ." For the benefit of his audience the compère rolled his eyes and appeared about to drool. "Very nicely too . . . And you're going to answer questions on, let me see, on folklore isn't it, that is correct, folklore?"

"Om orlready *tole* yer twice," muttered Granny fiercely. "You blokes do goo on, dunt yer?"

A gale of laughter. The compère rode above it. "And why . . . why this particular subject, Mrs. Thompson?"

"Ar, well," said Granny, settling onto more familiar ground. "Om a witch, see? Fact is we both are. Only she ent 'ad much of a charnst ter practice, seein' as she ent no age."

The compère's eyebrows rose and fell; it was his most famous expression and the audience promptly became hysterical. Anita hung onto her Granny's arm, feeling the old lady buzzing with rage. The longer she could avert the explosion, the better it would be when it came. The compère cut the amusement short. "Very well, then could we have the first question please on folklore? Thank you. Now Mrs. Thompson, and you too Anita, think very carefully, for one pound can you tell me . . . now think v-e-r-y carefully . . . Is a *leprechaun*. . . . is a *leprechaun* a little man, or a complaint of the foot?"

Granny drew herself up. "As fur as I know, it ent neither. . . ."

The quizmaster was anxious to help. "Now Mrs. Thompson, this is only the first question. Now think carefully, when an Irishman . . ." He winked roguishly at the audience. "When an Irishman sees a little man on a shamrock leaf, what does he call him?"

"They ent nothink like little men," declared Granny stoutly. "Little skinned-rabbit tatty lookin' things they are, orl 'ead. If yer'd seen one yer wouldn't be so free gooin' on about 'em." When the laughter had died down again she shot her final barb. "I dunt b'leeve yer knows wot yer *on* about. . . ."

The compère was delighted. He was certainly getting the company money's worth out of this pair. Beauty and character together, what a combo. . . . He would have liked to milk them some more but the clock was ticking on. He put his next question. "Very well, Mrs. Thompson, we'll accept you as an expert. It does seem you know exactly what a leprechaun is. Now for two pounds, *two* pounds, can you tell me three old-time cures for rheumatism? Any three you can think of now, any three at all...."

Anita thought she was going to burst. This was it, this just had to be it....

"Toads," snarled Granny. " 'Round yer neckit usually though yer *can* stick 'em practic'ly *anywheer*. I dunt 'old with 'em though. Sheep jollop's best, that kent 'ardly be beat...."

The compère's face changed abruptly. Up above, someone began a frantic signalling. "Yer dries it," bellowed Granny inexorably. "Then rubs it uvver anythink wot 'urts. That gen'rally answers. But if it *dunt*, try dug's wotsits...."

The quizmaster was aghast. The audience convulsed. "Only they ent so easy come by ner more," explained Granny. "They're the things though —"

"Mrs. Thompson, *please* —"

"You 'as ter spell 'em up," screeched the old lady. "Bile 'em. I kent tell yer the spells 'cos they're a trade secret but if yer teks my advice —"

The compère was trying to hustle them away from the mikes. He no longer looked suave. "I ent *finished*," fumed Granny. The great man spoke between his teeth. "You have lady, by God you have...."

"Dunt you blaspheme in my presence!" shrieked the elder Thompson. The stick was up at last, beating the air. Faint blue crackles emerged from its tip. "Tek yer 'ands *orf*," snarled Granny. She swung round. "An' stop pokin' that thing down our gel's *frock*...." The camera received a full charge from the spellstick, whistled backward and began making thunderous circuits of the stage. Hardboard flats fell apart; technicians removed themselves with more speed than elegance. "Whippersnappers," yelled Granny. "Shovin' an' pushin' young knows-it-orls. Never seen nothink like it, not in orl me days. Disbeleevin' lot ... If yer wants magic yer kin ev it...."

She flourished the stick and trails of fire leaped in the air like snakes, lights flashed, machines jetted smoke before collapsing into fragments. The old lady became surrounded by an aura of malevolence, blue and flickering. Galumphing noises sounded as the audience took to its heels. "Give y'orl summat ter larf at," howled Granny. Huge winds rushed about the studio performing indignities on everything; the control room panel imploded with a mighty whooshing, Anita's skirt blew up round her ears. She ducked and part of a ground row passed over her head, followed by the compère. Both began doing falling-leaf stunts over the stalls. The runaway camera careered by again, its superstructure decorated with an odd variety of objects: pieces of lath and rope, loops of cable, the remains of a canvas-back chair; and a shoe, solitary and rather forlorn, hooked over the top of the lens turret. The machine straightened,

10: IDIOT'S LANTERN

accelerated and vanished with a huge crash through the side wall.

Granny was well into her stride now; circles of blue light were splashing from the end of her stick and the tinkling and screaming round about were continuous. Anita concentrated desperately, trying to shut out the din. Her mind groped along wires, through junction boxes, found the great main fuses far off in the intake room. She screwed up her face, strained; there was a bang and a sputtering and the building was in darkness. Emergency lamps flared on almost at once; she killed those as well, grabbed her Granny's elbow and scurried for the stage door, using her bat-sense to dodge Unidentified Flying Objects and the clutching hands of technicians. The doorkeeper nearly had her; Anita threw a quick spell and his hat rammed itself down over his eyes with a soft, powerful sound. He blundered on past into the auditorium, which by now sounded like level four in the Inferno. Anita set a bank of fire extinguishers gushing as a diversion and panted round the corner of the building, still hauling Granny. There was a taxi; they bundled into it, Anita sweating nearly as much as she was laughing and Granny still clutching the spellstick and uttering horrible maledictions on everybody connected with television, hexcavators, quizzes, Lunnon and everything else she could think of. The hue and cry fell behind them rapidly and at Saint Pancras there was a train already waiting, first stop Kettering. Within minutes they were clear of town, and by nine o'clock they were home.

For the rest of the week the Thompson telly stayed silent. Granny did not deign either to mention it or glance in its direction; even her omnipresent duster passed it by with scarcely a flick. For Anita, it was bliss. She wandered about meeting old friends and making new ones. The nights were full of chattering again; she listened to foxes underground and badgers, the squeaks of mating newts miles off in the dewponds back of Brington Hill. She discovered an entirely new pipistrelle family and there were grass snakes in the copse now and a new boy at Debden's farm whose thought-patterns were very nice indeed. She could hear everything talking, owls and bats and insects, even the little creatures on the back of the moon. She collected a couple of newspapers and read about the odd technical accidents at a London television studio; the G.P.O. and the Electricity Authority were still investigating them. The police held the disturbance to be the work of practical jokers and were anxious to interview two people who had appeared on a certain quiz programme; but if there was a hunt it didn't reach as far as Anita and her Granny. Things returned almost to normal.

But not quite. A week later Anita sensed the old familiar tingling in the air and rushed home disappointed to find the telly on and her Granny settled in front of it as of old. But she need not have worried; the old lady's eyes were glittering ominously, her lips were compressed and she was gripping her stick in front of her. Round about were great books of magic, vats of odd liquids seethed and smoked and the cauldron was bubbling furiously with no fire beneath. Anita settled quietly in a corner. She could tell something remarkable was about to happen.

The quiz that had been Granny Thompson's favourite programme was announced. The compère appeared, urbane as ever, smiling and bowing as he introduced a fresh batch of victims. Granny sat stolidly until the questioning was under way. Then she leaned forward. As the quizmaster mouthed his second poser she raised her stick, pointed it at the screen and said slowly and distinctly, "Stuff...."

Anita watched open-mouthed to see if there would be any effect. Behind her the cauldron splashed and gurgled; she could feel the power gathered in the room. On the screen the gentleman did seem to stiffen a little; then he rallied and carried on. Granny Thompson increased the pressure. Sparks poured from the end of her stick, enveloped the television set with blue fire. On the cottage roof the aerial began to hum with strain. "*Stuff,*" said Granny with even greater firmness.

The compère stopped at that, and stared round him as if dazed. The sparks were hissing and roaring now, nearly blotting out the picture on the tube; something erupted from the thatch overhead, fled squawking. "Orter be took *orf,*" yelled the old lady triumphantly. "You ent wuth wotchin'. Dunt know wot yer *at*...."

The quizmaster appeared to wrestle with an inner compulsion. Then he turned and walked rapidly into camera, face twisted with rage. "You wicked old bat," he hissed. "I'll find you; and when I do I'll ram that stick so far down your gullet —"

For a moment the television appeared to swell. Then there was a flash and a shattering roar. Anita was bowled backwards. She got up slowly, half stunned and with her face covered with smuts. At first she couldn't see anything for the coloured patches floating in front of her eyes. Then she made out the blastmarks on the walls, the crater in the ceiling. The end of her bed hung through it precariously. The television was completely smashed, a blackened hulk from which smoke was rising in a column; there was a rich smell of burning insulation. Anita coughed, put a hand to her head and stared about for her Granny.

In the far corner of the room was a mess of furniture; protruding from it she saw a pair of shoes, sharp-pointed toes turned outwards. She rushed across terrified but before she had got Granny Thompson upright the old lady was cackling gleefully. " 'Ad 'im, gel," she shouted. "I 'ad 'im.... I didn't reckon I could 'ardly, 'ad ter work out a brand noo spell fer it. But I 'ad 'im. Tek 'im orf now they will, they'll reckon 'e's gorn orf 'is 'ead...." She slowly became aware of the mess. "Lor'-a-daisy," she said, shocked into profanity. And then with quick panic, "Gel, *wheer's me glasses*...."

For Anita, victory was complete. The destruction of the telly was like

10: IDIOT'S LANTERN

the death of an old enemy. There were disadvantages of course; they had workmen in the house for a month, and it took her even longer than that to find her cat and persuade him he could with safety return home. But Granny Thompson always stoutly denied the spell had gone wrong. "It were the telly," she explained. "It jist wadn't man enough for it." Then, with a sniff that indicated the subject was finally and completely closed, "Ought to 'a bin a *twenty-one inch*...."

KEITH ROBERTS

11: TIMOTHY

ANITA WAS BORED; and when she was bored odd things were liable to happen. Granny Thompson, who studied her granddaughter far more closely than she would have cared to admit, had been noticing a brooding look in her eyes for some days. She cast about for chores that would keep her mind off more exotic mischief for a time. "There's the 'en run," intoned the old lady. "That wants a good gooin'-uvver fer a start. 'Arf the posts orl of a tip, 'oles everywheer.... An' the path up ter the you-knows-wot. Nearly *went* on that, yisdey. Place gooin' orl of 'eap, an' yer sits there *moanin'* ..."

Anita sneered. "Chicken runs. Paths up to you-know-whats. I want to do something *interesting,* Gran. Like working a brand new spell. Can't we —"

"No we *kent!*" snapped the old lady irritably. "Spells, spells, kent think o' nothink but *spells.* You want ter look a bit lively, my gel. Goo on out an' earn yer keep, sit there chopsin' ... Goo on, git summat *done.* Git some o' that fat orf yer...."

Anita hissed furiously. She was very proud of her figure.

"Mackle up that there chair-back in the wosh'ouse," snarled Granny, warming to her theme. "Tek the truck down to old Goody's place an' git them line props wot's bin cut an' waitin 'arf a month. Git rid of orl that muck an' jollop yer chucked down by the copper 'ole a week larst *Toosdey.* Git the three o'clock inter Ket'rin', save my legs fer a change. 'Ole 'eap o' stuff we're run out on ..."

"Oh *please,* Gran, not today ..."

Granny Thompson softened a little. She didn't like going to Kettering either. "Well, goo on uvver to Aggie Everett's then an' git a couple of 'andfuls o' flour ... an' watch she dunt put no chiblins o' nothink in

[107]

with it. Aggie's sense o' wot's funny ent the same as anybody normal. . . . An' when yer gits back yer kin goo up an' git orl that bird's-nest muck out o' the *thack*. I ent 'avin' that game agin, wadn't the same fer a month larst time I went up that there ladder . . ."

Anita fled, partly to escape her Granny's inventiveness, partly because there was some truth in the crack about her weight. In the winter she seemed to store fat like a dormouse, there was no answer to it; she'd tried a summer dress on only the day before and there had been too much Anita nearly everywhere. She decided to make a start on the chicken run. Levitation and spellraising were all very well in their way but there was something peculiarly satisfying once in a while in taking ordinary wood and nails and a perfectly normal hammer and lashing about as vigorously as possible. She rapidly tired of the job though. The rolls of wire netting were recalcitrant, possessed of a seemingly infinite number of hooks and snags that all but defied unravelment; once undone, they buried themselves gleefully in her palms. And the ground was soaked and nasty so that worms spurted out whenever she tried to drive a post. Anita leaned on the somewhat dishevelled end frame of the run and yawned. She probed the mind of the nearest of its occupants and got back the usual moronic burbling about the next feeding-time. Hens are easily the most boring of companions.

Anita snorted, pushed back her hair, wiped her hot face and decided to go to Aggie's for the flour. She knew her Granny still had a good stock of practically everything in the larder and that the errand was only an excuse to get her out from underfoot for a while, but that didn't matter. She could take the long path round the far side of Foxhanger; perhaps the wood creatures were waking up by now.

She walked between the trees, well muffled in jeans, boots and donkey jacket. As she moved she scuffed irritably at twigs and leaves. She hated this time of the year with a peculiar loathing. February is a pointless sort of month; neither hot nor cold, neither winter nor spring. No animals, no birds, the sky a dull, uniform grey. . . . Anita hung her head and frowned. If only things would get a move on. . . . There were creatures in old tree stumps and deep in the ground, but the few she was able to contact were dozy and grumpy and made it quite clear that they wanted to be left alone for another six weeks, longer if possible. Anita decided she would like to hibernate, curled paws over nose in some brown crackling lair of leaves. Another year she really must try it; at least she might wake up feeling like doing something.

If she had expected any comfort from Aggie Everett she was disappointed. The old lady was morose; she had recently developed a head cold, had treated herself with a variety of ancient remedies and felt as she put it "wuss in consiquence." She was wearing a muffler knotted several times round her thin neck; her face was pale and even more scrinched-looking than usual while her nose, always a delicate

11: TIMOTHY

member, glowed like a stop-light. She confided to Anita that things "orl wanted a good shove, like"; her nephews would be coming down for the spring equinox and there were great plans for festivities but until then the Witches' Calendar was empty. The boys were away making cardboard boxes in far-off Northampton, and there was nothing to do at all. . . .

On the way back, weighed down by boredom and a bag of flour, Anita took a short cut across part of the Johnsons' land and saw Timothy on the horizon. Lacking anything better to do, she detoured so as to pass close by where he stood. She couldn't help noticing that Timothy looked as depressed as she felt. He had been made the previous spring to keep the birds off the new crops, so he was nearly a year old; and for nine months now he had had nothing to do but stand and be rained on and blown about by the wind and stare at the crown of Foxhanger Wood away across the fields. Anita nodded mechanically as she trudged past. "Afternoon, Timothy." But it seemed he was too tired even to flap a ragged sleeve at her. She walked on.

Twenty yards away she stopped, struck by a thought. She stood still for a moment, weighing possibilities and feeling excited for the first time in weeks. Then she went back, stepping awkwardly on the chunky soil. She set the flour down, put her hands on her hips and looked at Timothy with her head on one side and her eyes narrowed appraisingly.

His face was badly weathered of course, but that was unimportant; if anything, it tended to give him character. She walked up to him, brushed the lapels of his coat and tilted his old floppy hat to a more rakish angle. She made motions as if parting his wild straw hair. Timothy watched her enigmatically from his almond-shaped slits of eyes. He was a very well built scarecrow; the Johnson boys had put him together one weekend when they were home from college and Anita, who loved dolls and effigies, had watched the process with delight. She prodded and patted him, making sure his baling-wire tendons had not rotted from exposure. Timothy was still in good order; and although he was actually held up by a thick stake driven into the ground he had legs of his own, which was a great advantage. Anita walked round him, examining him with the air of a connoisseur. There were great possibilities in Timothy.

She moved back a few paces. Her boredom was forgotten now; she saw the chance of a brand new and very interesting spell. She squatted on her heels, folded her arms and rocked slightly to aid concentration. Around her, winter-brown fields and empty sky waited silently; there was no breath of wind. Anita opened her eyes, ran through the incantation quickly to make sure she had it firmly set in her mind. Then she waved a hand and began to mutter rapidly.

A strange thing happened. Although the day remained still something like a breeze moved across the ground to Timothy. Had there been grass it might have waved; but there was no grass, and the soil twinkled and shifted and was still again. The wind touched the scarecrow and it seemed his shoulders stiffened, his head came up a trifle. One of his outstretched arms waved; a wisp of straw dropped from his cuff and floated to the ground. The stake creaked faintly to itself.

Anita was vastly pleased. She stood and did a little jig; then she looked around carefully. For a moment she was tempted to finish the job on the spot and activate Timothy; but the Johnson farmhouse was in sight and scarecrows that talk and walk, and sing maybe and dance, are best not seen by ordinary folk. Anita scurried off with her head full of plans. Twenty yards away she remembered the flour and went back for it. Timothy stirred impatiently on his post and a wind that was not a wind riffled the ragged tails of his coat. "Sorry," called Anita. "I'll come back tonight, we can talk then. Besides, I'd better look up the rest of the trick, just to be sure." She skipped away, not turning back again, and Timothy might or might not have waved.

The sky was deep grey when she returned, and the swell of land on which the scarecrow stood looked dark and rough as a dog's back. Timothy was silhouetted against the last of the light, a black drunken shape looking bigger than he really was. Anita breathed words over him, made passes; then she undid the wire and cord that held him to his stake and Timothy slid down and stood a little uncertainly on his curious feet. Anita held his arm in case he tumbled and broke himself apart. "How do you feel?" she asked.

"Stiff," said Timothy. His voice had a musty, earthy sort of quality and when he opened his mouth there was an old smell of dry soil and libraries. Anita walked slowly with him across the furrows; for a time he tottered and reeled like an old man or a sick one, then he began to get more assurance and strode out rapidly. At first his noseless round face looked odd in the twilight but Anita soon got used to it. After all Timothy was a personality, and personalities do not need to be conventionally handsome. She crossed the field with the scarecrow jolting beside her, headed for the cover of the nearest trees.

She found Timothy's mind was as empty as a thing could be; but that was part of his charm, because Anita could stock it with whatever she wanted him to know. At first the learning process was difficult because one question had a knack of leading to a dozen others and often the simplest things are hardest to explain. Thus,

"What's night?"

"Night is now. When it's dark."

"What's dark?"

"When there isn't any light."

"What's light?"

"Er . . . Light is when you can see Foxhanger across the fields. Dark is when you can't."

"What's 'see' . . . ?"

11: TIMOTHY

Anita was on firmer ground when it came to the question of scarecrows.

"What's a scarecrow?"

"A thing they put in a field when there are crops. The birds don't come because they think it's a man."

"I was in a field. Am I a scarecrow?"

"No, you're not. Well maybe once on a time, but not any more. I changed you."

"Am I a man?"

"You will be . . ." And Anita leaned on the arm of the giant, and felt the firmness of his wooden bones, and was very proud.

Timothy was back in his place by first light and Anita spent some time scuffing out tracks. When the scarecrow walked he had a way of plonking his feet down very hard so they sank deeply into the ground. If old Johnson saw the marks he might take it into his head to wait up and see what queer animal was on the prowl, and Anita hated the thought of Timothy being parted by a charge from a twelve bore. She was only just beginning to find out how interesting he could be.

During the following weeks Granny Thompson had little cause for complaint. She rarely saw her granddaughter; in the daytime Anita was usually mugging up fresh spellwork, or trying with the aid of a hugely battered Britannica to solve some of the more brilliant of Timothy's probings; and at night she was invariably and mysteriously absent. Her Granny finally raised the question of these absences.

"*Gallivantin'*," snorted the elder Thompson. "Yore got summat *on*, I knows that. The question is, *wot?*"

"But Gran, I don't know what you mean. . . ."

"Kep me up 'arf the night larst night," pronounced Granny. "I could 'ear yer, gooin' on. Chelp chelp chelp, ev'ry night alike, but I kent 'ear nothink *answer* . . ." And then with a suddenly gimlet-like expression, "Yore got a *bloke* agin, my gel, that's wot . . ."

"Really, Gran," said Anita primly. "The very *idea* . . ."

"Anita, what's a witch?"

"I've told you a dozen times, Timothy. A witch is somebody like me or Gran, or Aggie Everett I suppose. We can . . . talk to all sorts of people. Like yourself. Normal folk can't."

"Why can't other people talk to me?"

"Well, they . . . it's hard to explain. It doesn't matter anyway, you've got me. I talk to you. I made you."

"Yes, Anita . . ."

"I've got a new dress," said Anita, pirouetting. Timothy stood stiffly by the gate and watched her. "An' new shoes . . . but I'm not wearing them tonight because I don't want the damp to spoil them. I've got all new things because it's spring." She held her hand out to Timothy and felt the brittle strength in him as he helped her over the gate. He had

[111]

a sort of clumsy courtesy that was all his own. "Anita, what's spring?"

Anita was exasperated. "It's when . . . oh, the birds come back from Africa, don't ask me where's Africa because I shan't tell you . . . and there's nice scents in the air at night and the leaves come on the trees and you get new clothes and you can go out and everything feels different. I like spring."

"What's 'like'?"

Anita stopped, puzzled. "Well, it's . . . I don't know. It's a feeling you have about people. I like you, for instance. Because you're gentle and you think about the things I think about." Overhead a bat circled and dipped and the evening light showed redly through his wings and for a moment he almost spoke to Anita; then he saw the gauntness walking with her along the path and spun back up into the sky. "I shall have to teach you about liking," said Anita. "There's still so many things you don't know." She pelted ultrasonics after the noctule but if he was still in range he didn't answer. "Come on, Timothy," she said. "I think we'll go to Deadman's Copse and see if the badgers are out yet."

"Spells," said Anita. "Marjoram and wormsblood and quicksilver and cinnabar. Mandrakes and tar and honey. Divination by sieve and shears. Can you remember all that?"

"Yes, Anita."

"You've got a very good brain, Timothy, you remember practically everything now. You've got most of the standard manual word for word, and I only read it through to you once. You really could be very useful. . . . I think you're developing what they call a Balanced Personality. Though there's so much to put in; I still keep remembering bits I haven't done. . . . Would you like to learn poetry?"

"What's poetry?"

Anita fumed momentarily, then started to laugh. "I'm tired of defining things, it gets harder all the time. We shall just have to do some, that's all; I'll bring a book tomorrow." And the day after she brought the book; it was one of her treasures, heavy and old and bound with leather. She opened Timothy's mind till he could read Shakespeare better than a man, then they went to Drawback to get a dramatic setting and Anita found Timothy's withered lips were just right for the ringing utterances of the old mad Lear. Next night they did a piece of *Tempest,* choosing for it the ghostly locale of Deadman's Copse. Anita read Ariel, though as she pointed out she was a little too well-developed for the part. Timothy made a fine Prospero; the cursing boomed out in great style though the bit about pegging people in oaks was if anything rather too realistic. When Timothy spoke the words Anita could see quite clearly how bad it would be to get mixed up with the knotty entrails of a tree as big as that.

The next day it rained, making the ground soggy and heavy. Mud

11: TIMOTHY

covered Anita's ankles before she was halfway across the field. Timothy looked a little sullen and there was a pungent, rotting smell about his clothing that she found alarming. "It's no good," she said, "we shall just have to get you under cover. I hate the idea of you standing out all the time; I don't expect you mind though."

"Anita, what's 'mind'?"

By mid-April Anita would normally have been busying herself about a hundred and one things connected with the field creatures and their affairs, but she was still mainly preoccupied with Timothy. Somehow she had stopped thinking of him as a scarecrow; the thing she had woken up was beginning to work by itself now and often when she came to release him he would bubble with notions of his own that had come to him in the grey time before the sun drained away his power. He asked her how she knew the names the bats called each other and why she was always sure when the weasel was too close for comfort; so she gave him a sixth sense, and portions of the seventh, eighth and ninth for good measure. Then she could leave him standing on watch in his field and scurry off on her own business and Timothy would tattle and wheeze out the night's news when next he saw her. He found out where the fieldmice were building, and how the Hodges were faring on their rounds; then one of the hares under Drawback was taken by a lurcher and Timothy heard the scream and told Anita stiffly, making the death seem like a lab report; and Anita angrily gave him emotions and after that the tears would squeeze from somewhere and roll down his football face whenever he thought about killing.

Anita came home with the dawn to find her Granny waiting for her. "This," said the old lady without preamble, " 'as gotta *stop*."

Anita flung herself down in one of the big armchairs and yawned. "Wha', Gran . . ."

"Gallivantin'," said Granny Thompson sternly. "Muckin' about wi' that gret thing uvver at the Johnsonses. *Ugghhh* . . . Giz me the creeps it does straight. . . . Gret mucky thing orl straw an' stuff, sets yer teeth on edge ter *think* on it. . . ." She crossed to one of the little windows and opened it. A breeze moved cold and sweet, ruffling Anita's hair. The room was shadowy but the sky outside was bright; somewhere a bird started to sing, all on its own. *"Gallivantin',"* said Granny again, as if to clinch matters.

Anita was nearly asleep; she'd used a lot of power that night and she was very tired. She said dreamily, "He's not a thing, Gran. He's Timothy. He's very sweet. I invented him, he knows about *everything* . . ." Then a little more sharply, *"Gran!* How did you know —"

Granny Thompson sniffed. "I knows wot I *knows* . . . There's ways an' means, my gel. Some as even you dunt know, artful though yer might be. . . ."

Anita had a vision of something skulking in hedgerows, pouring itself across open ground like spilled jam. A very particular vision this, it lashed its tail and spat. She said reproachfully, "You didn't play fair. You used a familiar. . . ."

Granny looked virtuous. "I ent sayin' I *did,* an' there agin I ent sayin' I *didn't.* . . ."

"It was Vortigern," said Anita, pouting. "It must have been. None of the others would peach on me. But *him* . . ."

"Never mind 'ow I *knows,*" said Granny Thompson sternly. "Or 'oo tole me. The thing is, yore gone fur *enough.* Any more an' I wunt be responsible, straight I wunt. . . ."

"But Gran, he's nice. And . . . well, I'm sorry for him. I don't like to think of him being left on his own now. It would be . . . well, like somebody dying almost. He's too clever now, can't just . . . *eeeooohhhh* . . . jus' leave him li' that. . . ."

"Clever," muttered Granny, looking at the wall and not seeing it. "That ent no call fer pity . . . You save yer pity fer the next world, my gel, there ent no place fer it 'ere. . . . Brains, pah. Straw an' dirt an' muck orf the fields, that's brains. Same with 'im, same with 'em orl. You'll learn. . . ."

But the homily was lost on Anita; she had incontinently fallen asleep.

She dreamed of Timothy that morning, woke and slept again to see if he would come back. He did; he was standing far away in his field and waving his arms to her and calling but his voice was so thick and distant she couldn't hear the words. But he wanted something, that was plain; and Anita woke and blinked, thought she knew what it was, and forgot again. She rubbed her eyes, saw the sunlight, felt the warmth of the air. It was lunchtime, and the day was as hot as June.

The fields were dark and rough and a full moon was rising. Anita crossed the open ground behind Foxhanger. A hunting bird called, close and low; she stopped and saw distant woods humped on their hills, looking like palls of smoke in the moonhaze. Timothy was waiting for her, a tiny speck a long way off in the night. When she reached him he looked gaunter than ever; his fingers stuck out in bundles from his sleeves, and his hat was askew. The night wind stirred his coat, moonlight oozed through the tatters and rags. Anita felt a queer stirring inside her; but she released him as usual and Timothy wriggled from the stake and dropped awkwardly to the ground. He said, "It's a lovely night, Anita." He took an experimental step or two. "After you'd gone this morning my leg broke; but I mended it with wire and it's all right again now." Anita nodded, her mind on other things. "Good," she said. "Good, Timothy, that's fine. . . ."

In February the ground had been bare and red-brown; now the harshness was lost under a new green hair. That was the corn Timothy had been made to protect. She took his arm. "Timothy," she said. "Let's walk. I'm afraid I've got an awful lot to say."

They paced the field, on the path that was beaten hard where the tractor came each day; and Anita told Timothy about the world.

11: TIMOTHY

Everything she knew, about people dying, and living, and hoping; and how all things, even good things, get old and dirty and worn-out, and the winds blow through them, and the rain washes them away. As it has always been, as it will be forever till the sun is cold. "Timothy," she said gently, "one day . . . even my great Prince will be dust. It will be as though He had never been. He, and all the people of His house. Nobody knows why; nobody ever will. It's just the way things are."

Timothy jolted gravely alongside; Anita held his thin arm and although he had no real face she could tell by his expression that he understood what she was saying. "Timothy," she said. "I've got to go away. . . ."

"Yes, Anita. . . ."

She swallowed. "It's right what Gran says. You're old now and nearly finished and there are so many other things to do. I haven't been fair, Timothy. You've just been a . . . well, a sort of toy. You know . . . I wasn't ever really interested in you. You were just something I made when I was bored. You sort of grew on me."

"Yes, Anita . . ."

They turned at the farthest end of their walk. The air was wine-warm on her face and arms and Timothy smelled faintly of old brass spoons and what he was thinking about it was impossible to say. "It's spring now," said Anita. "It's the time you put on a new dress and do your hair and find someone nice you can drive with or talk with or just walk along with and watch the night coming and the owls and the stars. They're the things that have to be done because they start right deep down inside you, in the blood. It's the same with animals nearly, they wake up and everything's fresh and green, and it's as if winter was the night and summer is one great long day. . . ."

They had reached Timothy's stake. In the west the sky was still turquoise; an owl dropped down against the light like a black flake of something burned. Anita propped Timothy against his post. He seemed stiffer already and more lifeless somehow. She put his hat right; it was always flopping down. As she reached up she saw something shine silver on his wizened-turnip face. She was startled, until she remembered she had given him feelings. Timothy was crying.

She hugged him then, not knowing what to do. She felt the hardness of him and the crackling dryness, the knobs and angles of his bits-and-pieces body. "Oh Timothy," she sad. "Timothy, I'm sorry, but I just can't go with you any more. There won't be any spells for you after this, I've taken the power off. . . ." She stepped back, not looking at him. "I'll go now," she said. "This way's best, honestly. I won't tie you back onto your stick or anything, you can just stand here awhile and watch the bats and the owls. And in the morning you'll just sort of fade away; it won't hurt or anything. . . ." She started to walk off down the slope, feeling the blades of new corn touch her calves. "Good-bye, Timothy," she called.

11: TIMOTHY

Something iron-hard snagged at her. She fell, rolled over horrified and tried to get up. Her ankles were caught; she wriggled and the night vanished, shut away by rough cloth that smelled of earth. "Love," croaked Timothy. "Please, Anita, love. . . ." And she felt his twiggy fingers move up and close over her breasts.

She looped like a caterpillar caught by the tail and her fists hit Timothy squarely, bang-bang. Dust flew, and the seeds of grass; then Anita was up and running down the hill, stumbling over the rough ground, and Timothy was close behind her, a flapping patch of darkness with his musty old head bobbing and his arms reaching out. His voice floated to her through the night. "Anita . . . *love* . . ."

She reached the bottom of the field tousled and too shocked to defend herself at all, cut across the Johnsons' stackyard with Timothy still hard on her heels. A dog volleyed barks, subsided whimpering as he caught the strange scent on the air. Back up the hill, a doubling across Home Paddock; a horse bolted in terror as old cloth flapped at his eyes. Near the hedge Timothy gained once more, but he lost time climbing the gate. Anita spun round fifty yards away. "Timothy, *go back! Timothy, no!*"

He came on again; she took three deep breaths, lifted her arm and flung something at him that crackled and fizzed and knocked a great lump of wadding from his shoulder. One arm flopped down uselessly but the rest of him still thumped toward her. Anita was angry now; her face was white in the moonlight and there was a little burning spot on each cheek and her mouth was compressed till her lips were hardly visible at all. "Scarecrow!" she shouted. "Old dirty thing made of straw! *Spiders' home!*" She'd had time to aim; her next shot took Timothy full in the chest and bowled him backwards. He got up and came on again though he was much slower.

Anita waited for him on the little bridge over the Fyne-brook. She stood panting and pushing the hair out of her eyes with each hand in turn and the rage was white-hot now and choking her. Round her, brightnesses fizzed and sparked; as Timothy came within range she hit him again and again, arms and legs and head. Pieces flew from him and bounced across the grass. He reached the bridge but he was only a matchstick man now, his thin limbs glinting under tatters of cloth. Anita took a breath and held it, shut her eyes then opened them very wide, made a circle with her hands, thrust fire at Timothy. His wooden spine broke with a great sound; what was left of him folded in the middle, tumbled against the handrail of the bridge. He fell feet over head into the stream. The current seized him, whirling him off; he fetched up twenty yards away and lay quiet, humped in a reedbed like a heap of broken umbrellas.

Anita moved forward one foot at a time, ready to bolt again or throw more magic; but there was no need. Timothy was finished; he stayed still, the water rippling through his clothes. A little bright beetle shot

[117]

from somewhere into his coatsleeve, came out at the elbow and sculled away down the stream. Timothy's face was pressed into mud so he could see nothing, but his voice still whispered in Anita's mind. *Please . . . please. . . .*

She ran again, faster than ever. Along beside the brook, across the meadow, through Foxhanger, up the garden path. She burst into the kitchen of the cottage, spinning Granny Thompson completely round. Took the stairs three at a time and banged her bedroom door shut behind her. She flung herself on the bed and sobbed and wrapped blankets round her ears; but all night long, until the last of the power ran down, she could hear Timothy thinking old mouldy thoughts about rooks and winds, and worms in the thick red ground.

12: COUSIN ELLA MAE

ANITA DIDN'T often sulk; but when she did, she made a job of it. She sat on the station platform, knees crossed and legs stuck out, fists rammed into the pockets of her denim skirt. Her brows were contracted into a scowl; her lower lip stuck out ominously. (Granny Thompson had warned her, as a parting pleasantry, to "wotch an' not trip uvver it.") She was waiting for the five o'clock from London.

A little wind blew, stirring her white shirt and lifting her hair. It whirled a knot of summer scents among the smells of diesel fuel and waiting-room dust, but Anita was not to be appeased.

"Trains," she grumbled. "Taxis, buses . . . an' *tunnels* . . ." The trip under the platforms, short as it had been, had played Hell with her delicate complex of senses. She pulled her chin in and screwed her mouth up oddly. "Time you learned, my gel," she mimed viciously. "Yer kent 'ave it orl yer own way. It wunt *wosh,* not wi' me. . . . *Wosh,*" she muttered rebelliously. "*Wosh* . . . an' it wasn't as if I wasn't busy either. And that was *important.* . . ."

She skittered to the edge of the platform but there was nothing in sight. To the south the tracks reached off till they vanished, wobbling in heat-haze. Across the way the big clock jumped to eight minutes past five. Anita mooched back, banged herself down on the seat again and put her chin in her hands. "That's all it needed," she mused bitterly. "Now the damn thing's late. . . ."

The cable had arrived a few days previously. It had sent her Granny into a fever of activity, dusting the immaculate tops of tables and sideboards, polishing that which already gleamed. Anita had ignored the signs and portents till the morning she discovered Granny

[119]

Thompson atop a pair of steps in the pantry cupboard, whitewashing its walls. Her felt hat and floral apron had suffered extensively from the backwash and there were even little blobs of paint poised fascinatingly in the old lady's eyebrows. Anita put her hands on her hips. "Gran," she called up, "what on earth's going on?"

"Well yer might *arsk,*" puffed the elder Thompson. "Young *varmint* . . ." *Splosh,* went the brush. *Splosh, slurp.* The raw, rich smell of whitewash filled the air. "If yer was 'arf wot yer mek out," snarled Granny, "yer'd be up 'ere earnin' yer *keep.* . . . Me rheumaticks wun't *tek* much more o' this, I'll tell yer. . . ."

Anita captured the brush. The comments weren't strictly fair; admittedly she did sometimes get tired of ordinary housework, but never of painting. She knew her Granny was just niggled because she'd resisted asking till now. Granny Thompson yielded her place with alacrity; Anita climbed aboard the steps and carried on. "If you'd just tell me what was happening, Gran," she said, "I might be able to help. . . ."

Granny Thompson had hobbled away; now she reappeared importantly, glasses perched askew on her nose, the cable flimsy in her hand. "It's yer cousin, Ella Mae," she explained. "Orl the way frum Americky. Yer cousin, wot you ent ever seed. . . . She's a-comin' next *Toosdey,* it ses so 'ere. . . ."

"Coming where, Gran?"

" 'Ere, o' course," roared the old lady. "Wot d'yer use fer *'ead.* . . ."

"Oh, no. . . ." Anita froze, shocked, holding the brush above her. A small river of whitewash coursed instantly down her sleeve, mapped out a complex itinerary under her jumper. She dropped the brush into the bucket and put her face in her hands. "Gran, she can't . . . not *now* . . ."

But the old lady had been adamant. Ella Mae was coming, all the way from America, for an indefinite vacation. Anita was to meet her and bring her back to the cottage, and that was the end of it.

Another cable arrived the following morning. Anita hoped fervently that Ella Mae had been lost at sea or depressurized at twenty thousand feet, but no such luck. The new message merely confirmed her departure and emphasized that she was "looking forward to meeting you-all, stop." So here Anita was, broodingly waiting for the train that would bring the unwanted visitor into her life.

One of Anita's major vices was that she was very bad with her relatives. Visitors were comparatively rare, but each one that arrived seemed more impossibly tedious than the last. The Thompson clan was widely scattered; she had gathered, from her Granny's somewhat woolly geographical ramblings, that Ella Mae came from somewhere in the southwest, but that was all. Anita had already decided what she would look like. She would be rather fat and disgustingly jolly, have white hair and predatory rhinestone glasses and keep saying "Wal, ah

12: COUSIN ELLA MAE

declare. . . ." There was an alternative version in which Ella Mae was tall and thin and dried-up like Aggie Everett and sat around all day knitting and saying, "Land *sakes,* girl," at everything Anita did. She shook her head and decided on the fat, jolly version. It would annoy her much more.

Far off a diesel shouted, with its voice made of brass and oil. Anita sat upright with a visible tremor. The train was coming at last; the next few minutes would finally decide her fate.

The coaches took the curve into the station with a twittering of wheelrims and a knifegrinding noise of brakes. Steam blew out from hissing unions, enveloping Anita completely. British Railways, in accordance with their own highly stylized sense of creature comforts, seemed to have decided to improve the amenities of the train on this sweltering day by heating all its compartments. A motley of somewhat bedraggled passengers began to descend, doors banged like cannon shots along the platform. Anita searched desperately, tacking about here and there. *Luggage,* she decided suddenly. Cousin Ella Mae would have about a hundred trunks and boxes, and keep dropping things and saying, "Wal, gol*durn* it. . . ." She searched for huge ladies with suitcases. There weren't any.

She dithered at the top of the platform steps. Unwelcome as the visitor might be, it would be disastrous to let her slip by; Granny Thompson would be sure it had happened on purpose. A large person bore down on Anita, sweating profusely and making noises like a foundering grampus. Anita gulped, facing disaster; but that wasn't Ella Mae either because someone met her and whisked her away down the steps. *She wasn't on it,* thought Anita with a sudden rise of hope. *She wouldn't just tear off, she'd expect to be met . . .*

The platform was empty, except for one girl. She was very attractive; she was wearing a nearly-white suit that didn't look crumpled at all, an odd-coloured blue-brown blouse, little shoes with neat inch-high spike heels. They set off her ankles superbly. She was carrying a single small case; her hair was dark blonde, nearly matching her skin, and worn in a neat coif at the back of her head. Her face was like a chiselled cat, just like Anita's picture of Bast in her great book of all the Egyptian gods; and her eyes were very blue, so blue they looked nearly crossed like Winijou's when he stared hard. Anita felt vaguely sorry for her, she was looking a little lost. She turned to leave; she was halfway down the steps when the strange girl called.

"Pardon me, ma'am. . . ."

Anita stopped, frozen. The voice, the great twang in it . . . But it couldn't be! She ran back, quickly.

"Yes . . . ?"

The girl who looked like Bast simpered. It gave Anita the oddest feeling; her mind started tapping out on several dark frequencies. "Ah'm sorry to trouble y'all," said the stranger. "But ah kind o' thought ah might be met . . ."

Anita nearly couldn't breathe. "I don't believe it," she whispered. "You're not . . . your name isn't Ella Mae, is it?"

"Wal, gol*durn*," said the girl, dropping her suitcase. "Yew must be Anita; ah've heard a lot about yew. . . ."

They embraced enthusiastically. They were both rather mussed up by the time they were through. *Beautiful,* panted Anita, not using her voice. Their minds had locked frequencies now. *I thought you'd be absolutely terrible . . . gosh, this is fabulous. . . .*

"Wal, goldurn," said Ella Mae again. "Y'ain't so bad y'sailf. . . ." She brushed a strand of hair from her eyes. "Gee honey, that crazy ole train . . . where do we go naow?"

Anita picked up her case. It felt very light. "I thought you'd be about ninety years old," she said, "and fat. I just can't wait for you to meet my Granny, we've been doing the cottage up for weeks . . . gosh, this is fabulous. . . ."

"Wal," said Ella Mae. "Wal, ah *declare.* . . ." Somehow, now, Anita didn't mind the phrase at all.

They sat at table; Anita, her Granny, and Ella Mae. In front of Ella Mae was a cup containing a light brown fluid. "We call it tea," said Anita a little apologetically. "We drink it nearly all the time."

Ella Mae concentrated; there was a *plink,* and a second cup appeared alongside the first. Its contents were much darker. Ella Mae picked it up and drank gratefully. "That's great stuff, that tea," she said. "But ah guess maybe ah'll take a li'l ole time t'git used to it. . . ."

Anita's eyes popped open very wide.

The two girls sprawled on the floor of Anita's bedroom. Between them was an Ordnance Survey sheet; blonde hair mingled with brown as they pored over it. Ella Mae had changed now, into a fluffy white sweater with vast initials on the front and absolutely crease-resistant slacks. "I shall have to show you . . . oh, absolutely everything," said Anita. "Gosh, there's thousands of things. . . . And you'll have to meet Aggie, and my cousins, and masses of people. . . . How long did you say you were staying?" she asked anxiously.

Ella Mae laughed. "Long enough, ah reckon. But Annie, don't yew let me put y'all t'no trouble. . . ."

"It isn't any trouble," said Anita. "It's *important* . . . Where do you want to start?"

"Well, what's this your Granny was saying, honey, 'bout this whaddya call it, this pub? Did ah git it right, did you say pub?"

Anita's face clouded a little. "Oh, that . . . Well yes, there's a sort of problem with it just now; we were all very busy. But it doesn't matter," she said quickly. "The others can manage."

Ella Mae lit a Lucky Strike, fanned the smoke away quickly as

12: COUSIN ELLA MAE

Anita's nose wrinkled. "Tell me 'baout this place," she said. "Might as well start somewhere."

Anita sat back on her heels. "It's a bit difficult," she said. "I don't really know where to begin." The cat-eyes watched her steadily. "It's going to be pulled down in a couple of weeks," she said. "They pull all sorts of things down now. It's a very old place. Anyway the co—" She stopped. She'd nearly said "coven" before she remembered. They weren't a coven, not any more; they'd had a circular about it the week before, now they were a Field Research Group. "The Group were working on it," she said. "Getting all the people out."

"People?"

"The ghosts," said Anita. "Poor things, they don't have anywhere to go, you see; and if they're still there when they wreck the place they'll go *crazy*."

"Uh-huh," said Ella Mae, eyes narrowed. "Go on, honey."

Anita floundered a little. "I don't suppose you get this sort of problem where you come from," she said. "I don't expect you're very interested."

Ella Mae blew smoke in a bright blue cloud and sat upright, crossing her long legs neatly. "Honey," she said, "ah'm here t' *learn*. Ah'm interested in ever' li'l thing. . . ."

Anita and Ella Mae strolled along Brington High Street. Ella Mae stared around as they walked, taking everything in. They passed ancient cottages, their walls wavy and leaning, their windows replete with painted shutters and boxes of flowers. Between the old houses were shops and supermarkets, set well back from the road. Fluorescent tubes glared out coldly into the dusk. "That's the Building Line," said Anita, pointing. "Everything's got to go back to it, they're knocking it all down."

Ella Mae held up her pack of cigarettes, squinted at it. There was a *plop* and a mild flash of blue light. Another pack appeared beside it in her hand. Doubling was her best trick; Anita, who couldn't do it at all, was still fascinated by it. Ella Mae opened the new pack and lit up. "Why'd they do that, honey?" she asked.

"Do what?"

"Push all this ol' stuff daown."

"I don't know," said Anita simply. "I think it's a Sign of the Times. Look, there's the pub. At the end there."

The Saracen's Head jutted forward at the road. On either side of it raw new building lots emphasized its isolation. Once it had leaned on the buildings to right and left; now, deprived of support, it seemed to crouch and shiver. Ella Mae looked up at it, saw bedroom windows she could reach and touch, insurance plaques still set in the pink-painted walls. "It's great," she breathed. "Jes' great. . . ."

Anita nodded. "It is beautiful, isn't it? The whole Group's been watching it for weeks now." She gripped Ella Mae's elbow. "There's one of our people, look. I'm taking over from him."

Ella Mae nodded. "It's okay, honey, ah can tell." Aggie's nephew sat outside the pub, astride a nearly-new Matchless. He waved his arm briefly; almond eyes burned before he pulled his goggles into place. He started up and crackled away, bending low over the handlebars.

Anita sighed dreamily, watching the young witch out of sight. "He's nice," she said. "Sometimes I think I could go for him. But then I like his brother too; and they're twins, it makes things difficult."

They went into the snug. Anita bought half a pint of bitter for herself and a large gin for Ella Mae. They sat looking round at old beams, walls glazed brown with nicotine. The windowcurtains moved in the evening breeze and Anita felt her back hair prickle. "We've got nearly all of them," she said. "We've moved them out to Foxhanger. There's only one left. He's sixteenth century, I think; he's *sweet,* but terribly shy. If we could only get him to materialize for long enough we could explain it all to him but he just won't . . . Do you have many ghosts in America?"

"One or two." Ella Mae shrugged deprecatingly. "Ol' Indian jobs; y'know honey, Winijous an' sech." She stared round her again. "Honey, you say they're pullin' this place *daown?*"

"Yes."

"We ain't got no sech places," said the American girl. "Not over theah. . . . What'll they put up instaid?"

"I don't know. A supermarket I expect."

"Why?"

"I don't know. There's one already. There have to be two so they can buy each other's sugar back."

"Honey," said Ella Mae seriously, "ah guess yew better start right from the beginnin'. There's a whole heap ah need fillin' in on." She bent down under the table and grimaced. Anita, peering curiously, saw she was taking her shoes off. Ella Mae grinned apologetically. "Sorry, Annie," she said. "Ain't rightly used t'these things yait. . . ."

Anita began to chuckle. They had so much in common it nearly wasn't true.

Ella Mae fitted in as if she'd been born in Northamptonshire. Some evenings she would sit and talk by the hour, entrancing Anita with stories about mountains and rivers and Winijous, motels and soda fountains, Cadillacs and soil erosion, Planned Obsolescence and Richard Nixon. "And once," she said, "y'know honey, once . . . ah met *him.* . . ." They were undressing in Anita's bedroom; Ella Mae sat with her hair down and the lamplight shining golden on her skin.

"Who?"

"Him. . . ." Ella Mae held a bright paperback against her chest. It was one of Anita's prized books. *"Bradbury,"* said Ella Mae, voice hushed. "It was in California one time, ah *met* him. . . . Leastways," she added, simpering, "ah touched his *coat.* . . ."

12: COUSIN ELLA MAE

"Gosh," said Anita, thoroughly converted. "Oh, *gee*. . . ."

Ella Mae's trick of doubling was certainly her major talent. Her suitcase might be small but it seemed to contain one of almost everything. Anita got so she couldn't face breakfast without maple syrup and fruit juice and coffee and a whole host of extras; she acquired a fluffy white sweater (she spent hours picking the monogram off the front and stitching A T in its place) and innumerable pairs of absolutely crease-resistant slacks. Transistors and deodorants, bubble baths and corn on the cob; the miracles were endless. In return she took Ella Mae on excursions; they saw Wicksteed Park and the Houses of Parliament, the Tower of London and the Triangular Lodge. But none of it solved the problem of the Saracen's Head and its one remaining ghost. The place had been easily the most haunted pub in Northamptonshire; its displaced inmates thronged Foxhanger so the little wood was full of chillings and whinings, even on a bright summer's day. Anita explained that part of the problem to Ella Mae. "It's the clearances," she said petulantly. "The new Controller's an absolute *dear*, but he's so clueless it just isn't true. The poor things don't like it here, they should have gone down ages ago. At this rate they'll be stuck for years . . ."

"Seems t'me," said Ella Mae pensively, "y'all could use some good ol' knowhow around heah. Git yoursel's a good Controller. . . ."

"We had one," said Anita. "He was so good," she added nastily, "they transferred him to the film business. . . ." She shuddered. "I think," she said, "we'll stick with the one we've got. . . ."

Some nights later Anita sensed a most unpleasant emanation. She rushed to the cottage and upstairs to her room. She flung the door open and gasped. Ella Mae sat on the floor beside her bed. Between her knees was a yellow plastic bucket; pressed firmly against the wall in front of her was a three-legged stool. She was pulling at the legs in turn, crooning softly to herself. The words were inaudible but Anita knew they were a spell. She had never seen one like it before but she had no doubt what was going on; tomorrow some perfectly innocent local farmer would find he had a herd of very dry cows. Anita snatched the stool away indignantly. "You can't do that. . . ."

Ella Mae looked plaintive. "Wal, goldurn it, Annie, ah gotta keep m'hand in somehaow. . . ."

"Well don't do it like that," said Anita tartly. "It looks revolting. If you really want to try some magic you can help us tonight at the Saracen's. We've had an idea."

Ella Mae dusted her hands and hitched at her slacks. "That's mah girl," she said approvingly. "That's what ah was waitin' t'hear. . . ."

The two hares scuttled cautiously across a moonlit waste of rubble, dived into thick shadow by the side wall of the Saracen's Head. They sat up, noses quivering, testing the air. They watched each other enigmatically for a moment; one was very dark, the other an odd corn-colour, nearly blonde. *So far so good,* Anita transmitted breathlessly. *What now?*

The window . . .

She looked up and nodded. She crouched, quivering; there was a *plop,* a momentary flash of light, and where the hare had been, was nothing. A bat flew from the shadows, zigged up to where a little window stood ajar in the warm night air. A moment's pause, and another followed it.

Small shapes moved down the stairs, along a corridor. Found the door at the top of the cellar steps, wriggled underneath and were gone. Inside, the place was pitch dark. There were unidentifiable sounds, two soft concussions; Anita sat up in the middle of the floor and looked around for Ella Mae.

She had materialized behind her. Anita shone a small torch. Ella Mae had dressed, very dramatically, in black high-neck sweater and black stretch pants. "You know," said Anita, "I love those trews. They really do something for you."

Ella Mae pushed back a wisp of hair from her eyes. "Ah'll double y'a pair in the mornin'," she said laconically. "Y' got the things?"

"I think so. . . ." Anita felt in her pockets, produced several sticks of coloured chalk. She started to draw. "Aren't eight legs rotten?" she asked over her shoulder. "You just can't manage them. I'd hate to get stuck like that."

She completed the first pentacle, started on another. "It's always been difficult," she said. "I've scratched these things in the yard dozens of times but they're never really strong enough. . . . Are they still asleep upstairs?"

Ella Mae snuffed the air like a bloodhound. "Ah think so . . . yep, they're okay." The elderly couple who ran the pub could almost be relied on not to interfere.

"Three. . . ." Anita sat back on her heels. "There you are. Do you think you can manage now?"

Ella Mae shifted her position. "Land *sakes,* Annie," she said, "don't yew think they train us over theah?" She concentrated, staring down; at her feet the dust of the cellar floor whimpered and scuffed. Another set of chalklines appeared beside the first; then another, then six together. Anita felt her skin begin to prickle. It was working; with each doubling, the power of the pentacle increased dramatically. When Ella Mae had finished, the spell was practically screaming to be let go. Anita transmitted quietly.

Ready, Gran?

Testily. *Git on with it, the pair on yer. I ent got orl night. . . .*

Ready, Aunt Aggie?

A cackling. *Let it goo, gel, I'll 'ave 'im. . . .*

Right!

Anita made a quick pass. There was a flash and a crackling. For an instant the cellar, the barrels on their stillions, the stacks of bottles in their crates, were brightly lit. The force snatched its inmate from his Parallel Plane, slammed him down inside the multiplied pentacle with a bone-shaking thump. Anita hugged Ella Mae. "It worked, Ella Mae, it *worked*. . . ." She scurried forward. "It's all right," she said. "Please don't be frightened, we won't hurt you. . . ."

The ghost sat trembling, unable to escape from the chalkmarks. He wore breeches and a ruffed shirt; his eyes were dark and huge, his hair fair and long, curling most attractively beside his ears. He hardly looked any age at all. Anita tried to take his hand but he snatched it away. "Who art thou?" he asked a little wildly. "Com'st thou from Heaven, or from Hell?"

Anita coughed. "We won't go into that now," she said delicately. "All that matters is, you're in a terrible fix. . . ." She started to explain what was going to happen. "You've only got one more day," she said. "Tomorrow's the last night. If you don't come with us quickly . . . *poof!*" She kept talking, desperately; with a part of her mind she could feel her Granny and Aggie Everett winding up what they would jointly have described as a right good 'un."

"Thou speakest of destruction," said the boy, bewildered. "What, shall some plague, some torment, fall then from the air?"

"It shall," snarled Anita. "They call them supermarkets. . . ."

Ella Mae put her hand on her arm. "Steady, Annie, you're confusin' the little guy. . . ." The ghost turned to her, brightening a little. "Thy garb is strange," he said, "but thou art passing fair . . . com'st thou from our colonies in the Americas?"

Ella Mae choked. Anita began to giggle; then *bang, pouff.* . . . The ghost screamed shrilly. Aggie Everett cackled, distant in Anita's mind. *That's got 'im . . . that's fixed 'im, Maude. . . .*

The spell was now non-reversing. Aggie had a major talent, too. . . .

The ghost had drawn a little dagger. He swung at Anita, terrified. She knew he couldn't hurt her; she jumped back nonetheless, not wanting to hurt his feelings. Then a voice called and grumbled sleepily; and a light gleamed at the top of the cellar steps.

The place became a whirl of activity. Three figures scurried frantically, flung themselves down behind a stack of crates. Anita lay with her arm round the boy's shoulders. He smelled sweet and dry, like all old dead things. The voice called again; a torch swept the walls in a perfunctory manner, clicked off. The publican, relieved, tramped back upstairs to bed.

The three disengaged themselves slowly. The boy held Ella Mae's hand rather longer than was strictly necessary. She stared into his face, correspondingly dazed. "Gee," she said. "Gee, ah'm still tryin' t'git over it. Gee whiz, a genu-ine English ghost. . . ."

"You're all right," said Anita breathlessly to the lad. "Ordinary people still can't see you, it's just you won't be able to play that silly hyperspace trick again."

Ella Mae laughed. "What's your name?"

The boy was still confused. "D-Dickon, an' it please thee. . . ."

She chuckled again. The sound rang musically in the cellar. "Well, Dickon, ere a fortnight make thee older —" She passed abruptly onto another wavelength. Anita retuned but by the time she'd caught up the message was finished.

She said curiously, "What did you say?"

"Nothin'. . . . Honey, we'd best scram before the ol' guy comes back with a scattergun. You comin', Dickon?"

The boy shook his head, frightened again, and drew back.

"Leave him," said Anita gently. "It always takes them a little while to get used to moving. But you must be ready for us next time, Dickon. We'll come again tomorrow. All right?"

He nodded, dumbly. She wanted to hug him but it would only upset him again. "We'll be back tomorrow," she said. "Goodnight, Dickon. . . ."

" 'Bye naow. . . ."

Twin flashes. *Things* scuttled up the stairs, eased their way under the door.

All three bars of the pub were packed to capacity. On the counters were placed pints of beer, their taps facing outwards for people to help themselves; it was like New Year's Eve. There was much talk and laughter and chinking of glasses. Outside in the yard machines like primitive beasts waited, their yellow claws quiet; in the morning they would come, and there would be dust and nothingness.

The younger members of the coven had congregated in a corner of the saloon; Anita was there with Ella Mae, and Aggie's two cousins. The boys were resplendent in bright, fringed shirts and cowboy boots, worn in honour of Ella Mae; Ella Mae was as elegant as an American saying goodbye to an English pub can be expected to be; Anita was wearing a tiny white summer dress with matching handbag and shoes. She was rather flushed; Ella Mae's trick of doubling had already been performed a dozen times on a miniature bottle of gin and she was feeling most of the effects.

Dickon had joined the group for a time, greatly daring; but once the hooch started to circulate he had slipped away. Anita was conscious that somewhere at the back of her mind a thoroughly annoyed Granny Thompson was hammering for admittance; but somehow she couldn't seem to get the old lady tuned in.

Ella Mae was in splendid form. "So this guy," she was saying, "goes up to the bartender, he says, 'Ah wanna Martini made mah way. Pour me . . . yea much gin.' " She held up three fingers. " 'Then lean over the glass an' say, very gentle, *Vermouth*. . . .' "

"Ella Mae —"

12: COUSIN ELLA MAE

"Shut up, Annie. So the bartender leans over the glass, he says very soft, 'Vermouth.' And the guy picks up the gin, he tastes it, rolls it round his tongue, he eyes the bartender an' says, 'Loudmouth. . . .' "

"What?"

"Loudmouth," said Ella Mae, looking pained. "Hey, Annie, have a slug of rocket fuel. . . ."

Anita collapsed backward onto a pile of coats. She sat giggling and fanning the air with her hands. "*Loudmouth,*" she said helplessly. "*Loudmouth. . . .*"

One A.M.

Granny Thompson sat stolidly in the cottage, eyes on the big clock on the mantelshelf. She lifted her head, turned it; her ears swivelled slowly. There was a noise of singing, tiny and far-off.

Two figures crossed the brook below Foxhanger, balancing precariously on the stepping-stones by the bridge. On the far bank one of the revellers, dressed in white, paused to pirouette unsteadily. The sound came again, sweet and wild. Sufficiently drunk, Anita could make like Callas.

"It was a lover and his lass,
"With a heigh and a high and a ho,
"That o'er the green cornfields did pass,
"In springtime, in springtime,
"The only pretty ring time. . . ."

In the cottage Granny Thompson rose and began to roll back her sleeves.

"When birds do sing hey ding-a-ding-a-ding. . . ."

"That's right," said the old lady. "Ding-a-ding away, my gel. . . ."

"Between the barley and the rye,
"With a heigh and a high and a ho. . . .
"Those pretty country folk did lie. . . ."

Granny hefted her spellstick. "Not only does she 'ave ter goo slummockin' *orf* 'arf the night," she muttered fiercely, "she 'as ter chelp *on* about it. . . ." She whirled the stick, flicked her wrist. Something fizzed out of the cottage, through wall and thatch. There was a bang from the copse and a chittering, followed by unrepentant squeals of laughter. The door opened abruptly; Ella Mae staggered in, encumbered by Anita. Anita's feet were plaiting and she was a little scorched. "Gee Hell, Granny," said Ella Mae in awe. "Blew her pants clean off. . . . How in tarnation'd ya do it. . . ."

Anita, unimpressed by her sartorial disaster, was put to bed.

"I dun't know I'm sure, my gel," said Granny Thompson. "I dun't know at *orl*. Wot the world's comin' to, I jist dun't *know*. Not out o' me sight 'arf a minute you ent but wot yer up ter yer pranks. Slummockin' orf, comin' 'um in States.... Never seen nothink like it, not in orl me born *days*...."

Anita sat delicately, holding her forehead with her fingertips while the old lady's voice clanged around inside her skull. Ella Mae, fresh as a daisy, sat by the fireplace in a gingham frock doubled from a Northampton shop window the week before. "Gran," she said, "ah guess it was all mah fault...."

"You keep *out* on it," said Granny Thompson fiercely. "Wot you does an' wot you dun't do ent my concern. Though if yer was mine I'd lay 'airbrush round yer, dun't think I couldn't...." She prodded Anita violently in the ribs. Her granddaughter moaned. "Slummockin' orf," said Granny for about the hundredth time. "It's 'igh time you young uns learned some *risponsibility*. 'Ole pack on yer down there there were, an' wot 'appens?" She struck a dramatic pose. "*Nothink*...." She started to bang pots and pans about, increasing the percussion effects behind Anita's eyes. "If yer wants summat doin'," said Granny Thompson bitterly, "do it *yerself.* That's wot I says. Kent trust non on yer...."

Anita raised a ravaged face. "But Gran," she said weakly, "it was the last night. And it was such a lovely old place...."

"Weer's yer shoes?" bellowed Granny. "Noo pair they were, an' orl. ... And yer 'andbag. An' that there frock, wot you were at ter git it in a state like that I kent imagine.... Leastways I can but I *wunt*.... An' ter cap it orl, *weer's that sperrit*...."

Anita sat bolt upright, mouth a circle of shock. "*Heavens,*" she said, shocked into profanity. "Poor Dickon ... we *forgot* him ... !"

The crane was poised over the roof of the Saracen's Head. The pub seemed to crouch even lower as though trying to avoid the monster's attention. A great iron ball was winched slowly back; the heads of the spectators turned to watch it, flicked round again as it was released.

Boom....

Dust flew, and chips of brick. The pub shuddered; a great bruise showed on its plaster side.

Anita struggled through the crowd. She was feeling better now; Ella Mae had given her two raw eggs beaten up in sherry and milk and she had taken them and it had been all right till Ella Mae told her what she had drunk but she really was better now. Ella Mae jostled behind her, eyes searching, anxiety showing on her golden-cat face. Anita called, with her mind.

Dickon.... *Dickon*....

12: COUSIN ELLA MAE

He was there somewhere; she could hear him crying.

She plunged into the dustcloud. The iron ball swung again; somebody started to shout.

BOOM....

Ella Mae clutched at her shoulder and pointed. Anita saw the ghost running away. Her face was streaked with dust and sweat, his hair glinted in the sunlight.

DICKON...!

They caught him, one girl gripping each wrist. He writhed and heaved. They clung desperately. "It's all right," panted Anita. "Dickon, it's all right. . . . Oh gosh, we should have come before . . . we completely let him down...."

"Well, get him out the gate...." Ella Mae sounded desperate. "Honey, let's scat *outa* here...."

"Oi...!"

The man was huge and redfaced and in a towering rage. "Wot the 'Ell are yer playin' at comin' up 'ere...." He ran toward them through the dust.

Anita's chest started to heave. She raised her free hand, eyes bright blue and burning. Ella Mae dragged her wrist down. "Annie, doll, not *naow*...." She headed for the gate, wrestling with empty air as she lugged Dickon after her.

Part of the pub roof caved in with a thunderous roar. More dust boiled in the air. There were shouts from the crowd; pieces of brick and chimney pot hummed over Anita's head. "That's all they want to do," she foamed. "Get something an' smash it up just because it's old...." The foreman was close behind them as they panted through the gateway. They swerved and jinked, losing themselves in the crowd.

An hour later they staggered into the cottage, Dickon still quivering from the shock of being forced onto a United Counties omnibus. Anita collapsed in the first available chair and fanned herself vigorously. "Well at least," she said, "we've got him. He'll be all right now. And you know, I think it's going to be nice having him around...." She turned to eye the ghost, appraisingly.

Ella Mae was talking to him and soothing, one arm round his shoulders. "Yew'll go over great, Dickon," she was saying. "Why, yew'll jest love the li'l ol' U.S. of A...."

Anita sat up slowly, eyes glowing. "Ella Mae," she said gently, *"what did you say?"*

Ella Mae looked awkward, possibly for the first time in her life. She stood on one foot then the other, pouted, scratched the back of one ankle with her toes. "Well, Hell, Annie," she said. "Hell, ah'm sorry. It jest kinda slipped out...."

"Dickon," said Anita, in a voice like crackling icicles. *"Is that what she said to you the other night? When she tuned out on me?"*

The boy nodded unhappily. "Fain would I stay with thee," he said. "But there is no place for us in this little land. . . ."

Granny Thompson tottered in from the vegetable patch, a trowel in one hand, a skip of fresh lettuce in the other. She paused halfway through the door, sensed disaster and edged back carefully from the probable line of fire. Anita's lips tightened slowly. Their red turned to pink, then white; then it looked as if she had no lips at all. Her brain was working furiously. "You had it all planned," she said to Ella Mae. "You were in it too, Gran. . . . She isn't my cousin at all, is she? She's nothing to do with us. . . ."

The silence was eloquent.

"I've heard about people like you," said Anita. "But I never believed it. Not till now. You come over here and m-mess us up with your soda fountains and chewing gum and juke-boxes and H-bombers, but that isn't enough. You haven't got anything of your own, not really. So you take what belongs to us. You chop our c-castles up in little bits and take them away and put them up on your horrible ranches, you take p-people away from us and paintings and animals, you think you can b-buy anything you want and what you can't buy you take anyway . . . Now you want our *ghosts* . . . I hate you," she said. "I *hate* you, Ella Mae. . . ." Her chest was heaving rapidly and tears were not far off; but they were tears of rage. "You —" she said. "You — you — *Okie*. . . ." It was the only truly Transatlantic insult she could think of, she'd got it from reading Steinbeck. She launched herself across the kitchen; Ella Mae sidestepped, but she wasn't quick enough by half.

Granny Thompson scuttled through the back door, nimble as a lizard; Dickon jumped, trembling, onto the windowsill. Two bodies rolled about, kicking furiously; there were slappings and punchings and yelps.

Ella Mae, hair tousled, knelt astride Anita's back. Anita wriggled convulsively but both her wrists were pinned, she couldn't do a thing. She lay face down still panting with rage. "Listen," said Ella Mae. "Listen, Annie, y'crazy bitch. . . ."

A convulsion. Ella Mae thumped her victim firmly and Anita subsided. "What in tarnation's gotten into yew?" said Ella Mae plaintively. "Jes' a straightforward li'l business deal. . . ."

"You couldn't be straightforward," panted Anita, nose in the cocomatting, "if you tried for a month. You're all the same. When you die they'll have to s-screw you in, you . . . *Yank* . . . *yeech*. . . ."

"Annie, child," said Ella Mae sorrowfully, shifting her position with care, "y' wonder me, y' truly do. . . . Listen," she said. "Jes' listen. How many dark corners y' got left in this poor li'l land? How many places f'r *ghosts*? How many places they kin run wild, an' see the clouds. . . . Why, Annie, they jest don't belong no more. Honey, we cain't help not havin' no castles, that ain't our fault a-tall. Why that poor li'l guy he tol' me straight out, he lived in fear an' tremblin' for years waitin' for jest that thing t'happen. This place is dyin', Annie, y' showed me y'sailf.

12: COUSIN ELLA MAE

You're jest shuckin' off things like ghosts, y' don't want 'em no more. Let 'em go, honey, don't hold up now...."

Granny had reappeared; she was hovering uncertainly in the doorway, trying not to titter. Dickon crept forward to pat Anita's shoulder. "There is much truth," he said sadly, "in what my sister says...."

"Annie," said Ella Mae. "They went off afore. There was the Great Flit, from Dymchurch. It's all put down in a book. An' again, on a great big boat. Sturgeon wrote 'bout that. It's jest another time, is all. There'll be plenty still left here...."

Granny Thompson lifted a finger. Her eyes glowed oddly. *"Listen,"* she said. *"Listen...."*

And there was a pattering, a rushing. A whispering, a moaning, a sighing. The trees of Foxhanger creaked, the bushes waved to a complicated breeze; grass dimpled where no feet ran along. The house was surrounded, enfolded; and more came, and more. "He *tole* 'em," said Ella Mae. "An' they're comin', jest listen to 'em come.... Honey, it wasn't me. They *want* to go, the poor ole things. Don't stop 'em now...."

Anita was quiet awhile. Then, "Ella Mae," she said. "Tell me ... what's the current price of an English soul, in quarters an' dimes ... ?" Her shoulders started to shake; it was a minute or more before they realized she was laughing.

The leavetaking was a scenty, messy affair, beautifully spangled with tears. Anita waved as Ella Mae walked to the great airplane. She stood staring, arm still above her head, long after the ambassador had gone from sight; and the great throng that poured behind her across the tarmac waved, and waved, and waved.

The skipper of BOAC flight two seven nine, out of London Airport for Gander and Kennedy, confided to his first officer his opinion that the Boeing was flying like a solidly-constructed comfort station. (He didn't in fact use those exact words.) Although the airliner was visibly nearly empty she took over an hour to wallow up to operational height. His report in the log was more restrained; the company spent several thousand dollars pulling the aircraft's engines apart, but they never found a thing that was wrong.

KEITH ROBERTS

13: SANDPIPER

ANITA WALKED UP the garden path, damply happy from a night spent foraging in the woods. She paused at the kitchen door. Granny Thompson was displeased; she could feel the old lady's annoyance positively ebbing out through the wood. She frowned, wondering what she had done wrong recently. Skipping the housework was usually the surest way to start her Granny ticking. She tried to remember if she'd missed out on anything yesterday. But no; she'd changed the beds, done the floors, dusted through; whatever was wrong, it wasn't that. She shrugged, lifted the latch delicately and ducked inside. She would find out soon enough.

The kitchen table was set for breakfast, but nobody was there. Anita walked through to the living room feeling thoughts tweaking and rapping at her mind. Far from friendly thoughts. She pushed the door open. "Gran," she said, "whatever's the matter? I had a lovely — *egghh* . . ."

Her Granny sat by the window, rocking gently, spellstick across her knees and wearing an expression of far from patient martyrdom. Opposite her sat a girl. At first sight she looked to be Anita's double; Anita, recoiling, saw with her second glance that she was. "Gran," she said, "what on earth . . . Have you been spellraising?"

The elder Thompson let out a whoop that a destroyer captain would have envied hugely. "Yer young *varmint*. . . . She 'as the nerve . . . she 'as the brass-bound impert'nence to arsk *me* if I bin *spellraisin'* . . . ." She fell back, gobbling faintly, momentarily deprived of words. Then she was up, and her stick was beating the air between her and her granddaughter. Anita backed up, feeling the wind of the old lady's invective. "You jist tek a look," snarled Granny Thompson, wagging an ancient, lumpy and indignant finger at the apparition. "You jist tek a look; an' then tell me, yer cheeky young cat, 'oo yer think 'as bin spellraisin' . . . an wot's more ter the pint, *why*. . . ."

The not-Anita stood up gracefully and walked forward. "Hello," she said coolly, in a voice just like Anita's own, "I've been wanting to see you again for a long time, darling." There was an inflection there somewhere that Anita just didn't like.

She circled the creature cautiously, ignoring the outstretched hand. "It's name's Piper," said Granny Thompson with some asperity. Then, suddenly losing her temper again, "Goo on, yer'd think it were a *guessin' game*. . . ."

The newcomer corrected her suavely. "*Sand*piper, please . . ."

Anita frowned. Sand. . . . Something was tugging at her memory. That was exactly what the girl looked like, a thing made from sand. She had just the right sort of tawny tint to her skin; and her hair, though it was nearly like Anita's, was lighter somehow, more creamy. As if she'd taken a wodge of sand and . . .

Realization came flooding. A holiday, a beach, a bad-tempered witch who wanted to go under the sea and couldn't, a hasty game of mud pies. . . . Anita groaned, loud and long. "Gran, I can explain —"

"Yis," shrieked the old lady, dancing with temper. "An' so kin *I*. . . . Arter wot you said an' orl . . . gooin' slummockin' orf wi' them *things*, leavin' — this — leavin' yer pore old Gran . . . Om seed you git up ter some bits, my gel, but I ent seen nothink ter match *this*. Ter see the way om brought yer up an' orl . . . jist look at yer. Deceitful, deceitful ent in it . . . sly young cat . . . pokin' fun at yer old Gran wot yer dun't think knows no better —"

"But Gran, it wasn't like that —"

"I knows wot it were like, so dunt gi' me none o' yer *chelp*. . . ."

"But I had to go, it was fabulous, it was another world like fairyland . . . I'm sorry, Gran —"

"Sorry?" screeched the old lady, her voice becoming positively ultrasonic. "Well yer kin jist sorry it back orf *out,* an' tek that . . . *thing* . . . with yer. Om got me work ter do; it's bad enough wi' one on yer loungin' about on yer backside 'arf the day, but two . . . goo on, git *out*. . . ."

"But Gran, I haven't even had my cornf——"

"*Out!*" bellowed the old lady in a voice that brooked no argument. "Om seed enough on it, an' you . . . comin' up 'ere bold as brass, yer should jist've *seed* it. 'Wheer's me sister?' it wants ter know. 'Wheer's Anita?' it sez. 'Om bin walkin' months lookin' for 'er. Om 'um now.' Um, *bah* . . ." The door slammed behind both of them.

Anita looked at Piper sorrowfully. "You needn't have done that," she said. "Just walked up and peached on me to Gran. You might have known it would cause trouble. I wouldn't have done it to you."

Piper smiled enigmatically. "I'm sorry," she said. "But I'd been searching for you for so long. Ever since you sheered off and left me in Dorset. I knew your name of course, and that you'd made me, but that was all. I had a terrible time finding where you lived."

Anita tucked her hand in the double's arm, trying to be friendly. "It's all right," she said. "I don't suppose you realized. I'm sorry, I should have disbanded you again after I'd done. I just forgot . . . You must be worn out."

Piper shook her head. "I don't tire easily. . . ." For some reason, the words sent goose shivers up and down Anita's back.

They walked through Foxhanger, out to the main road and back, with Anita chattering all the way. She was trying to bring the conversation round to disbanding, but the sand girl didn't seem interested. So she talked boys instead; she presumed it would be a safe subject. "There's a super one at Hollis's farm, he's just started there. I was going to see him, he's got the tractor out and I know where he stops for lunch. . . ."

Piper's strange eyes glowed. "Good," she said. "I'll come with you."

Anita was suddenly wary. "As a matter of fact I've just remembered, today's the day he works in the yard. We can't go there because of the manager. . . . We'll go round to Deadman's Copse instead, there's badgers. You'll love them. Have you ever seen a badger?"

Two hours later Anita was feeling like screaming with frustration. Piper still glided beside her. She'd frightened off everything in sight; the badgers, the birds, a whole warren of rabbits, the Hardacres' dog. The badgers she had simply picked up in her strong hands, regardless of how they struggled and nipped. They hadn't seemed able to hurt her. She had apologized, after the entire family had taken to its heels, but Anita was sure she'd done it deliberately. She was feeling totally cut off; she could sense all manner of things two or three fields away but they wouldn't risk coming any closer while Piper was there, she pinched. "You'll just have to be more careful," said Anita, fuming. "You have to realize you're . . . well, a little bit different. They'll need time to get used to you."

Piper threw her head back and laughed, showing teeth as golden as her skin. Her eyes had yellow flecks in them too, Anita realized suddenly; they were cold, and glittered with something that was not amusement. "Why should I worry?" she asked pleasantly. "Nothing can hurt me, nothing at all. You made me, but you can't change me back. So I'm not afraid of you either."

"That," said Anita through set lips, "remains to be seen. . . ." She had already selected her position, a knoll in a field that overlooked Foxhanger. It was the highest spot for miles around; she always liked spectacular settings for her important spells. She led Piper there, made her sit down and backed off a few yards. She began to wind up. The sand girl watched her with a hint of amusement. Anita wondered if she knew what was coming to her. She brought the spell to boiling point,

[137]

crouched on her haunches, straightened, and threw it at the annoyance with all her force.

The air around Piper spat and crackled. Blue flames developed; lights of various sorts weaved and bobbed. Anita put her hands on her hips. So that was the end of the bother. It was a pity really; but if the simulacrum hadn't been so uncooperative
She saw the magic rebounding and prudently fell flat. Lightning fizzed and sputtered over her head; she sat up feeling scorched. Piper was still watching her. "Have you finished, darling?" she asked acidly.
Anita could only gasp.
The sand girl rose and walked toward her, hips swaying. She put her hand out and helped Anita up. Her fingers felt like steel. "By the way," she said. "Something I forgot to mention. On the way here I met an old lady. A Mrs. Everett, I think her name was. I told her about myself, and I think she was sorry for me; so she made me —"
"Non-reversing," moaned Anita, holding her head. It was just the sort of thing the sworn enemy of the Thompsons *would* do.
"Yes, dear," said Piper sweetly. "So now I can't be disbanded, not by anybody. So I shouldn't waste any more energy. There, look at you. . . ." She clicked her tongue and started to flick pieces of grass from Anita. "Keep still, you've got yourself all dirty. I'll do your back."
Anita wriggled away. "I'll do my own back, thank you. . . ."
"Don't mention it," said Piper urbanely. "Shall we go and have some more fun now?"
Anita gritted her teeth. "Somehow, I don't quite know why, nothing's fun any longer."
The smile didn't leave Piper's face. "No," she said sympathetically, "life isn't all sunshine, is it? I haven't been around all that long but even I know that. It was fun in Dorset, when you made me. And it was a big giggle helping fool your Granny. I liked you a lot then. I thought you were very lovely, and that you were my sister. But you went away. You didn't think about me any more, you didn't even bother to unmake me. And I didn't have anywhere to go, I walked the beaches in the storms and didn't have a home or anybody to talk to. But that's over now, because I've found you. I'm home. Only somehow, I don't think I love you quite so much any more." Her voice became softer, but kept its nasty edge. "Shall we go," she said, *"sister . . . ?"*
They walked the rest of the day without going near the cottage. Anita couldn't face it. She had a whole coven of familiars there; she knew she wouldn't keep them long if the sand girl had her way. For Piper, who didn't eat worth mentioning, the time might have passed pleasantly; but Anita's stomach had been used to more regular treatment. Deprived even of its breakfast cereal, it began to complain loudly. When she couldn't stave things off any longer she turned back to Foxhanger.
She got a few minutes alone with her Granny while Piper was outside

13: SANDPIPER

washing her face. " 'Ad a nice day, gel?" asked the elder Thompson pleasantly, banging out dishes on the table.

Anita put her face in her hands. "Gran, you've got to help. She's an absolute beast; and she's non-reversible, Aggie did it . . ."

"Did she now?" Granny Thompson looked thoughtful. "Now, let's see. Two places is it, or three? You orter know. . . . I esspect she acted fer the best. You knows Aggie; allus one fer doin' a good turn whin she could. . . ."

Anita stamped. "Gran, you're a beast . . . you know Aggie never did anybody any good if she could help it. She only did it to spite me. . . ." She tried again. "Gran, *please*. . . . She drove all the badgers out of the wood, nothing will come *near* me. . . ."

Granny Thompson, cutlery in hand, favoured her granddaughter with a long, cold stare. "There's some round 'ere," she pronounced, "wot thinks they're *smart*. An' I wouldn't need a long stick ter touch 'em, neither. . . ." She dug Anita in the shortribs with a bony forefinger. "You knows wot om a-gooin' ter say ter *you*, my gel. Yore made your bed; you jist *lie* on it a bit. It wunt 'urt yer. . . ."

And that was all she would say on the matter.

The girls shared Anita's bedroom. It wasn't comfortable as the room was tiny to begin with. Piper sat on the bed, resplendent in a pair of Anita's pyjamas, picking things up, commenting on them, tossing them down again. Anita, who could see herself spending the night on the floor, was bubbling with rage.

"What's this?"

"A *book!*"

"I can see that. What sort of book?"

"My Shakespeare."

"Pooh. Looks dry to me. What are these?"

"Fossils."

"Dirty old things. Why do you keep them?"

"*Because I want to!*"

Piper raised her eyebrows. "Don't shout, darling. I don't mind; it takes all sorts to make a world." She yanked open a drawer. Inside were dolls; tiny, beautifully made, some of them a little outrageous but all very precious. She said, "What on earth are these?"

"If you touch those," said Anita, panting, "I'll scratch your eyes out. . . ."

Piper dropped the figurines back disparagingly. "You'd wear your nails out trying," she said. "I wouldn't bother if I were you. . . . Well, I'm going to sleep. Put the light out when you're undressed, it bothers me. Good night. . . ."

Anita couldn't answer for fear of choking.

She had a surprise next morning.

She was pacing beside an old quarry with Piper in tow, and

absentmindedly turning over ideas for shoving her down it, when she saw a man some distance off in the bushes. He wore a big straw hat that shaded his face, and appeared to be sketching. Curiosity had always been one of Anita's major vices; she tiptoed up to him and for once the sand girl didn't spoil things. Anita got to within half a dozen paces before the stranger looked round. By then it was too late; she was already on the way. She yelped, "Sir John. . . ." and flung herself happily into his arms. She hadn't seen Sir John Carpenter since the day she made a time charm work for him and almost shot him out of all possible dimensions in the process. Now here he was, in the flesh, as handsome and large as ever. She hung on happily, crooning and doing things to his beard.

He struggled to get free; the easel went over with a crash, paints and brushes flew in all directions. He was shouting something; it took some time for it to get through to Anita. When it did, she let go as if he had become electric. "What?" she said. "What d-did you say?"

"I'm not John," he bellowed. "I never was, and I don't want to be. And I'm not a Sir, I'm just plain Charles . . . and look at my painting, it's wrecked. . . ." Somebody's heel seemed to have gone through the canvas.

Anita said dazedly, "I'm terribly sorry, I thought . . . Oh dear, you're so like him. . . . You've got his colouring an' . . . an' everything," she finished weakly.

The stranger smiled. "Well," he said in a kinder voice, "I suppose it was understandable. We are pretty much alike; matter of fact y'see, John's me twin brother."

Anita was entranced. "Oh, how wonderful. I never knew, I had no idea. . . ."

"I don't suppose you did," said Charles Carpenter, picking up the easel. "Not many people do know. John's the famous one o' the family; always has been."

"How is he?" asked Anita breathlessly. "Is he all right? I thought when I didn't see him again I'd killed him with that time trick. I was so worried. . . ."

"You damn nearly did," said Charles. "He went to Tibet to find wisdom again. But he's all right now. Matter of fact, he asked me t'look you up. Sent his very warmest regards. . . ." He twinkled at her suddenly. He was amazingly like Sir John when he did that. "You are Anita, I take it?"

Anita put her hand to her throat. "Gosh, fancy him remembering. . . ."

"He did more than that." Charles reached into his pocket, held out a necklace. "He sent y'this. I was goin' to bring it round soon as I got settled in properly. He says it isn't magic as far as he knows, but it'll replace the one you lost."

Anita hugged him again, meaning it this time. "Oh, how sweet. . . ."

13: SANDPIPER

Then she remembered something. She gulped, and turned hastily. Piper was watching the whole affair with a sour little smile. "This is . . . this is my cousin from Weymouth," said Anita. "Piper, this is Charles Carpenter. . . ."

"Charmed," said Piper, and had the nerve to curtsy.

Charles twirled his moustache. Apparently the habit ran in the family. "Delighted t'meet you. Yes, delighted. . . . You must bring her round to the house sometime m'dear. I shall be there six months or so. Got a lot of work to catch up on. Writin', stuff like that y'know."

"Not on your nelly," muttered Anita, resentment making her unladylike. Then aloud, "I should love to, Charles, I really should. But right now we'd er . . . better be going. Thanks very much for the present. . . ." She backed off, holding the dally.

Charles Carpenter called after her. "Got some more for you at home, m'dear; whole bag o' trinkets. John said they'd keep you amused. . . . Come round and see me, come for the evening. Don't leave it too long."

"I'll let you know," said Anita, gulping again. "Yes . . . 'bye, Charles . . ." She fled, with Piper trotting alongside. Any other time she'd have been thrilled to small fragments, but right now the news that there was a Carpenter within reach made her more miserable than ever.

They stopped half a mile away. Piper wasn't even out of breath. She said, "Why did we run? I think he's nice. When are we going to see him?"

"Soon," gritted Anita. "Very soon."

"Well, don't leave it too long. Otherwise I might make my own arrangements." Piper smiled nastily. "I'm beginning to think you don't want me to have any fun. When are we going to see that farm boy . . . ?"

Anita went to see Aggie Everett. She had to trail Piper along, of course; she hadn't had her out of sight for a week. On the way the sand girl caught a frog and did something positively revolting to it. Anita scolded her furiously. "If you'd only try and be nice . . . you don't even *care!*"

Piper tossed her head. "Why should I care?" Her voice sounded very bitter. "I wasn't made from things that care. I'm the sand and the sky, the wind and the hot white sun. I'm the rocks, and the sea that gnaws them away. I'm foam, and slime on breakwaters, the great weeds the sea throws up when there's a storm. . . . How can I care?"

Anita had to admit to herself she'd never looked at it that way; she could almost feel sorry for Piper, but it didn't make any difference. One way or another, she just had to go.

She sat facing Aggie in the small living room of her cottage. "Aunt Aggie," said Anita reproachfully, "I just don't think it was fair. There wasn't any need for it, you hadn't had a row with Gran for weeks."

Aggie looked uncomfortable. "Fact is, gel," she confided, "I wadn't quite meself at the time. 'Ad a touch o' the jimjams I 'ad, an' the twingin' screws ter goo with it. Then this 'ere young gel come up — least, I thort it were a gel till I 'ad a proper look — so I thort 'Right,' I thort, 'there's that there young Anne dancin' round a-thinkin she owns the place, I'll show 'er,' I thort. An' I done it afore I thort. . . ."

Anita scowled. "Well it was beastly of you. She just isn't nice. She's upset everything; I think she positively enjoys hurting things. And she doesn't feel anything herself, and she can't be unmagicked, so there's just no way of teaching her a lesson. . . ." She glared through the window to where Piper was lolling against the front gate. Round her legs pressed a strange apparition, an enormous pink and mauve cat. "*He's* the only one that likes her," she said bitterly. "An' that's proof, because you know what *he* is. He's being horrible too. He's positively wrecked my room three times this week, an' she says . . . if I touch him she'll punch me, an' she would too an' . . . she'd hurt!" Anita's lip quivered; she was approaching the end of her tether. "Isn't there any way of reversing that thing you put on her, Aggie? Any way at all?"

The old lady shook her head mournfully. "No way known ter mortal or witch or 'Im Wot's Down Under," she admitted. "I dunt reckon as 'ow I'll use ner more on 'em. I reckons they orter be put by special. Like a sort o' Hultimate Detergent."

"That's all very well," said Anita. "But it doesn't help me much, does it? I've just *got* to do something, she's driving me crazy. . . ."

"You ent the only one," said Aggie. "Look at 'im. . . ." She pointed and Anita saw a small and shivery familiar crouched in the corner of the room under a chair. She ran to him and picked him up, cooing. "Poor little thing . . . what's the matter with him?"

"Wunt goo out," said Aggie. "Reckons 'e can sense 'er. Ent bin outside fer more'n a week. No more ent none on 'em. Om at me wits' end, I can tell yer. . . ."

Anita stroked the little creature's fur. *Hole where no hole should be,* it confided quaveringly to her mind. *Wrong sort of space. . . .*

Anita hugged it. "Never mind. . . . The worst thing is, Aggie, she goes everywhere with me. Just *everywhere.* . . . There's that boy up at the Hollis's, I've been trying to see him for days but she keeps saying she'll come as well and I just daren't. I've had an awful job keeping her away, I just can't imagine what she'd do to a human. . . ."

A light kindled suddenly in Aggie's eye. "Gel," she said, "om thort o' summat. Come 'ere. . . ." She whispered rapidly. Anita inclined her head to listen; her eyes grew rounder and rounder with shock. "No," she breathed, when Aggie had finished. "I don't believe it. . . ."

Aggie sat back triumphantly. "I tell yer, gel, it's the only way. That'll do it; I'd put me pension on it. 'Course, yer gotta pick somebody wot knows wot they're *at,* if yer foller me meanin'. But that shouldn't be no trouble fer *you;* if you kent do it nobody can. . . ."

"It seems awfully mean," said Anita thoughtfully. "I mean, I know

13: SANDPIPER

she hasn't behaved very well and all that but . . . It's a low-down rotten trick really, Aggie, isn't it?"

"She'd play wuss on you," declared the old lady. "I knows these similacras when they git gooin'. Mean ent in it . . . wot were she, ter start with?"

"Sand, mostly. . . ."

"I knew it," said Aggie. "Sand 'uns are the wust."

"But sand people are usually dreamy and gentle. All the others I've made have been."

"Well they might be," said Aggie wisely. "But they needs a-shakin' an' a-siftin' now an' then ter keep 'em ter rights. She's 'ad time ter *settle*. . . ."

Anita's last twinge of conscience vanished that night. After they'd gone upstairs Piper took her shirt off and sat examining herself critically. Then she looked Anita up and down. "I must say, darling," she said sweetly, "if I was supposed to be a simulacrum you didn't make a very good job of me. Or perhaps you were a little optimistic; I seem to have a much better figure than you. . . ."

Anita chittered softly with fury but managed to control herself. She could wait.

Next day she shut herself in the living room while Piper was outside playing with Vortigern. She got out pen and paper and wrote a hurried note. *Will see you tonight without fail,* she scribbled. *Please don't be out, as I'm so much looking forward to it. Sir John was sweet, and I'm sure you're the same.* . . . She signed it with a flourish, folded it and addressed it to Charles Carpenter. Then she looked round for a familiar. It had to be somebody totally trustworthy, somebody who knew exactly what they were doing.

There was a little pressure on her knee. She looked down and Winijou was standing upright, one paw on her leg, the other raised. His eyes were fixed on her face. They said, *I know what you want.*

She fondled him thoughtfully. "Do you, Winijou? Do you know *exactly?*"

Yes, said the superb eyes. *Give it me, I'll go.* . . .

Anita made her mind up. She fetched his collar, a-tinkle with fetiches and bells, fixed the note to it by a rubber band and slipped it around his neck. "Be careful, Winijou," she said softly. "And thanks. . . ." He crooked his tail at her, leaped onto the windowsill; then he was through and away, like a cream shadow.

Anita, walking through Foxhanger Wood that night in her newest dress, never knew what sort of trap she stepped in. There was a *thunk,* a sensation of falling, a brightly-coloured cloud of stars; she came round as she was being dragged to a little hut and recognized it as a place the gamekeeper used to store food for his pheasants. It was empty now, and the door stood ajar. Anita was lugged inside; there was a flare of light as Piper lit a candle. She got to her knees and tried to scuttle through the door. The sand girl was too quick for her; she hauled her back and Anita felt her wrists being tied, nastily, with baling wire. She tried to struggle, but Piper was horribly strong. She fixed her ankles the same way, then rolled her over and sat her up. The look on her face was appalling. "Now I'm going to have some fun," she said. "But before I go to Charles' house, let's just see if you can get away. I haven't any magic of my own, as you know; but some things are better."

Anita flailed about convulsively till it became obvious that she couldn't escape.

Piper set her up against the wall again. "I shouldn't do much more of that," she advised, gloating. "You'll only cut yourself. . . . You just stay here and be good and I *might* let you out tomorrow." Her eyes blazed suddenly. "If I *think* of you again. . . ."

Anita wriggled miserably. She said, "How did you know . . . You must have caught Winijou . . ."

Piper shook her head. Her grin became worse than ever. "As a matter of fact, I didn't need to. He *brought* your note to me. There's your little friends for you."

Anita's shoulders drooped. A tear escaped from one eye and trickled artistically down her cheek.

"Well," said Piper, "I'd like to stay and talk, but I've got fun to have. Goodbye, Anita. Think of me. . . ." She pinched the candle out, slipped through the door and ran swiftly away through the wood.

Anita stayed where she was, shoulders shaking slightly, till the footsteps had died away. Then she pulled herself together, concentrated. Strange things happened to the baling wire. When she pulled her wrists apart it stretched and broke like toffee; its molecular bonds were shot to Hell. She bent to pick the rest from her ankles, then trotted back through the spinney, quivering with laughter.

She had her first good night's sleep for a fortnight. When she woke at half past seven she could tell instantly that Piper wasn't around the cottage. In fact the combination of her nine major senses suggested strongly that Piper wasn't around anywhere any more. She sat up gleefully; and her smile turned to a scowl. Sitting facing her atop the chest of drawers was Vortigern. He looked at her, sneered and proceeded, insolently, to wash an ear. Around him the room was once more a shambles. Drawers and cupboards had been emptied; all the clothes Anita owned, skirts, woollies, slips, headscarves, ribbons, anklesocks, bras and pants, lay scattered in heaps; and everything had received at least one lovingly-imprinted and jet black footmark. The familiar had obviously been silently busy most of the night.

Anita rose and approached him. "I'm awfully sorry," she said pleasantly, "but your little friend doesn't seem to be back. Nor do I think . . ." There was a brief scuffle as she seized his scruff. "Nor do I think," she continued amiably, "that she *will* be back again. Ever. . . ." She carried Vortigern to the door, and opened it. "It's not the act," she said sadly. "It's the thought behind it that hurts. . . ." She drop-kicked Vortigern just as far and as hard as she could. He flattened like a furry penny, sailed across the landing and fled squalling. Anita dusted her hands. It was the best she'd felt for days.

There was better to come; or worse, depending on the viewpoint. Anita had breakfast, fobbing off her Granny's questionings as well as she could, and rushed out, heading for Charles Carpenter's home. She met him halfway there; she waved when she saw him and leaned on a stile till he reached her. He began to run, whirling his arms and shouting. It was only when he got very close that Anita realized how angry he was; but by then it was too late. She tried to bolt; but he caught her twenty yards across the next field, rolled her over his knee and spanked till he was tired. Then he tumbled her onto the grass.

Anita sat up, tousled, rubbing herself indignantly. His hand had fallen heavy. "If you weren't John's brother," she said, "I'd kill you, and I'd take *hours*. . . . What on earth was all that for?"

He was still in a superb temper. "For?" he bellowed, jumping about. "You know very well what it was for. For sending that . . . that *thing* last night. I thought it was you. John warned me about you, he said you needed watching, but I never dreamed you'd do a thing like *that*. . . ."

Anita could feel laughter bubbling up inside her. She managed to keep her face straight. "What do you mean?" she asked concernedly. "Piper . . . you didn't . . . *strain* her, did you?"

"Strain?" Charles Carpenter howled to the sky. "Strain? I was the one who was strained. If only there'd been a warning. But there wasn't. Not a thing. We'd been . . . getting along very well, very well indeed, then suddenly, *puff, bang* . . . ugghh!" He spat disgustedly at the memory. "*Puff, bang* . . . no warning at all . . ."

Anita could no longer contain herself. "Poor Piper . . . she wasn't as . . . tough as she thought . . . the excitement, poor thing . . . Aggie . . . said it would, but I could hardly believe it . . . Charles, please listen, I had to do it, I can explain honestly — *ouch*. . . ."

He had caught her by the wrist, and was lugging her across the field. "You can do your explaining at the house," he said. "I've got some work for you."

Anita skittered along, trying to keep pace. "I'll do anything I can. . . ."

He stopped suddenly, used his free hand to twirl his moustache. Then he twinkled at her. "Yes," he said reflectively. "There's a lot of things you can do for me, m'dear. . . . But first of all you can help me get what looks to be at least a ton and a half of sand out of my *bed*. . . ."

KEITH ROBERTS

14: JUNIOR PARTNER

THE TALL YOUNG LADY tacked down the street, slightly encumbered by a large Persil box. From the box came ominous sounds. She paused outside the surgery, regarded the door and tried to enter. Frontways was impossible, she couldn't get hold of the catch. Sideways was a little difficult as well; she eventually made it backwards, arriving inside more than a little tousled. She plumped down on the bench that ran around three sides of the waiting-room, set the box beside her and puffed vigorously. Several pairs of eyes regarded her stonily; she simpered, adjusted her dress, crossed her knees sedately and composed herself to wait. From the box came a thud, followed by a long and muffled howl. She rapped the thing sharply. "Vortigern," she hissed, *"behave yourself. . . ."*

The box seemed oblivious. It bulged in several places; then a steady chewing began. Across the room a little old lady, clutching an ill-wrapped bird cage, began to look apprehensive. "My dear," she said nervously, "is that a . . . cat you have there?"

Anita nodded sombrely. "I suppose you could call it that. . . ."

The corner of the box gave suddenly, and a weird head protruded. It was tinted a delicate lilac colour and fairly large. Its ears were small, pointed and set rather too close together on top of its skull. Its eyes were most strange. A quick glance would have suggested they were invisible; a second would have confirmed it. The old lady squealed; Anita brought the apparition a smart thump and it vanished. There were further sounds of destruction from within. "It's quite all right," she explained airily. "He doesn't like birds very much; they give him hiccups —"

The old lady squeaked again and vanished precipitately through the door. Anita stared after her vaguely surprised. As her Granny was fond of insisting, there was "no accountin' fer 'oomans...."

The inner door opened. Anita's heart skipped a few beats, settled back to its normal position. The dress she was wearing didn't simplify the operation. A boxer came out with its ear bandaged, and Anita saw a bit of *him*. Just his hand actually, holding the door; but he had lovely nails. "Next, please," he called.

She had to wait a considerable time for her turn. She was preceded by an unhappy Alsatian with a hacking cough, a Basenji with eczema, a Labrador puppy come for his Epivax Plus and something indeterminate with a long whippy tail that had got its fool paw shut in a door. When she finally penetrated the inner sanctum the street door was closed against further callers and the soapbox was showing definite signs of fatigue. Mr. MacGregor, the junior partner, was very sympathetic; but for some reason Anita found it hard to speak. He was quite tall and had a sort of long solemn face and a little dark-blond moustache and the saddest, most Celtic-blue eyes....

The carton sat between them on the table, vibrating with rage. "It's always the same," gulped Anita. "It's boxes, I think. They sort of send him into a delirium —"

Mooowwww ... ppttthhhh....

"Aye," said Mr. MacGregor, circling cautiously. "Aye, it's a ... cat, then...."

"Yes," said Anita. "Well, actually ..."

The question was solved once and for all by the appearance of Vortigern. The box, having done all that cardboard could be expected to do, gave with a sigh. Vortigern bobbed, spat, slashed at Anita, missed, contacted Mr. MacGregor more satisfactorily, squalled again and left the table with something of the speed and fury of a Polaris missile. Anita shrieked. "Vortigern, *please*...."

The next few minutes were hectic. Bottles smashed, cupboards reeled, blood was shed brightly on the neat-tiled floor. It ended with Vortigern, tired of exhibitions, lying in Anita's lap purring like the bastard he was while she rubbed his tummy. Mr. MacGregor approached him carefully. "Well, Hell," he said, shocked into profanity. "What the Devil d'ye call *that* ..."

"Vortigern," said Anita stoutly. "He's *sweet* really but he's ... er ... rather shy with strangers." She simpered again. "Not very good with men," she added brightly.

The patient showed signs of renewing battle. Anita hissed in his ear. "I'll tell *Gran*...." Vortigern subsided.

Mr. MacGregor rubbed his face. His thumb had nearly stopped bleeding now; he was in command of the situation again. "Well ... what would ye say's the matter wi' him, Miss ..."

"Thompson," said Anita rapidly. "Anita Thompson. We live at the back of Foxhanger. We haven't got an address really but if you take the Wellingborough road up by Wicksteed's Park and turn off at —"

14: JUNIOR PARTNER

"Aye," said Mr. MacGregor. "The . . . er . . . the cat. . . ."

"Oh, of course. Silly. . . . Well, he's . . . off his food," said Anita. She looked slightly anxious; she'd known this would be the difficult bit.

The junior partner frowned, cocked an eyebrow and looked stern. He made as if to prod Vortigern in the paunch. Vortigern said very plainly, "*Don't.*" He didn't.

"Aye, well," he said. "Well, we'd best hae a wee look. Can ye put him on the table there. . . ."

Five minutes of cautious testing, and Mr. MacGregor pronounced his opinion. "He's awfu' fat," he said. "But there isna a thing apart frae that, that I can see. . . . He wilna hurt noo, for gaein' *shorrt.* . . ."

Anita bridled. "He's got his nerves bad then," she cooed. "Poor little thing. There, wouldn't the nasty man help 'oo den? Come to mummy. . . ."

"I didna say that," corrected the vet hastily. "Mebbe he cuid stand in need of a wee *tonic*. . . ." He vanished into a cupboard, emerged with a bottle of pills. "About three times a day," he said. "We'll have him . . . er . . . fit, in noo time. . . ."

Anita looked rapturous. "Oh, Mr. MacGregor," she said. "I just *knew* you'd put him right. . . ."

Re-crating Vortigern proved a problem. His original container was evidently past useful service; Mr. MacGregor grubbed about till he found a cat basket. Anita promised joyfully to return it the following night. "Have ye a car, Miss Thompson?" asked the vet as he saw her out.

"Oh, no. . . ." Anita looked dejected. "We're rather poor, we can't afford anything like that. And I suppose I've missed the last bus now." She brightened. "But it's all right, it's only six miles. We'll be there in no time. Come on, Vortigern . . . g'night. . . ."

"Here," called Mr. MacGregor hastily. "Here, I say. . . ."

The Lagonda was superb. She had a fabric body, which suited Anita nicely. As a rule she detested car riding; steel is uncomfortably like iron, and at the best of times she hated being surrounded by metal. Mr. MacGregor drove her almost to the cottage door. He would have come further, but Anita demurred; Granny Thompson was a disconcertingly light sleeper. Anita watched the headlights from her bedroom window as they lurched back toward the main road. *He's so masterful,* she thought as she unhooked her bra. *And just fancy him having a car like that, oh he's perfect.* . . . She slid into bed, wriggled, mumbled, kissed the pillow; a moment later she sat upright in the dark. "His *colour,*" she said, awed. "An' his *eyes.* He didn't even ask me about his eyes. I must have made a hit. . . ." She subsided again, dreamily. *I can't possibly* spell *him,* was her last conscious thought. *He's too sweet, it just wouldn't be fair.* . . .

Granny Thompson was up first in the morning, by an hour or more. Anita, wandering downstairs to breakfast, sensed an atmosphere and waited guardedly for the storm to break. It didn't take long.

" 'Oo were that bloke," demanded her Granny sternly, "wot brought you 'um larst night?"

Anita addressed herself to her cornflakes. "Just a friend," she said vaguely.

No answer. She looked up. Granny Thompson was standing regarding her with a certain expression on her face. "His name was Mr. MacGregor," said Anita hastily. "He's very swe——"

"MacGregor?" The old lady yelped spectacularly. *"MacGregor?* Ent there enough blokes down 'ere for yer but wot you 'as ter goo orf consortin' wi' *furriners.* . . . Gret 'ulkin' car there thumpin' an' rattlin' arf the night, kent get no sleep fer love ner —"

"He's *not* a foreigner," said Anita, stung to the quick. "He's the vet. Well, the junior one. . . ."

"*Vet?*" Granny Thompson whooped, clutching instinctively for her stick. "Vets, vets, wot do we want with a *vet.* . . . Ter see the time om put in on yer an' orl; spells, they come out yer *ears,* an' you cavortin' with a *vet.* . . ." She paused, suddenly anxious. "Gel," she said, "wot were up?"

"Ohh. . . ." said Anita. "Oh, Gran, really, you're impossible. It wasn't me, it was Vortigern."

A sudden light came into the old lady's eye; Anita should have been warned but for once she didn't notice. "May I *arsk,*" said the elder Thompson with ominous politeness, "wot were up with *'im* then?"

"He's off his food," said Anita, playing the lie to the last. "Poor little thing, he could hardly drag himself outside to —"

"Food?" Granny Thompson's voice rose several octaves; a window pane buzzed in agony. *"Food?"* She collected herself with difficulty. "I'll 'ave you know, my gel," she said, seething, "this mornin', it should 'a bin kippers. Only 'Is Majesty, 'im wot kent *et,* scraunched 'is way inter the pantry cubbard and 'ad the *lot,* an' weer 'e is now I'd give ten years o' me life ter *know.* . . ."

Anita imagined a plate of hairy kippers glaring up at her and smiled beatifically. Even Vortigern couldn't be evil all the time; accidents were bound to happen.

"Well," said Mr. MacGregor. "He's a mair *ordinary* sort of creature than yon . . . what did ye say the name of it was?"

"Vortigern."

"Aye," said the vet. "Tell me, Miss, the . . . er . . . *colour* of him . . . how on earth . . ."

"He had a little accident," said Anita tartly. "With some dye."

"Aye," said Mr. MacGregor, not very happily. "Aye, I see . . . noo what's the matter wi' this one . . . ?"

Anita stroked Winijou's back. He wriggled and fawned, kinking his tail, blinking his shocking eyes. At least Winijou had been no fuss; he'd

14: JUNIOR PARTNER

got into the basket straight away, as soon as he'd realized what she wanted.

"He isn't mousing," said Anita promptly. "And you were *so* good with Vortigern, he's getting so much benefit, I just had to —"

"Aye," said the vet, rubbing his jaw. "Aye, I see . . . Miss . . . er . . . Thompson, was there no a wee bitty commotion when ye arrived. . . ."

"It wasn't his fault," said Anita quickly. "This silly great Samoyed poked its nose into his basket and . . . Well, you wouldn't like it either, would you?" she finished defensively.

"Hmm. . . ." said Mr. MacGregor. He was touching Winijou gently, prodding and kneading. "And his trouble ye say is, he canna catch a moose?"

"Not one," said Anita. "He used to get . . . gosh, seven or eight a day at least but it's been positively *weeks* now and I told Granny and she said it was all right but I just sort of had to bring him along because I'm sure it isn't natural and I was afraid he might be pining or something awful and you were so good with Vortigern I thought if there was anything wrong you would be bound to know and I was so *sure* you could put him right, I mean. . . ."

"If ye'd just hold him a wee minute. . . ." Mr. MacGregor was inspecting ears.

"Of course. . . ." Then, tentatively, "Mr. MacGregor. . . ."

"Yes?"

"Did you . . . get home all right? Last night?"

"I got stuck in a ditch," said the vet shortly. "I got home at three o' the mornin'. It took twa cranes an' a breakdoon truck tae get me oot. . . ."

"Oh, gosh. . . ." Anita gulped and blinked her huge eyes. "I'm *terribly* sorry. . . ."

"There's no a discairnable thing wrong wi' this animal," said Mr. MacGregor sharply. "Noo have ye considered the possibility that ye've simply and straightforwardly run oot o' *meece?*"

"Oh, we can't have done. We can hear them . . . scampering . . . all over. . . ." Anita's voice tailed off. Her lower lip trembled momentarily. She looked down, then back to Mr. MacGregor. She said hopefully, "Nerves . . . ?"

"Nairves," said the vet, walking toward his cupboard. "Aye, of course. There's always *nairves.* . . ."

Vortigern's tablets had been bright blue; these were white, with little pink splodges all over them.

"I'm awfully sorry," said Anita again. "I've put you to an awful lot of trouble."

"Aye," said Mr. MacGregor uncompromisingly. "Tell me, Miss, have ye many *mair* animals?"

She nodded happily. "Hundreds. . . ."

He winced. "Well . . . aye. If ye have any further trouble, just come

[151]

along and see me, or Mr. Hodge-Sutton...."

Anita looked shocked. "Oh, I'd never do *that*. I'm very satisfied with you...."

"Aye," he said gruffly. "Well, ye'd best run on the noo, Miss Thompson; ye have a bus at . . . let me see, eight thairty-two I believe...."

Anita left on the wings of the blast.

It hadn't been too bad though. After all, he had looked up her bus times, that must prove something. And there were compensations. She hadn't expected the car trick to work twice anyway; and Winijou, riding home on her shoulder, caused a most satisfying sensation.

"In the ol' days," said Granny Thompson with heavy sarcasm, "afore we orl *knew* 'ow iggerant we were, we used ter mek our own jollop. An' wot's more, it *worked*.... Wot 'e needs," she said, warming to her theme, "is a right good turnout...."

"Gran, don't be *beastly*." Anita was attempting to restrain something in a wicker basket. Oddly-shaped limbs protruded, apparently at random; she pushed the last one inside, shut the lid and fastened it gratefully. A mewing began, terminating in a series of little concussions like squeaky barks. The basket bulged as its occupant brought a few pairs of legs to bear. "Never 'eard nothink *like* it," muttered the elder Thompson. "Wot are we orl supposed ter be 'ere fer, that's wot I'd like ter know. Jumped-up young blokes smart-aleckin' about tekkin' the bread out of our mouths.... An mind you ent *late*. An' dunt bring that gret *charrabang* . . . back uvver ner more...." Her voice rose as Anita receded down the garden path. "Else I shall tek 'and in things, my gel, an' if I do yer'll *both know summat*...." She slammed the kitchen door, hobbled back to the living room and her abandoned crochet work. "*Vets*," she muttered balefully. "I knows wot 'er game is ter *start* with. It ent *them* wot needs lookin' to," she continued, banging herself down in her chair. She picked up her work, smoothed it and began again, old fingers nimble. "Well, the sooner it's uvver," she soliloquized, "the sooner we kin *orl* git some peace...."

Winijou, sitting by the empty hearth, washed an ear and agreed.

Mr. MacGregor peered into the basket and recoiled. "*Guid God*," he said faintly. "What *is* it?"

Anita pulled the little creature out. It had an indeterminate number of arms and legs, all kicking. Several pairs wrapped themselves instantly round her wrist. Admittedly it wasn't one of her Granny's more attractive efforts; but it did have nice fur, and its eyes were rather lovely. There were four of them, placed in pairs one above the other. "It's Jarmara," she said. "And she's very sick. She's got a tummyache, she told me...."

Mr. MacGregor produced a pair of horn-rimmed glasses, polished them and put them on. They made him look divine. The inspection, it seemed, hardly helped; he took the specs off again, shuddering, and put them away. Jarmara squalled; then an arm that seemed possessed of telescopic properties shot out, clamped itself firmly on the junior partner's tie.

The situation began to deteriorate almost at once. Mr. MacGregor, thoroughly upset, began plunging and snorting; Jarmara, even more alarmed, let go and climbed onto her mistress's head, wailing to be taken home. Anita backed, convulsively; and there was a vast and complicated crash. A cupboard tipped sideways; bottles rolled, filling the surgery with a rich stink of ether. Jarmara promptly forswore all human contact and took to the wall, along which she ran with surprising speed. Anita wailed, sensing disaster, and made a flying grab. She missed, and became somehow entangled with Mr. MacGregor. The familiar reached a ventilator, hissed with disgust and vanished through it; galumphing noises sounded instantly as a well-packed surgery took to its collective heels. Children yelped and skittered; old ladies clutching mewing containers to their bosoms hobbled grim-faced away. In the doorway a small, nervous-looking man, encumbered by an overweight spaniel, collided briefly with a distraught person with Eton crop and jeans, in charge of a deeply disturbed bull-mastiff. The creature vanished rapidly into the middle distance, its owner clinging to the lead and digging her heels in as brakes; her attitude somewhat resembled that of a water-skier behind a motor boat. A final flurry of exiting bodies; and peace descended at last.

Anita sat up puffing. Her hair had fallen across her face; and her skirt, she knew already, had split up to her behind. Mr. MacGregor seemed equally dazed. His collar had burst from its stud, his tie was awry; and something exceedingly violet had splashed across the front of his shirt, creating an interesting Palm Beach effect. He eyed Anita silently; Anita watched back. In the quiet there was a scraping sound and a faint mew. Jarmara, tired of the outside world, reappeared at the ventilator, squelched happily down the wall and bounced into her mistress's arms. Anita simpered, opened her mouth, closed it and tried again. "Please, Mr. MacGregor," she said in her smallest voice, "I think she's better now...."

Anita broached the whole business of Mr. MacGregor to her Granny. "It just won't sort of develop," she said unhappily. "It went like a bomb to start with, you know, the car an' that; but things have just got worse. Last night was awful, Jarmara was a positive little beast. I've been dozens of times now, I've taken all sorts of things, and he's terribly sweet but I just can't get any *further*. . . ." She hung her head. "I just ... don't think he *likes* me. . . ."

"Stuff," said Granny Thompson irritably. "Never 'eard nothink like it, not in orl me born days. Wot, you, with orl the powers yore got, moonin' an' mullockin' about . . . om a-tired of 'earin' yer goo on. Clap one on 'im, my gel, if yer kent do it no other way. Come ter think on it, I'll do it for yer meself. Keep me 'and in. . . ." She rose, hitching at her sleeves. "It's bin a year or two since I were called on fer anythink like this," she said grimly. "But if I kent sort 'im out, my name ent Maude Thompson. . . ."

Anita yelped. "No, please!" She hung onto the old lady's spell-arm. "You just don't understand Gran, you can't do that. I should *die*, it'd be *awful*. . . ."

"Well, yer'll 'ave to do *summat*," snapped the elder Thompson. "Om fed up wi' yer *maungin'*, straight I am. Grown gel like you, never come acrorst the like. . . . If it ent *one* bloke," said Granny maliciously, "it's *another*. An' if it ent 'im, it's somebody else. . . . Gel'll be the death on me yit. . . ."

"I shall just have to try again," said Anita desperately. "But it's awful, Gran. He's told me so much about himself, about wanting his own practice and all that; and he's so clever, he really deserves it but he'll never do it while he's with that awful Mr. Hodge-Sutton, he's supposed to be a partner but he's positively *working* for him. And I hate him, all he cares about is walking round the cattle-market on Friday with those awful leather gaiter-things and he's got horrible light-blue eyes, all cold. I don't think he even *cares* about things getting hurt an' that, he's only in it for the money. Mr. MacGregor is so much better than he is but he'll never get a chance. . . ." She brooded, chin in hands. "I don't suppose I've really been much help either," she finished sadly.

Granny Thompson fixed her granddaughter with a beady eye. "No, my gel," she said with some asperity. "I dun't esspect you 'ave. . . ."

The surgery seemed more deserted than usual. Anita wandered about, looking at pictures and diplomas, holding the paper bag clutched in her hand. She was in a high state of nervous tension; when she put her hand on her dress below the bosom she could positively feel her heart thudding. The only way though was to *tell* him, just tell him straight out, and let things sort themselves out. . . .

She was uncomfortably aware that the lack of clients had to do with her own frequent visits. She revolved in her mind, gloomily, various means of setting things to rights. A few malicious spells scattered about would soon increase the flow of patients again but she hated casting them, she had to be really worked up and in a rage before she could be efficiently evil. She was too preoccupied to hear the surgery door open though the "Yes, please," penetrated her awareness. She trotted in, clutching the bag, which by now had begun to writhe. "Mr. MacGregor, I just had to come and see you," she started breathlessly. "I found a poor little — eeeghh. . . ."

She gulped, eyes wide, hand to her mouth. Mr. Hodge-Sutton stood

14: JUNIOR PARTNER

smiling in a very nasty way, stroking his chin and glittering at her with his little icechip eyes. Anita backed instinctively; but it was no use, she was caught. "Mr. MacGregor was called out rather suddenly," said Mr. Hodge-Sutton. "So I'm taking surgery for him. Now if you'd be good enough to close that door, young lady, we can have a little chat. I've been wanting to meet you for some time...."

"So that's that," said Anita miserably. "He was *awful*, Gran. He said I'd . . . spoiled his p-practice playing practical jokes, an' he'd . . . put the police on us, and sue us and everything. An' he said . . . if I went back any more it would only cause trouble for Mr. MacGregor, an' then Catch got out an' Mr. Hodge-Sutton got his ear bitten, you know what Catch is like when he's scared, an' I ran away an' . . . it was *awful*, just *awful*. . . . An' I . . . can't see Mr. MacGregor any more, not ever, an' I feel so . . . awful, I'm going to wail and wander and . . . oh, I shall probably die...."

The air-tremblings ceased. Granny Thompson's knitting needles clicked on unabated. *Stuff,* she said silently. *Om tole yer wot ter do orlready, only yer too sorft. Yer wunt ketch no sympathy orf me. If yore too big, my gel, that's yore lookout. I shent worrit, one way or the other....*

Silence.

Anita? The thought hung on the air, questing. There was no answer.

Granny Thompson hobbled to the cottage door, peered out. The trees of Foxhanger hung silent, their leaves like new green coins. A spring wind moaned among the branches, swept into the fields and away across the wet red earth. The old lady shut the cottage door with a bang. "Jist git *on* with it then," she muttered balefully. "Yore'll come 'um when yer've 'ad enough. . . . 'Oomans, bah. More trouble than they're wuth, the 'ole pack on 'em." She settled back in her chair. "It's the time o' year, I esspect," she said. "Allus the same, the gel is. *Mooney,* no good ter 'erself or 'oomans or 'Im Wot's Down Under.... Jist git *on* with it, that's orl om gotta say...."

Far away, the wind wailed in pain.

The mantel clock ticked the hours, and the quarters. Scufflings sounded in the thatch and cupboards of the cottage. The place was full of familiars; Anita's activities had brought them in from miles around. "Allus trippin' uvver *summat,*" muttered Granny fiercely. "Nearly *went* four times yisdey. 'Edge'ogs orl day *Satd'y,* the day afore that it were snakes . . . an' that there thing on the stairs this mornin', wot that were I *dunt* know...."

Silence redescended.

It was an odd thing; Anita was never noisy, yet without her the cottage seemed hushed as a graveyard. The tickings and scrapings and rustlings didn't count somehow, there was no aliveness. Granny champed irritably, threw her knitting down, picked it up, made two stitches, dropped one, and tossed it down again. She looked at the clock and frowned.

A sudden squalling fight broke out behind the sofa. One at least of the combatants was clearly recognizable. Granny's face lit with sudden resolve. She rose, reaching for her stick. "Vortigern," she said pleasantly, "come out 'ere a minute, will yer?"

Pssshhh . . . fffftttt . . .

"Out," snapped Granny. "Yer gret square'ead. . . ."

FFFTTTT . . .

Granny Thompson made a pass with her stick. A small ball of blue light appeared, balanced on its tip. "When I sez 'out'," she remarked amiably, "I means *now,* not a week come *Toosdey.* . . ." She flicked the spell across the room. It whipped under the sofa; there was a muffled bang and an explosion of cursing. Vortigern appeared, slightly scorched and with more haste than dignity. He crouched in front of Granny flattening his ears and glaring with his nonexistent eyes.

"That's more *like* it," said the old lady sternly. Then, "Wheer's orl the others, cat? The big 'uns? Pyewacket, Ilemauzar, Vinegar Tom?"

Vortigern stamped, waving his tail. He indicated many directions; north and south, east and west. "Orlright then," said Granny Thompson determinedly, the light of battle in her eye. "Goo on orf an' fetch 'em. Om got a job for yer; it'll tek orl on yer there is. . . ."

Mr. MacGregor had got home late and bad-tempered from a whole series of emergency calls, all foisted on him for one reason or another by his senior partner. The flat over the surgery seemed cheerless and cold despite the mildness of the spring night. He yawned, searched the fridge for the last of yesterday's chicken, and made himself a mug of coffee. He undressed, brushed his teeth and took the meal to bed with him. He read through the terrier notes in *Dog World,* checked certain small interests in the *Financial Times* and finished the day with an Ian Fleming. At midnight he yawned and shut the book. He put the light off, rolled over and was asleep within minutes. He felt, literally, dog-tired.

The noise startled him upright. He sat listening in darkness. The telephone? No, please God. Not the telephone. . . .

The sound came again. It certainly wasn't the phone. It sounded, in fact, like one of the original Bells of Hell. Mr. MacGregor rose hastily, tied his dressing gown around him and padded downstairs, switching on lights as he went. He found nothing. A window behind the surgery was ajar; he closed it and plodded back upstairs, yawning prodigiously. He got into bed, clicked off the light and composed himself luxuriously for sleep.

Booowwwww . . . pssstttzzzzzz . . .

Mr. MacGregor bounded up again with an oath. The noise repeated itself, accompanied this time by a vast, tinkling crash from the next

14: JUNIOR PARTNER

room. The junior partner dashed onto the landing. He was in time to see a large, impossibly-coloured form vanishing down the stairs.

"That bliddy girl," howled Mr. MacGregor. "And her bliddy mogs. . . . And the whole bliddy —" He passed, abruptly, into Gaelic. He began a futile pursuit; futile because Vortigern had never before had the chance to do so much damage in such a good cause, and was putting his heart and what passed for his soul into it. Lights swung, cupboards crashed, furniture reeled; the familiar finished his act by flying up the waiting-room chimney, leaving Mr. MacGregor enveloped in a cloud of long-accumulated soot. The vet rushed back upstairs; by the time he reached the landing incidents were taking place in a dozen different corners of the building. There was wailing, chittering, plopping, scratching, clucking, maunging; something improbable was scuttling giddyingly round the bedroom ceiling, something else had gone to ground beneath the tallboy and was now apparently trying to heave the thing onto its back while a process taking place in the bathroom was giving rise to sounds that defied analysis.

Mr. MacGregor, eyes popping and face crimson with rage, began hauling on his clothes. The investiture was not without incident. Something divebombed him as he stooped to lace his shoes, another oddity scuttled between his feet and nearly sent him sprawling. *Things* appeared to have taken over the entire property. The vet dived for a cupboard, backed out carrying a treasured possession — a walking stick, gnarled, silver-mounted and extremely heavy. He straightened up breathing furiously, and the war started in earnest.

An hour of furious activity served to evict all but the most determined of the invaders. Then Mr. MacGregor, still seeing commonplace objects as if through thin sheets of pastel red, ran for his garage, grabbing up keys and car torch on the way. This affair was going to be settled once and for all.

He stopped the Lagonda nearly an hour later, seething with rage and hopelessly lost. He'd taken the right turning off the main road, he was sure of that; but in the moonlight the woods and the maze of little gated byways that wandered through them were hopelessly confusing. He switched off engine and headlights, reached for the doorcatch. A few yards back he'd seen a signpost. If he could get his bearings again, that would be something; he'd deal with the rest of the matter in the morning. He opened the door, swung his feet to the ground.

Something furry and infinitely long went past and went past and went past. Mr. MacGregor, hoisted unexpectedly onto its back, waved his stick wildly in attempts to keep his balance. Granny Thompson had worked well; she had enlisted the aid of Aggie Everett's troupe of familiars, some of which were even more improbable than her own. This one seemed to be possessed of innumerable pairs of twinkling feet; it also had a distressing trick of vertical undulation. Mr. MacGregor landed a dozen yards away feeling he'd had a free cruise on the Loch Ness Monster. He straightened carefully, breathing through his nose. Once more the night was scarlet and pink; through the veils he saw, dimly, the Thing humping across a field. Round it a score of lesser shapes skittered and bobbed.

In the junior partner's veins ran the blood of wild ancestors; in fact in his cups he had been heard to boast of his descent from the great Rob Roy himself. "*Yaarrr.* . . ." he bellowed, beside himself at last. "*Hoots, yaheerrr.* . . ." He whirled the stick like a claymore, and dashed in pursuit.

He came round slowly, to the accompaniment of numerous groans, and opened his eyes. Above him, infinitely far away, hung a sky spangled with stars and milk. His head was resting on something soft; it moved when he did, whimpering faintly. He raised himself further, wished he hadn't and fell back. Hands touched his face. "I thought you were dead," sobbed Anita. "I th-thought you were dead. . . ."

He sat up again, more carefully. Her hair was across her face; tear-tracks marked her cheeks, glinting prettily in the moonlight. "You s-slipped," she said. "You must have caught yourself an awful bang. . . ."

Mr. MacGregor touched his brow, carefully; then memory returned with a rush. "*You!* What the Hell did ye mean, sendin' those . . . creatures tae plague a man. . . ."

"*I didn't!*" She jumped to her feet furiously, breasts heaving under her ragged, thin old jumper, fists clenched. "*I didn't!* I saw you r-running, an' then you slipped, an' I thought you were dead an' now — now I wish you were. I know you hate me," she went on rapidly. "An' . . . an' I don't care. I hate you as well, so there. . . ."

Something strange happened; some effect, maybe, of concussion and moonlight. Mr. MacGregor took her shoulders, shook her. "Here," he said. "Here, noo . . ."

"Go away! I hate you, I don't want to see you again ever. I don't know what happened, I think G-Gran sent the things but I don't care. I'm glad you bumped your head, I hope your car gets stuck again as well —"

"Miss Thompson," he said desperately, "please. . . ." He drew himself up, straightened his collar. "I wish ye'd desist," he said. "I have something tae say tae ye. . . ."

"*Don't want to know!*"

"Aye," said Mr. MacGregor sadly. "Happen ye don't, but I'll say it no'withstanding. I have a . . . cairtain feeling for ye, Miss Thompson, and it distresses me tae see ye cry. . . ."

Anita stopped abruptly, raising a ravaged face. "Gosh," she said. "You . . . said it, Alex. You said it! That was what was wrong all along, you were shy. . . ."

14: JUNIOR PARTNER

She launched herself precipitately. Mr. MacGregor tried to jump aside, but he was far too slow.

The surgery was neat and bright. Red tiles covered the floor; there were businesslike ranges of cupboards, there was a shiny table that wheezed obediently up and down at the pressure of a variety of levers. Above it was a big lighting fitting that could also be swung about to suit. Mr. MacGregor was hard at work bandaging a spaniel's paw; Anita hovered at his elbow, immaculate in a spotless white overall, its top pocket full of Biros and thermometers. She handed pads and bandages with an air of detached professionalism; when the job was finished she lifted the animal down, restored it to its anxious owner. The last patient of the day was admitted, a disgruntled Pekinese that had swallowed a ball of string. Leastways its owner said it had swallowed a ball of string, and it had been coughing for hours.

Anita concentrated. "Yes," she said. "That's right enough, the silly little thing. I can see it all knotted about." She made a quick pass with her hands. The air around the table became faintly luminous; the animal's coat jumped in several places. "It's all right now," she said. "It's all in bits, it won't cause any bother."

Mr. MacGregor looked vaguely unhappy. "Y'know," he said thoughtfully, "though I wouldna deny the *help* ye are, I tak' tae wonderin', sometimes, aboot the *ethics*...."

"Pooh," said Anita. She tossed her head. "You've got your new surgery, and you're famous already. You deserve to be anyway, you're miles better than old Hodge-Sutton. And what about *my* ethics?" She untied her coat and stretched. "I'll just go and phone Mrs. Featherington-Massey to tell her Chang Poo's all right. Then you can take me home. Unless you can think of something better...." She grinned maliciously, and was gone.

She picked the phone up and dialled, waited till it was answered. While she was waiting she smirked once more at the wall. She was finding life extremely interesting these days; she'd always fancied herself doing something like this, it was a sort of Florence Nightingale complex with a leg at each corner. And after all she'd always believed in the relief of suffering — especially her own.

KEITH ROBERTS

15: THE MAYDAY

THE MESSAGE CAME with a chittering and piping. It seethed through the old high grass of downlands, thrilled and rustled in the leaves of trees. Furry feet thundered it, strange creatures yapped it at the moon. It swung from the skirts of stormclouds, clanged in summer hail. It came a weariness of miles; but always, wherever it moved, noses pointed, tails twitched, wings with feathers and wings with thumbs waved it on toward the north. It faltered and weakened, threatened to disperse, boil away to nothing. It was a suggestion, a whimper; but finally, at long last, it reached its destination.

Anita was walking in Deadman's Copse. She stopped and stiffened; her ears twitched, her nose tasted the air. Above her the trees stirred; the unease came again. The bright sky pleaded, silently.

She trotted to the edge of the wood, badly bothered; stood turning her head and frowning, tuning her ears till they might have heard a needle drop on the moon. The message came again, stronger, then dying, ending with a *wash, crash,* like an undertow half a lifetime away. Waves beat on an inland hillside, creamed and murmured and lost themselves again. Anita and her Granny sat tensely in the living room of the cottage. Evening had come but the lights were not turned on. In Anita's hands the oldest magic of all hummed and burned; the crystal ball winked, throwing back reflections of a sky banked with the pink-tipped clouds of sunset. Deep inside the little globe other lights flashed and moved. "It's still there," said Anita breathlessly. "And it's a Mayday, I can tell. But it isn't coming through Channels. . . ."

"Ssss. . . ." Granny Thompson was rocking, eyes hooded, one thin finger raised. "Shut up gel, om *trackin'*. . . ." High above the cottage a bat fluttered desperately, sideslipping to keep in station. His electric ears turned and probed; through his eyes both witches could see the darkening countryside, the high grey smoke-palls of the woods. "Left a bit," muttered the old lady. " 'Old it . . . bit more, jist a *smidgin'*. . . ." Anita turned, holding the crystal on her knees, lining up body and ears and brain, hardly daring to breathe.

"*Got it!*" Granny Thompson rapped her stick sharply. "Yer lined up, gel. Weer's it *comin'* from, though. . . ."

It was Anita's turn to shush. She stepped up the power in the crystal, feeling the impossibly faint vibrations twanging against her mind. The spell locked on; the bat, released, fell away gratefully, took an insect with a snap of his tiny jaws and scuttered off into the dark like a flake of burned paper. In the cottage, the crystal lit up; blue reflections burned on the ceiling, glowed on Anita's awed face. "*Gosh,*" she said, forgetting herself in her excitement. "Gran, it's the *Jennifer.* . . ."

Granny Thompson wrinkled her nose, assuming an automatic expression of disgust; then she so far compromised her dignity as to peer over Anita's shoulder. "Direck transmission," she muttered feverishly. "By 'Im Wot's Down Under. . . ." She licked her lips, eyes glittering. "Yer wun't 'old it, gel, not fer no time. Yer *kent.* . . ."

"*Shhhhh!*" Anita raised the crystal level with her eyes. The mermaid waved desperately; a flicker of interference blotted her out, then she was back. "What is it?" asked Anita urgently. "Jennifer, what's *wrong?*"

Under water, tears couldn't show; but they were there. The sea-girl's flukes trembled, her small breasts heaved. Her voice lisped and twanged in the sphere, like an insect caught in a raindrop. "*Gosh,*" said Anita again. "Oh, *no.* . . ."

The Jennifer arched about, rocking with misery. The interference came back; Anita was nearly blinded. Earth was swinging, the moon tugging at the sea. The mermaid was drifting with the great pull of the tide, moving out of range. Anita retuned, to the farthest limits; the globe seemed to swell till the room was filled with the restless night ocean. "That's *awful,*" she said. "Gran, it's one of her sisters. She's been *caught.* . . ."

"Wot, by *'oomans?*"

"Yes. Listen, she's telling us . . . oh, the poor thing . . . They've got her in some sort of beastly box or cage. Gran, this is terrible. . . ."

"Eh?" Professional concern for once rattled Granny Thompson's calm. "That ent ever 'appened afore," she muttered, shaking her head. "Not in livin' mem'ry it ent. . . . Wot were it a-doin' of, ter git caught. . . ."

"I don't know, I can't hear. . . . But she wants help. She says . . . she says our people down there can't do anything. Something about the Dorsetshire Controller says it's irregular, it's got to be referred to a Lower Authority. . . . You can see what it is," said Anita bitterly. "Another departmental muck-up. They're scared of having their knuckles rapped because sea-things aren't under their jurisdiction. An' I

15: THE MAYDAY

suppose while they're sitting there deciding who's to do what the story's spreading everywhere. That's why she called me, I'm the only one she knows on land. Though what she thinks I can do I don't . . . *What?* But they can't, they wouldn't dare. . . . Yes, Jennifer, of course I will. Please don't worry, it'll be all right. . . ."

The mermaid held her arms out; she started to say something else and there was a surging, a bang, a ringing black void. Anita just stopped herself tumbling mind-first into it. The glow died from the crystal; it became once more just a quiet grey ball of glass. Contact was broken.

Granny Thompson sat back with a self-satisfied air. "Well," she said, smirking. "Well. Direck contact. . . . 'Ow fur d'yer reckon that were, gel? One up on Aggie Everett anyways. . . ." She picked the globe from Anita's unresponding fingers and patted it affectionately. " 'Ad 'ers *transisterized* larst week she did, jist ter show orf, now she kent even raise *Titchmarsh* with it. . . ."

But Anita wasn't listening. "Gran," she said, "I shall have to go down there. It's vital. . . ."

Anita wandered down the High Street of Compton Holywell, a suitcase in her hand. It was a very smart case; it had been bought new in Kettering only that morning. As she walked she stared around her at the old buildings and the bustling traffic and people. The afternoon light warmed the greyness of the ancient stone, sparkled from the paintwork of doors and window-shutters. Anita stopped outside a pub. Barrels crowded with flowers stood to either side of the door; there were old insurance plaques on the walls, the roof was steep and lichened. She could have reached up and touched the jettied windows of the upper floor with her hand. Its sign proclaimed it the Mermaid Inn and there was a saucy painting of a Jennifer; she was a little too full-bosomed for Anita's taste but she had a sweet face. Anita shrugged and stepped through the partly-open door. One place was as good as the next; and the sign might prove to be an omen.

Getting a room was easier than she had expected. The landlord told her she was lucky, he'd had a last-minute cancellation. Anita liked him on sight. He was short and jolly-faced, and some physiological accident had robbed him of hair, even to his eyebrows. He put her in mind of a pink celluloid Puck.

He showed her the room. It was in the front of the pub, facing the street, and had one of the neat little windows she had admired. It was small, neat and bright; its white walls were set off by old twisty timbers, there was a chest of drawers and a dressing table with mirrors poised above it like a nest of geometric butterflies. Anita proclaimed it perfect; the landlord nodded and smiled, and said he'd leave her to "get settled in, like." He bounced off down the stairs humming to himself, and she was on her own.

[163]

KEITH ROBERTS

She swung the case onto the bed, opened it and sat staring somewhat helplessly at the contents. The thoroughness of the packing showed her Granny's hand very clearly; left to herself Anita would have panicked and scumbled half the contents of her wardrobe and then not been able to shut the lid, and would still not have had anything she really wanted.

She lifted out a small stack of undies, and another of handkerchiefs. She felt round inside the space she had made, and took out the crystal. She sat with it in her hands feeling it throb first hot then cold; then she put it aside resolutely and started putting her things away. She hadn't brought much with her. There was no need; by this time tomorrow everything would be sorted out one way or another.

As she worked she tried to ignore the buzzing deep inside her that meant she was scared. She had never been this far from home on her own before; she'd wanted her Granny to come with her, but it had been impossible. The old lady had recently, to her unconcealed disgust, been made "area secertry" in charge of various dark matters, and there was a coven meeting later in the week that had to be attended as a matter of policy. She had worked out a spell, an odd little taradiddle of her own, to blanket the emissions from Anita's ragbag of extra senses; the tiny locket that held it was hanging round her neck right now. But that was all the help Granny Thompson had been able to give. From here on, Anita was on her own; and there was disaster in the air, she could smell it.

She wished she could have brought a familiar at least. Winijou had wanted to come but she'd been forced to say no. She wanted to attract no attention; a seal-point Siamese on a jewelled lead would scarcely have helped in that respect. She might have managed one of the tiny ones, somebody like Dickon or Jill, they could have travelled in her pocket or her handbag; but they would be no use on a job like this and in any case they were too flighty, apt to scent mischief and scuttle off and get involved in it. Anita didn't feel justified in taking risks, not when there was so much at stake.

She finished unpacking, pushed the suitcase under the bed and lay down with her arms behind her head. She closed her eyes and felt the room still swaying slightly. That was because of the train; she used railways so seldom their effects took a long time to wear off. She opened her mind, cautiously; and at once the bed seemed to reel. The West Country was thick with magic; she heard the soundless roaring of the hills as they butted at the sea, felt the rage of giants lying buried, all buckled and distorted by the strata, their pictures carved above them like x-rays in the turf. Old voices rang from the barrows atop windy downs, thudded from underground where fossils lay like coiled watchsprings in the rocks. She sensed the power of the Great Henge away to the north, the dumb stone anger of Corfe; and from far in the west, where the place-names clashed and tinkled like ancient weapons, came the blue shouting of the Great One, the Thing men sometimes

15: THE MAYDAY

call Merlin. She closed her mind with an effort, sat up feeling half drowned; she reminded herself, unhappily, that they really batted in the big league down here.

She picked the crystal up, sat holding it against her chest. She daren't try to transmit; she was here without a work permit, in fact without a clearance at all. If the Dorsetshire folk triangulated on her, all Hell would very literally break loose; and she could hear their voices everywhere, the syllables rolling and tilting like the contours of the hills. She could receive though, surely. She concentrated, narrowing her eyes. The globe beneath her fingers clouded, and cleared; she saw a line of hills, a great heath clean with wind. She extended her range; and the picture began to alter, like the changing view from the window of a helicopter. She crossed a town, then another, lost herself in Wiltshire and struggled to re-orient. She swerved round Salisbury spire, sharp and thin as a needle; then pop, flutter. . . . The images were gone, dissolved back to greyness. Anita bit her lip, feeling close to tears. She needed, more than anything else, a glimpse of the flat fields and red earth of Northamptonshire. If she could only see the cottage and her Granny and Winijou maybe, just for a second. . . . She tried again and reached Berkshire, recognized the Great West Road, but atmospheric conditions were bad up there, she was already near the limit of her power. She took a breath, beamed her mind for a final effort; and somebody tapped on the door.

She gasped and nearly dropped the crystal. She set it down hastily on the dressing-table and flung a woolly over it. She clenched her fists, shivering a little; and her voice when it came sounded all wrong and wobbly.

"Y-yes . . . ?"

The door opened a fraction, then wider. A shining pink face beamed through the crack. "We was just havin' a bite, like," said the landlord. "Reckoned you might like a cuppa. . . ."

Anita's held breath escaped with a whoosh. "Gosh," she said, "thanks. Thanks very much. . . ."

There was more than just tea; there was a tray with sandwiches and cakes, as much as she wanted to eat. When she had finished she took herself for a walk round the little town. The evening air was fresh and sweet; it put some colour back into her cheeks, and after an hour of watching the people and the boats in the harbour she had almost forgotten her homesickness. She went back to the Mermaid as dusk was falling. The place was crowded now, and the landlord in fine form; he was beaming round a long, rank-smelling cheroot, and bouncing from end to end of his little domain like a ball on a piece of elastic. Anita settled herself in a corner of the Public and drank half pints of bitter and watched and listened as hard as she could. All the customers were locals, and most of their talk was of the sea. There were tales of boats and torn nets and shoals, tides and cuttlefish and a buoy that had come

[165]

loose from its moorings; but no word, no whisper anywhere, of a captured mermaid.

Anita began testing, cautiously. That man at the bar now, the big one in the reefer jacket and jeans and heavy boots. She probed his mind; it was filled with a tinkling blue susurration like the sea, through which his thoughts came swelling up easy and calm and big, like rollers or the rolling crests of downs. She even found his name, tucked in a corner of his brain: John Strong. But there was nothing else, nothing at all. John Strong hadn't heard about the Jennifer.

She watched him nonetheless, fascinated. His face was so seamed and tanned by the wind his eyes looked paler than they really were; they watched out from under black swatches of eyebrows like chips of quiet blue ice, while his voice went rumbling on and on and his hands worked steadily, haggling tobacco from an ounce of iron-hard twist, teasing the hard little chips into a ball of fibres. He lit the pipe and drew, steadily, tamping the glowing tobacco with a calloused fingertip; and Anita heard about the day a Stuka shot his Dad up while he was making a hayrick, and how they saw the bodies in the water after Jerry tried to invade and got burned up with oil. There was anger still in John Strong when he thought about the war, but that was a recent thing. This was the land Judge Jeffreys clawed, boiling and cutting, selling children for stitching the hems of flags; and behind his red ghost tramped others, knights and shadowy minstrels, Normans and Saxons and Romans. Beyond were others and still more, the old men who lugged the magic stones up to the downs, left them there for the rain and wind to harden. Anita, entranced, lost track of time; she was amazed when the landlord started calling for the glasses. The evening was over; and John Strong swallowed down the last of his beer, and rolled out the last of his words, and rolled off into the night. She heard his van start up and drive away.

She collected the glasses from the tables, helped her host wash them and hung the teacloths up to dry. After supper she talked awhile with the landlord and his wife, about Dorset and the sea and the old things still alive in the West. But she was keyed-up now; she excused herself as soon as she could, went to her room and shut the door. She lay down on the bed. The sheets smelled of lavender and were cozy and snuggly but she knew she daren't sleep. She read instead from the one book she had brought with her, a collection of the essays of Richard Jefferies. It was the only thing that could calm her down once she got really panicky and upset. The lovely balanced sentences and the quiet thoughts under them had their usual effect; in an hour she was nearly relaxed again.

She set the book down and listened. It was well past midnight, and the town was quiet. The curtains across the window stirred in a breath of wind, making a little clicking of rings; but there were no other sounds. She tested carefully; the landlord and his wife were both asleep. She turned the light off, tiptoed to the window and peeped out. The

15: THE MAYDAY

moon was up, silvering the fronts of the High Street buildings; but nothing moved.

She changed in the dark. At first haste made her fumble; she forced herself to slow down again. By the time she was ready it was nearly one o'clock. She crept across the room and opened the door. The landing was pitch-dark. A burst of sonar located the head of the stairs. She reached the saloon bar, using her bat-sense sparingly, trusting to the charm round her neck to scramble the emissions. The Dorset folk were busy tonight; the air around her hummed silently with messages, instructions, snatches of laughter. Near the door she stiffened, knowing for the first time her journey hadn't been for nothing; she heard quite plainly the talk about a captured Jennifer. The speakers were some way away, and were plainly very worried. Anita set her lips and began working on the side door of the pub.

Easing the bolts seemed to take an age and she was terrified all the time; the landlord and his wife had lived in the place for twenty years and folk who stay that long in one house come to know every squeak and creak it can make. Shapeshifting would have been the answer but she daren't even think of it; the great splash of energy would have given her away instantly. She got outside at last and risked a low-level spell to cover her tracks. She drew a finger slowly across the door, heard the slithering inside as the bolts closed themselves. She edged out into the High Street, keeping to the shadows.

She was feeling spooky again now. She had dressed all in black — black sweater and trews, black ankle socks and pumps, a black chiffon scarf for her hair. That on its own had been enough to start the shivers. She felt a little better when she reached the open space of the harbour. She circled it, found a place where she could get to the beach. She dropped down and started to run. She still had a long way to go. Seen at night, the bay was nothing like she remembered. The great mass of the headland loomed threateningly, looking a mile tall; round it the sea creamed and seethed, flashing with phosphorescence as the waves smashed themselves against rocky teeth. The ocean was full; Anita could feel the rage in it, the swilling and piping and unrest.

She reached the headland at last, ducked into the cave at its foot. Inside, masked by the rock, she could at least use her sonar freely. She reached the inner pool and knelt on wet rock, calling and shivering. She hadn't dared try to contact the Jennifer again; she could only hope the sea-girl would remember where to meet her. The minds of sea-things are strange and wandering at the best of times, they just don't work in predictable ways; and the mermaid was dreadfully upset, she might do anything. Anita asked herself, with another shiver, what would happen if she lost her head completely.

The sea rolled and bawled; the cave was awesome and black as a cathedral, filled with a great harsh smell of salt. She called louder, risking detection, beaming her mind out from the coast. And there was an answer, a thin crying that moved and wavered uncertainly then homed and locked and began to streak in toward the land. Anita held her breath. Nothing, nothing human, could move that fast under the sea. Nothing except for a great fish or . . .

The mermaid surfaced. Anita's normal sight picked up the swirl from the water, her abnormal senses heard the bursting shout from the sea. She jumped off the rock impulsively, felt the lithe strength of the Jennifer. Arms locked round her neck; lips pressed her cheek, hair swirled across her eyes. She writhed about, spitting. "Steady on. . . . Jennifer, you'll drown me. . . ."

The sea-girl was panting. "You *came*. . . . I didn't believe you would, none of us did. I waited hours, it was terrible. . . ."

"It's all right. . . ." Anita managed to stand up. "Jennifer, what's happening? Where's your sister . . ."

"I don't know." The Jennifer sounded half choked. "She's in a . . . *piuf* . . . bay just along the coast but . . . *owf* . . . we can't get near. . . ."

Anita was struggling with her clothes. "What's wrong, you sound terrible. . . ."

"Sewers," said the sea-girl viciously. "Horrible great . . . *owf* . . . pipes and things everywhere. We can't come in any more, we get choked. . . ."

Anita tried to hurry. Sea pollution was new since she was last here; she could imagine what it must be like for gillbreathers. "Will you be all right?"

"For a few minutes. But be quick."

Anita rolled her clothes up, tucked them out of the way under a ledge of rock. She felt the mermaid grip her round the waist. "Don't try to swim," said the sea-girl. "And mind your head. . . ."

Anita ducked, sonar working overtime; rocks flew by close, then they were in the open sea, heading out from the coast. The mermaid moved fast, great mackerel tail beating the water. Anita tried to keep her head up but it was no good, she just wasn't streamlined enough for this sort of thing. She called to the Jennifer to slow down but she ignored her. "They're taking her away," she said. "We think it's tomorrow. . . ."

"Where . . . where is she?"

"In a cage, the stupid little thing. That's all we can tell. We don't even know how she got caught. She isn't very old," piped the mermaid. "She just hasn't got the sense she was *born* with. . . ." She slackened pace at last; Anita dog-paddled while their bright wake died away to blackness. They had come miles; the land was a dark humped outline a long way away. The Jennifer pointed. "She's there somewhere, I can hear her; but you'll have to hurry. She's getting weaker, I don't think she's been feeding. . . ."

Anita nodded, feeling the tide tug at her. "I'll do what I can. . . ."

"You'd better. . . ." The Jennifer's eyes glowed suddenly, like moons; and Anita was frightened without knowing why.

"What do you mean?"

15: THE MAYDAY

The sea-girl brushed her hair back from her face and grinned, showing bright pointed teeth. "There'll be some trouble . . ."

"What . . . what do you mean? What sort of trouble?"

"There's hundreds of us here already," said the Jennifer. "Listen, and you'll feel us. The Wardens are backing us, they say it's time. . . ."

"W-what?"

"We're tired," said the mermaid. "The sea was ours to live in, once. But the humans spoiled it. They mined it for coal and drilled it for oil and fished in it and let horrible great bombs off in it and killed us. . . ." Her eyes burned blue with rage. "We want our kit back," she hissed. "Tregeagle is awake; and Fingal muttered in his sleep. We've sent for the Serpent. . . ."

"What will the S-serpent do . . . ?"

"Breach the Chesil Bank. And we're working on the storms. . . ."

Anita saw it all, instantly; the Dorset folk doing what they had always done, fishing and cutting stone and making butter and bread; and the wall of water coming bluely, smashing up from the coast. She gulped, swallowed salt and spat. "Jennifer! You mustn't. . . ."

"It won't just be here," said the mermaid. "It will be all over the world. All the magic in the sea, all the magic that's left, working together. We've waited too long already. . . ."

"Please," said Anita. "Please listen. . . . Jennifer, all humans aren't bad. . . ."

"It'll be all of us together," said the mermaid. "Coming up the rivers, letting in the sea." She arched in the water, breasts gleaming. A wind howled round her, scumbling the waves, smashing spray from their tips. "I've brought my comb and glass," she said. "Do you want to hear me sing?"

Anita screamed; and the wind was gone, as quickly as it had risen. "I'm sorry," said the mermaid. "Please try and get her back. She's so small . . ." She turned away, sinking into a trough of foam; and Anita paddled toward the land. She didn't trust herself to speak again.

The bay she finally reached was semicircular, guarded at each side by great bulging headlands. The whole of the foreshore was littered with boulders, some of them over a yard across. She splashed between them carefully, stood up when the water would no longer cover her and waded the rest of the way to the beach.

There was no mistaking now where the mermaid was; thin distress-pipings from her jangled Anita's already overstretched nerves. There were people on top of the cliffs too, her people; she fingered the amulet round her neck, hoping the salt hadn't ruined the spell.

Everything stayed quiet. She walked to where she could see a gleam of light. It came from a small, humped cottage set a few yards back from the water. She moved forward again, half-crouching and ready to bolt. There was a slip for launching boats; beside it were piles of clumsy black baskets. She recognized them as lobster pots; they were like the

[169]

eeltraps she had seen sometimes at home, only bigger. The crying was coming from behind them.

The cage was half submerged in the sea, anchored to the beach by thick chains. Old sacks had been flung over it; Anita lifted them away and instantly a threshing and boiling started inside. Foam flew; she called desperately, trying to tune in on the panic- emissions. "It's all right, stop it. . . . Stop, you'll hurt yourself. . . ."

The threshing subsided. A wild, heart-shaped face glared out, small teeth gnashed. Anita pushed her arms through the cage, risking being bitten. The Jennifer was so little; she wanted to hug her but she couldn't because of the bars. She stroked her hair till she was quiet, making soothing-noises and watching the cottage windows worriedly. There was a man inside, she could feel him moving about. "It's all right," she said again. "Oh, you poor little wretch . . . how did you get into a mess like this?"

The kit gripped the bars with her small fists and gazed up wonderingly. "Who are you? You're not one of us."

"Your sister sent me," said Anita. She lied gallantly. "Well, you *are* pretty. You're even prettier than she is."

The Jennifer threshed her tail. "Get me out. Please. . . ."

"I'm trying. . . ." Anita was fumbling over the bars; but she knew already it was useless. They were solid iron, it hurt her even to touch them. There was a lock, but it was huge and old and stiff. She pried at the wards but they wouldn't budge; they burned her mind and she had to let go. No spell she could raise would take on them, she was sure of that. She leaned on the cage panting a little. "How did you get caught?"

The little Jennifer lowered her eyes unhappily. "It was my own fault, I shouldn't have done it. I was close in to land, sis kept telling me. I was just being greedy. . . ."

"How?"

"There was this l-lobster. A great fat juicy one. An' I . . . wanted it, it looked easy. I put my hand in the pot and got hold of it then the boat came and the man started pulling it up and I didn't know what to do, I couldn't think. . . ."

"Oh, no," said Anita. "Like monkeys with gourds. . . . You silly little thing," she scolded. "Why didn't you let go?"

The kit looked more miserable than ever. "I don't know," she said. "I think I was too scared to work it out. . . . And then he got me and . . . it was awful. . . ."

"Gently," said Anita. "Gently, it'll be all — ssss. . . ."

A bright oblong showed in the night; the opening door of the cottage. Anita flicked the sacks back over the cage and wriggled away desperately. She slid into the sea just in time. A torch flashed, picking out boulders; and a voice rasped and grumbled.

"Who's *there* then. . . ."

The fisherman was only a silhouette behind the bright silver eye of

15: THE MAYDAY

the torch but Anita hated him instantly. She began to hiss with rage. He turned back and she heard a stick rattle against iron. Water seethed as the mermaid tried to get out of the way. "Quieten down, damn 'ee," said the man. "Scuttle as much as ye likes, ye woan't get out o' there. . . ." There was more rattling, and a squeak of fear. The torch moved forward again to the edge of the water, quested suspiciously among the stones. The man waited another five minutes, silently; Anita could see now the long shape of a gun under his arm. Then he swore to himself and spat, hitched at his belt and stumped back into the cottage. The door shut with a slam.

"I've been sold," said the mermaid. "I know just what's going to happen, I can tell nearly everything he thinks. . . ."

Anita nodded. "Don't worry about it," she said. "Tell me what he's going to do. It's very important."

The kit mewed plaintively. "There's a lorry coming, tomorrow night. It'll have a tank on it, they're going to take me to what they call a r-research laboratory. They're paying him a huge lot of money. He didn't know what to d-do with me at first then he wrote to them and they didn't believe him so he cut a piece of my hair off and two men came in an awful state and bought me on the spot. He's very clever, he didn't breathe a word to anybody else —"

"It's all right," said Anita. "I often make noises like that, don't be scared. . . ." A plan was forming in her mind; it was wild and vicious but she couldn't think of anything better. "You'll just have to be brave till tomorrow," she said. "I can't possibly get you out of this thing but I think I can fix the truck."

The mermaid looked frightened. "What will happen?"

Anita knelt upright, staring at the cottage. "I might have to kill somebody," she said stonily. "But don't worry, you'll be all right. . . ."

Anita had chosen the spot carefully. The road wound across the shoulder of a chalk hill; she lay hidden near its summit, in a clump of bushes. From her ambush she could see nearly half a mile in the direction from which the truck would come. It had passed once already, an hour ago; it should be back any moment. This time it would be carrying the Jennifer. She strained her ears for the sound of its engine, ran through the spell a final time to make sure she had it just right. She wouldn't get a second chance.

Her ears twitched suddenly. She frowned, concentrated, and was sure. The lorry was coming at last, moving fast. Her mind touched the mind of the kit reassuringly; then she got to her feet and began to wind up in Granny Thompson's best tradition. By the time the truck came into sight the grass around her feet was alight with blue cracklings. They would register as interference across half the county but that couldn't be helped; she would just have to make sure to be away from the area before the local folk arrived. She tensed, choosing her moment; then rose, lifted her arms and threw the spell down the hill with all her strength.

It took like a thunderclap. It was a thoroughly nasty charm, the worst she'd ever worked singlehanded. When the smoke had cleared, there was a crater in the road a yard or more deep. Anita put her hands on her hips and waited for the truck to come to a boneshaking halt.

She had completely misjudged the speed involved. The truck swerved desperately as its driver saw the obstacle; then its front wheel struck the edge of the pit. Anita's hands flew to her mouth; but it was too late. The truck hit the bank almost below her, tearing a long wound in the grass and sending earth and stones flying. A tyre exploded with a sound like a gunshot; then the vehicle was gone over the edge of the road, plunging away down the slope beyond. The crashing seemed to go on for an age; when the wreckage came to a halt flames leaped up brightly.

Anita jerked out of her trance and started to run. As she neared the truck two men staggered away from it toward the road, their hands to their heads. She ignored them; all she could think of was the Jennifer.

The truck was lying on its side. She climbed in over a litter of old boxes. The kit was threshing about among the junk. Anita hauled her to one side, coughing. The sea-girl was heavier than she looked. She got her to the tailboard, tumbled her outside. The Jennifer lay on the grass, flopping and gasping; Anita lugged her to a safe distance and ran back. Water from the spilled tank was streaming out of the truck; she soaked her headscarf, scurried back to the Jennifer and wrapped it round her throat. The kit's breathing eased as the dampness touched her gills. Anita picked her up and staggered away; behind her the fuel tank of the truck exploded, sending up a column of sparks. The heath was lit almost as brightly as day.

Half a mile was all she could manage. By then her knees were wobbly and she was gasping for breath. She laid the Jennifer down in a grassy hollow and sat beside her hanging her head and panting. The sea was still miles away and the kit's breathing was becoming laboured again. Her mind wheezed at Anita. *I think I'm going to die....*

Anita snapped, "What rot." But she knew it was true. She put her face in her hands. Everything had gone wrong, from start to finish; she'd made a mess of it all, she had no right calling herself a witch. She couldn't go to her own people, not now; the trouble that would result wouldn't only involve her, Granny Thompson would be for it as well and that just wasn't fair. If the worst happened and the Area Controller revoked her licence she'd lose her cottage, her living, everything. It just didn't bear thinking about.

She sat up, eyes glowing. If the witch world was closed to her, then there was only one other way.

"Listen," she said. She caught the Jennifer's wrists and shook her to make sure she was taking it in. "I can't carry you any farther myself

15: THE MAYDAY

but I'm going to get you back to the sea. So I'm going to fetch a . . . a friend. Will you be all right?"

"I'll try," said the Jennifer faintly. "Please don't be long. . . ."

Anita hugged the kit quickly. Bits of dirt and grass were stuck all over her; she looked terrible. "Try not to worry," she said. "I'll be as quick as I can. Lie quiet, you won't need so much air. . . ." She jumped up and started to run again, like the wind.

Compton Holywell was over two miles away; by the time she reached it she thought her lungs were going to burst. She'd been meaning to shapeshift and fly back but she hadn't dared; patrols of her own people were out already, quartering the entire area, hunting angrily for whoever had been wildcatting. She reached the main street finally, turned left past the Mermaid and right. There was a line of little cottages; she ran to the nearest and banged the door.

Lights were on in the sitting room but nobody came. She hammered again, desperately; then backed off and shouted as loud as she could.

"John Strong . . . *John Strong.* . . ."

The door opened abruptly; he stood silhouetted against the yellow glow. "Who the Devil might that be. . . ."

Anita came forward again till he could see her. Her chest was still heaving and her hair had flopped across her face. "Please," she said, "it's me. I . . . need help, it's terribly urgent. Can I come in?"

It seemed he stood for an age, legs spread; she couldn't see his face but she knew he was scowling. Then he moved back, gesturing curtly with one great hand. Anita scurried past him gratefully, flopped on the nearest chair. The cottage room was plain and small, smelling of tobacco. An old wireless set stood in the corner and there was a cupboard with china on the shelves. An alcove housed coats and a pair of waders. There was a table, with the remains of a meal; an old spotty picture of a man o' war, and a spray of wax flowers under a glass.

John Strong shut the door behind him and leaned on it, still frowning. He was even bigger than she remembered; and his eyes watched unwaveringly. Anita gulped, patted at a strand of hair, tried to simper, gave it up and started to talk.

What she said she could never really remember. Certainly there were enchantments in it, witches and fairies and glow-worms and hills full of fossils and Gods; the things that have always been and always will be, till the sea comes mumbling in and ends them all. Sooner than he realized, if he didn't help. "Fisherman," she said, swallowing, "if I told you there was an . . . old thing, out on the heath, and that it needed your help, that it had to . . . get to the sea, would you help? Please?"

He didn't answer; his face was as set and black as when she had started. She looked at the floor and twined her fingers, feeling very small and lost. "You think I'm mad," she said. "Don't you. . . ."

He still stood and stared; then he reached slowly for his coat, shrugged himself into it. "I reckon," he said, "I reckon you might be, easy." He picked a torch up from the sideboard. "But I reckon I might just go an' see for myself. . . ." He gripped her elbow and raised her; she felt the strength in his fingers as he propelled her through the door.

The pickup bounced across the grass, its headlights cutting wild swathes through the darkness. Anita banged the fisherman's arm to make him stop; she was out of the cab and running before he'd pulled up. She had grabbed an old tarpaulin from the truck; she wrapped the mermaid in it and lifted her over the side. The kit was still breathing, but she was very sick. They didn't have long.

The truck moved back fast the way it had come, through the little town to the harbour. John Strong's boat was tied up at the end of the quay; a sturdy forty-footer with a single stumpy mast. Anita climbed down into it carrying her burden; while the fisherman was starting the engine and casting off she loosened the scarf around the sea-girl's throat, dabbled it over the side and tied it back again. Infected water was better than none at all.

The engine settled to a steady puttering; the lights of the town fell away astern, the boat started to lift and roll to the movement of the sea. Anita hugged the Jennifer, feeling angry thoughts pinging at the bottom of the hull. *A human has her still . . . She trusted another human. . . .*

Once through the harbour mouth the sea breeze revived the kit. She began to chirp and wriggle, struggling to get free. Anita clung to her, feeling the voices thrill through the water. The sea folk were converging in their scores, coming from all sides. She told herself desperately, "It's all right . . . it's going to be *all right.* . . ."

The engine noise died abruptly. The boat lost way, rolling slowly on the waves. John Strong walked forward and stood staring at Anita, feet spread on the deck. The sea slapped and chuckled; there was no other sound. The fisherman pursed his mouth, looked up at the sky and back to the dark loom of the coast. "All right then, miss," he said. "I done what 'ee wanted; I reckon this be far enough."

Anita felt her mouth start to go dry.

"What you'm got there?" said John Strong deliberately. "What is it as matters so much to 'ee?"

Anita tightened her grip on the bundle. "I . . . I can't tell you. Honestly. Please start the engine again."

He rubbed his face, watching her, jaw set like rock. "I carried some funny stuff in my time," he said broodingly. "It wouldn't do to deny it. But I likes to know what I'm about, see? I reckon that's fair. . . ."

Anita blazed at him. "You *promised* . . ."

He shook his head slowly. "No I never. I said I'd come an' see for myself, didn't I? What I does now is up to me. . . ."

Around them the sea was holding its breath. "Fisherman," said Anita

15: THE MAYDAY

reluctantly, "do what I said. Otherwise . . . I'm sorry, but you won't ever get to land again."

He laughed at that, long and slow, throwing his head back, showing his even white teeth. "That's as mebbe," he said. "But I says this. No man dies afore his time; an' if it's come to that time, it's no good arguin' anyway. . . ." He moved quickly, quicker than Anita would have believed. His hand gripped the edge of the tarpaulin, yanked; the mermaid yelped despairingly, rolled across the bottom of the boat. She lay staring up and panting, her long silver tail trembling against the boards.

Anita froze with horror; around them, the sea dropped to a millpond calm. At the edge of the circle of quietness, spots of fire slid and glittered; there was a howling and a sighing, spray curled up in white fountains in the moonlight. If John Strong saw, he paid no attention; he stood with the tarpaulin still gripped in his hand, and sucked air slow between his teeth. The thick muscles of his throat moved and writhed as he swallowed. "Well, damn I," he said finally. "Damn I . . ."

Anita gulped, not daring to move. "You've seen what you wanted," she said. "You've seen far more than you should. *Now start the engine. . . .*"

The fisherman still stood staring down, immovable as a cliff. The noise from the sea increased; waves slopped and cheered far out in the night. "Look at that," said John Strong. "Just look at 'en, lyin' there. Think what a thing like that'd be worth. . . ." He rubbed his jaw, slowly, and shook his head. "A man could work the sea all his days," he said, "and never see the like o' that again. . . ."

Far away, the strange wind increased its force. The boat began to rise and fall once more; Anita clung to the gunwale to keep from being flung across the deck. They neither of them had very long now; the sea-folk were raising the storm. "I thought you were different," she said bitterly. "I thought you would understand. . . ."

He faced her directly, for the first time. "Now listen t'me, miss," he said. "This is my boat. I worked for her, an' I earned her, an' I doos with her what I choose. I doan't take no orders; 'cause that ain't the way. An' I says this. I work wi' the sea. It's my livin'. That's the way it always has bin, that's how it always will be. An' what's took out o' the water, that's mine by rights to do what I want with. You wouldn't get nobody else t'say no different."

He moved again, equally fast, scooped the mermaid up before she even had time to bite and held her over the side. "I doan't want nobody tellin' me what's right and what ain't," he said, looking back at Anita. "Not even you, miss. . . ." He lowered the kit gently into the water. "Get *out* on it," he said. "Afore I changes my mind. . . ."

The sea seemed to explode. Green flames reared, hissing; Old Things pranced and thundered, things made of bubbles and weed, things of foam, things of deep-sea slime. The boat tilted, shocks banging at her planks. The light increased; and Anita leaped to her feet, stood arms raised, the wind tearing at her dress. "You heard what he said!" she shouted. "You listened to him, you saw what he did. You've got your kit back, that was what you wanted. Now go away. Turn the monster; *let these people be. . . .*" And slowly, slowly, the noise faded and sank, boiling away, the lights trembling and darkening, vanishing with a sound of deep blue bells, sliding deep and deeper into the everness of the sea. The night was still at last, and quiet.

Anita did the silliest thing of her entire life. The strain she'd been under, the power she had used, the sudden relief, were just too much. She clapped a hand to her forehead, moaned something indistinguishable, turned round twice dramatically and passed out like a light.

The boat chugged back slowly toward the land. Anita lay in the crook of John Strong's arm, his coat round them both, feeling the firmness of his great gnarled fingers. Her eyes were closed, dreamily; and he was talking about fish suppers.

"Lobsters now," he said. "There's only one way to have 'em. Have 'ee ever tasted 'em fresh from the sea, straight out the pot? That's how 'ee eats a lobster. . . ."

Anita pulled a face. "I think it's beastly. They squeal when you drop them in the water. . . ."

"I reckon," said John Strong solemnly, "somebody told 'ee wrong. They doan't make a sound. . . ."

Anita wriggled, fitting herself against him more firmly. "In that case," she said, "I might just consider it. . . ." She opened one eye far enough to see the moon sinking, throwing a quiet silver track across the sea.

KEITH ROBERTS

16: THE CHECKOUT

THE OLD LADY stood belligerently, glowering round her at the well-stocked shelves of the supermarket. She wore a black and shapeless coat, from beneath the hem of which coyly protruded an inch or two of bright floral apron. An equally shapeless hat of faintly mildewed felt completed her *ensemble*. Her feet, in their black, insecty shoes, were planted a trifle apart; and in one brown, gnarled fist she gripped a heavy stick, which she twitched from time to time with an air of vague menace. " 'Arf 'our om bin stood 'ere," she announced to the air around her, "and nobody en't bin *neer*. Call this *service?*"

"Oh, Gran," said Anita, appearing from behind one of the tempting arrays with a well-filled trolley, "don't be so silly. It's a supermarket, you know that very well. You have to serve yourself."

The elder Thompson emitted one of her inimitable whoops. Several shoppers faltered, and stared round in alarm. "Serve *yerself?*" she said incredulously. *"Serve yerself?* Wot's the world comin' to, I'd like ter know. Very idea, servin' *yerself*. In *my* young days —"

"Well, it was you who wanted to come in," said Anita, reaching past. Another jar joined the heap in the trolley. Shopping in the biggest supermarket in Kettering had been a mistake in more ways than one; she always had been a sucker for strawberry conserve. "I told you we'd do better in the village."

"Well, om a-gettin' *out*," pronounced the old lady. "Orl them things there blarin' an' 'ollerin', meks yer *'ead* goo funny." She glared at the nearest of the wall loudspeakers, from which, interspersed with Muzak, poured cheerful spiels about the Latest Reduced Lines. "Ayya got orl them bits?"

KEITH ROBERTS

Anita pushed her hair back. The day was warm and sticky; and as ever in a town she was feeling niggly and fretful. Her Granny's current mood, culminating in her noisy insistence on finishing the shopping in "one o' them noo-fangled places," had hardly helped matters. "I couldn't get any frogs legs," she said. "They just don't stock them. Would *escargots* do instead?"

"An' *wot*," said Granny Thompson fiercely, "might they be, when they're at 'um?"

"I don't know quite. Snails, I think."

"Then why dunt they *say* so?" muttered the old lady belligerently. She fumbled in various pockets, failed to locate her glasses and produced instead a much-creased scrap of paper, which she held about a half inch from the end of her nose. "I esspect we shall atter mek do," she said. "No, we kent. *Noot's* eyes, we kent do without them. . . ." She peered round as if expecting the absent commodity to materialize before her. "Dunt tell me they ent got none o' them neither. . . ."

"Try the delicatessen counter," said Anita nastily. Then she gasped. The old lady had set off at remarkable speed for the rear of the premises, where pâtés and gooey cheeses, rollmops and hams and smoked salmon slices displayed themselves in cabinets lit by coldly-glowing fluorescent tubes. Anita pattered after her. "No, Gran, please! They won't *understand*! It was a *joke*. . . !"

Her Granny waved the list, dancing by this time with temper. "No *noot's* eyes?" she bellowed. "No *noot's* eyes? Them there tiger bits I din' 'ardly esspect, not these days. An' snake fillets is 'ard I know, on account o' the winter we 'ad. But call yerselves a *shop*? Everythink, yore supposed t'ev. But you ent wuth comin' to. . . ."

"Get the Manager," said a stout, anxious lady in a bright-checked apron. Anita grabbed her Granny's arm and began to haul her away by main force.

"Dunt you bother," spluttered Granny Thompson to the small, interested crowd that had begun to gather. " 'Cos *I* dunt want ter see 'im. I ent comin' 'ere ner more; an' yer kin tell 'im that from me. . . ."

The rest was really all Anita's fault. As a thoroughly modern witch, she always had believed in labour-saving devices. A low-level spell, laid almost one-handed, had rendered the shopping trolley much more manageable. The thing had in fact been driving itself, with only the lightest of touches to steer it round the corners. In her anxiety to reach the checkouts, she clean forgot to degauss the charm; and the trolley, as if scenting victims, accelerated toward an immense, redfaced person in a tent-like floral dress. Anita clapped a hand over her eyes. "Do like forces *attract*," she moaned, leafing mentally through her physics, "or do they *repel*. . . ." The matter was rapidly resolved. The clash of metal was followed by a flash of bright blue light; the second trolley shot off in a parabolic fashion, shedding its topload of vegetables as it went. A small man reeled backwards, felled, it seemed, by a cabbage; eggs by

16: THE CHECKOUT

the dozen met sticky collective dooms; the immense lady, arms whirling, sat down decisively in the narrow bit by the first of the checkouts, where she instantly became irretrievably wedged. At which point the Manager appeared. Anita had never really believed the thing about banana skins; as it turned out though, it was exactly true. He shot past much in the fashion of a water skier, emitting a thin, high wail of despair; and a large stand of Cut Price Lines disintegrated, like metallic hail.

"Oven stuff," yelled Granny Thompson, struck by a sudden thought. "That there oven stuff, gel. We need it fer the *catalyst*. . . ." She darted aside; then paused, glaring up at the nearest of the offending loudspeakers. Anita whipped her spell-arm down; but for once she was a fraction too late. The assaulted machine whooped to itself, emitted a loud crack and a cone of bright yellow smoke. The effect sped on round the walls of the great shop, unnoticed in the still-growing din; till a stray charge bridged a gap and the burglar alarms set up a merry and gigantic clamour. Instantly, and with appalling speed, the chain reaction spread outside. It had all proved too much for the posse of discouraged dogs who usually sat tied to the rail by the door. Boxers and Alsatians put their heads back and howled; and a Basset Hound broke his lead and bolted. A small car screeched to a halt; behind it, a large green United Counties omnibus did not. The world became a place of crunching metal and rolling, jangling hub caps; and Anita leaned against the wall and covered her eyes once more. Far off, her keen ears had detected a distant *bee-bah, bee-bah* sound. Perhaps it was the police. Or the fire brigade. Or both.

Granny Thompson had finally, after much fruitless fumbling, located her glasses. She perched them askew on the end of her nose and peered at the scene of carnage with every appearance of bewilderment. "Lor-a-daisy," she said at length. "They must 'ave orl gorn orf their 'eads. . . ."

"Well," said Granny Thompson complacently, "I still dunt see wot it was orl *about*. Allus did think that Ket'rin' lot was a bit funny. Now I *knows* it. . . ."

Anita brushed at her skirt and snorted. "Well, I think we were lucky not to get arrested."

"Arrestid?" said the old lady in great surprise. "Wot *for? We* 'adn't done nothink. It were that there manager bloke wot started it, knockin' orl that stuff down uvver. It ent safe I dunt reckon, none on it. *Supermarkits*. . . ." She snorted. "Then that there gel a-sniftin'. Wadn't no call fer that. . . ."

"It wasn't us, Gran," said Anita. "I've never *seen* anybody so unhappy, her vibes were *awful*. There's something terribly wrong, I'm sure of it. . . ."

"Yer kin say that agin," said the old lady grimly. "An' I knows wot *with....*"

The bus ground to a halt; and Anita manœuvred the large shopping bag from under the stairs and jumped down gratefully. She set off down the rutted track that led to Foxhanger Copse, towing it behind her. Out of sight of the main road she stopped and took a breath. A quick pass, and the air around the basket became full of little twinkling lights. The thing rose to shoulder height, uncertainly at first; then oriented itself and zoomed off through the trees like a small, somewhat oddly shaped helicopter. She watched it go, then ran to the old lady. "It's no good, Gran," she said, "I shall have to go back."

"Back *weer?*" said Granny Thompson suspiciously.

Anita tossed her hair. "To Kettering, of course. Probably this afternoon. I want to find out just what's going on."

"Ent you ever 'ad enough?" groaned the elder Thompson. "Orl that squawk an' kerfuffle; you wot *started* it orl, it were. Run y'in next time, put odds on it. An' *I* shent bail yer...."

But the accusation, unfair as it was, fell on deaf ears. Anita was wholly preoccupied. Girls with violet eyes and brown hair to their waists shouldn't have to sit at supermarket checkouts. And they certainly shouldn't *weep*. "She's super," said Anita breathlessly. "Sort of mediæval nearly, I've never seen anybody *like* her. An' working in a place like that...." She opened a gate. "I shall have to borrow Jarmara," she said. "Or one of the little ones, the ones that can creep under things. I've got to find out exactly who she is...."

"Linette Hope," said Anita, chin in her hands. "That's lovely too, it really *suits* her. And she lives near Cransley somewhere. Leastways that's the bus she catches an' she only buys a tenpenny. She's supposed to be on some sort of training scheme, she was only supposed to be on checkout a week. But they won't let her off, they say she isn't good enough now. And it's driving her *crazy,* she's really *intelligent,* she's worth so much more than that. The others say she's stuck up an' it serves her right, two of them were talking in the lunchtime. But she's *not,* she's *not.* An' she daren't leave because of getting another job, her father says he wouldn't keep her, he'd put her in the *street.* He sounds absolutely *awful.* An' she can't get a flat or anything because they don't pay her enough. An' the other girls all hate her, they positively *hate* her. Just because she's pretty...."

"Wot stuff an' nonsense you do sometimes *tork,*" snapped Granny Thompson irritably. "Bin' pitchin' yer a fine yarn, she 'as. An' yer've *swallered* it...."

"She hasn't," said Anita, stung to the quick. "We haven't exchanged a single *word*...."

"Well, yer'd better soon start," snarled the old lady. "Sooner yer start, sooner yer'll find *out.* Linette this an' Linette that, mornin', noon an'

16: THE CHECKOUT

night. Allus were mooney, yer were; if it wadn't this, it were that. An' if it wadn't that, it were *summat else*. An' yer dunt git no better; yer gits *wuss.*" She wagged an ancient and lumpy finger at her granddaughter. "There's more ter that, my gel, than meets the *eye*. I knows these 'oomans; an' they ain't wuth both'rin' with, none on 'em. Om tole yer times enough; but yer dunt ever *learn*. . . ."

"She *isn't* human," said Anita defensively. "She's more like one of *us*. . . ."

Granny Thompson flung down her crochet work and grabbed for the evening paper. "While we're *on* the subjick," she said, "not as we're ever *orf* it, wot's orl this in the Tellygraph, about 'em 'avin' to 'ave the rat blokes in?"

Anita peered at the headline. PEST CONTROL OFFICERS VISIT LOCAL SUPERMARKET, it said. She swallowed. "It wasn't anything really," she said. "It was just that Jill got spotted. It wasn't her fault," she went on quickly. "I know what she's like, but she really was working *hard*. An' there was this great lout of an assistant trying to *hit* her with a piece of *wood*. So Jarmara just *had* to run between his legs, she didn't even *bite* him. Then Lin saw Sugar climbing out of her handbag an' nearly had a fit; an' that scared Jill so she went up the Manager's trouser leg an' . . . I mean, you can't *blame* her," she finished lamely. *"Can* you . . . ?"

Her Granny moaned. "Operatin' Familiars without a Prior Orthority," she said. "Get us both struck orf yer will, then weer shall we be? Yer knows wot they're like, since they 'ad that there *compooter*. . . ."

Anita frowned. There was justice in the old lady's complaint, she realized that. These were hard days for a freelance witch; all operations were supposed to be cleared in advance by Central now, and sometimes it took weeks. "Well," she said, "we shall have to do *something,* Gran. They've got this awful down on her, just because she's a girl. That Manager's a beast as well, you should hear the way he sometimes talks to her. If we're caught I shall just have to put it down to Private Research. . . ."

Granny Thompson looked up sharply. *"Wot* were that gel?" she said.

Anita looked puzzled. "I said I'd have to put it down to Private Research. . . ."

"No," said the old lady testily. "Afore . . ."

"What? Oh, about Lin. I said they pick on her because she's a girl. There's laws about it now; but they just don't take any notice. . . ."

A certain light had come into the old lady's eyes. "Gel," she said thoughtfully, "I dunt reckon as 'ow that's fair. . . ."

"Gran," breathed Anita in disbelief. "You're a Womens' Libber!"

"I dunt know about that," said the old lady sharply. "I dunt 'old wi' them noo-fangled notions, an' well you *knows* it." She cast around her. "Git me that jar o' jollop orf the *shefferneer,*" she commanded. "An' that noo book, that one wot come *Toosdey*. . . ."

[183]

"But Gran," said Anita, "what about the Clearance? You know what you just said. . . ."

Granny Thompson gimleted at her. "If I wants ter do a bit o' Privite Reserch," she pronounced, "it ent nobody's affair but *mine*. Om gotta keep me *mind* active, en' I?"

"Gran," said Anita some time later, "what are you *doing?*"

Her Granny held a small vessel to the light and stirred vigorously. She took out the teaspoon, shook it; and the bowl drooped in a rubbery sort of way from the stem. " 'Ackles a bit," she muttered. She added three drops of darkish liquid from a vial; the potion gurgled and began to emit puffs of steam and a far from aromatic smell. "I dunt *'old* wi' folks bein' passed *uvver*," she went on. "So we gotta attract some *attention* to 'er, ent we? If more guz through 'er till than anybody else they'll *atter* notice 'er, *wunt* they?"

"I don't know," said Anita slowly. "It sounds all right, I suppose it'll work . . ."

" 'Course it'll work," said Granny Thompson emphatically. "Dunt yer trust yer old Gran ter be right? Not even *yit?*"

"Of course, Gran! But —"

"There ent no but about it," said the old lady, immersed once more in her book. "Now let me see. . . . Git me them there *hiscargots* out the pantry. I reckon they'll come in 'andy arter orl. . . ."

Anita was thoroughly lost. "But Gran, what *is* it?"

"*Ferry-moans,*" explained the old lady with some pride. "Jist found out about 'em, they 'ave. Orl them scientist blokes. Jumped-up bits o' kids most on 'em, reckon they knows the lot. But they ent 'ardly started. . . ."

The kitchen table was covered with vials and bottles; it seemed the entire stock of the potions cupboard had been called into use at one time or another, Anita had never seen such a complicated spell. Also there had been much chanting and drawing of cabalistic signs; both witches had been kept more than busy. But the brew was finally finished. Granny Thompson held it up. "Well gel, wot do yer think?"

Anita took the tiny vessel carefully. Mysteriously, the potion seemed to have shrunk during manufacture; her Granny had explained it away airily as "a controlled *foosion* process." Now there didn't seem to be more than a thimbleful; but it was very magic. Tiny tides moved in it, little coruscations of light played across its surface. Anita sniffed cautiously. At first there was nothing; just a sweet, powerful scent that reminded her a little of sandalwood. There *was* something else though. She inhaled more deeply; instantly she was falling head over heels through space, accelerating faster and faster to a very strange destination indeed. She rocked; her Granny snatched the little vessel away and by degrees the room stopped spinning round. Anita swallowed, sat up and wiped her face.

16: THE CHECKOUT

"Gran," she said in a small, admiring voice, "that's *awful* . . . !"

Linette Hope could never work out afterwards just how she got to be in Deadman's Copse. She didn't even know at first that was its name. She ran out screaming when it all just got too much, and she thought she got on the Cransley bus but obviously she couldn't have because this one brought her in the opposite direction, right up by Wicksteed Park. Then the conductor came and said that was as far as she could go and she hadn't got any more money because she'd left her purse behind; so she just jumped down and ran as fast as she could, not looking back. When she did look round the road was out of sight. Before her a long swell of land was crowned with trees; she walked on into the little wood, not caring. The trees were hung with fresh spring green and birds were singing everywhere, but it made her feel worse than ever.

It had been a bad day right from the start. There had been a row at breakfast, a really awful one, the worst so far; she ran out of the house, walked halfway to Kettering before the bus caught her up. Then Mr. Foswick said he couldn't have her at the checkout in jeans, what on earth was she thinking about coming to work like that, so there was another scene. They were lovely jeans too, new and dark blue and flared and bottom-hugging. But she still had to borrow an old frock from another of the girls and it was miles too short and they all started laughing, she nearly walked out there and then. Then the strange girl came in, the one who always seemed to be watching her. She was very pretty, she had brown hair and dark blue eyes and a really super figure, but she stared so hard sometimes it made Lin feel uncomfortable. She was nearly the first customer; and something got spilled all down the side of the checkout, she said it didn't matter but the girl still ran away. She didn't look back but Lin knew she was laughing too. Then the rest all started.

She didn't realize at first, just thought they were busy for a Monday. She kept her head down and worked the till as fast as she could but the noise kept growing till suddenly she looked round. The other checkouts were deserted, the whole line of them; Mrs. Creswell and the rest sat glaring and tapping their fingers. Behind her though was this enormous crowd, getting bigger by the minute. They were fighting each other too, all trying to be first; fists and feet were flying, bottles and cans raining down all over. It was like about fifty rugger scrums all going on at once. Others were running in off the street; then Mr. Foswick got through somehow with his collar pulled all out and his tie up round one ear and started shouting about it being the Last Straw, and not putting up with any more of it. Then this woman started yelling about who did he think he was trying to take her turn and all the rest started off as well and she quite lost sight of Mr. Foswick under the heap of bodies though she could hear him shouting from time to time and making gurgling noises. Mrs. Creswell had been rammed into a shopping trolley somehow and couldn't get out, she was making an awful row and kicking about and cannoning off shelves and things. Then the police ran in and they started on them as well and she left the till and everything all unlocked and fled; and now she was here and she could never go back and the world had collapsed into little tiny pieces.

She looked up. She had reached the foot of a great gnarled oak tree crowning a little knoll. It seemed the king of the place almost; but it didn't care about her. Nobody cared about her, not in the whole wide world. She flung herself down by its huge, spreading roots and began to cry. The sobs got louder; and her shoulder was touched. She sat up wildly, glared round ready to bolt; then her face changed. "*You,*" she said bitterly. "What do you want now? Just leave me alone. . . ."

Anita swallowed. "I'm sorry," she said. "I only used a few spots too, I didn't realize. Gran did say it was strong . . ."

Lin jumped to her feet. "So it *was* you," she said furiously. "I knew it all along. An' I suppose you set those rats loose too. . . ."

"They're *not* rats! It was only Jill an' Jarmara, they're nothing *like* rats. They're nothing like *anything* really," said Anita. They're my Familiars. . . ."

Lin clenched her fists. "You must be mad," she said. "And now you've played this trick I can't go back, not ever. I'm going to drown myself or jump off a building, I haven't decided yet. An' I hope you'll be *satisfied.* . . ."

"But we were only trying to help —"

"Is *that* what you call it," shouted the checkout girl, chest heaving. "I'm glad you *told* me. . . ." She started to run. "I don't want to *see* you again, not ever. If I do I'll . . . I'll kill you. . . ." She vanished among the trees.

There was something decidedly odd about the wood. It had seemed small enough when she entered it, but now it was endless. She walked and walked, for hours it seemed; and rage gave way to tiredness. She finally came to a little stream. The water looked cool and inviting. She drank from it, hoping vaguely it would give her typhoid. A little farther on she reached the edge of the trees at last. Beyond was a broad sunny meadow. A small whitewashed cottage sat peacefully, smoke rising from its chimney. In front of it she saw the brook again, winding between low banks. There were stepping stones, round which the water chuckled pleasantly, and a clump of twisty old willows. By the first of them a pretty, brown-haired girl sat on the grass, her head in her hands. Beside her, anxiously, squatted a sleek Siamese cat. From time to time he put his paw on her knee, peered up to see into her face. Lin approached, soundlessly.

"But Winijou," the brown-haired girl was saying, "you just don't

16: THE CHECKOUT

understand. She's beautiful. An' when I saw how sad she was I wanted so much to help. An' . . . now she hates me, she said I got her sacked, an' she'll never speak to me again an' . . . I want to *die.* . . ."

It had come to Linette that what she had decided earlier on was true. Nobody *did* care, nobody in the entire world. She had no friends at all now, except one. And Mr. Foswick slowly vanishing under a flood of excited ladies really had been very funny. She sat down beside Anita. "It's all right," she said. "I'm not mad at you any more. Whatever it was you did, I know you were trying to help. . . ." She felt in the pockets of the borrowed dress, and found a tissue. "For heaven's sake," she said, "this isn't doing anybody any good. Just *blow.* . . ."

"She's super, Gran," said Anita enthusiastically. "I've never met anybody *like* her. She's so clever, she knows about absolutely everything. She was going to University, she was going to do History, only her father said they couldn't afford it, she'd got to earn her keep. That's what's so *awful.* But she still knows about . . . oh, Kings an' that, the Crusades, *everything,* she's lent me some super books. Did you know you can tell how old a hedge is by the trees that grow in it? It's *fascinating.* . . ."

You can tell how old a hedge is by asking the creatures who live there, or divining the nobbly roots of the hawthorn itself; but Anita, it seemed, had conveniently forgotten. She prattled on. "They've taken her back as well, she was really scared they wouldn't. But the Manager said he didn't suppose it *was* her fault, not really, she was just scared running off like that. She says he isn't really too bad at all, not when you get to know him. She says —"

"Gorn *back?*" said Granny Thompson incredulously. "Arter wot 'e *said* to 'er an' orl?"

Anita frowned. "Yes," she said. "But you see she reckons —"

"Well, *I* wouldn't," said the old lady roundly. "Nor wouldn't nobody with ounce o' self-*rispect.* That there lot orl *chelpin'* at 'er; an' them there things blarin' an' 'ollerin' orl hours, wouldn't stick it five minutes I wouldn't. Ner more would you. . . ."

Anita nodded. "It *is* sort of odd," she admitted. "There's masses of other jobs, I looked in the paper, she could do so much better. And she wouldn't have any trouble. I mean, she's . . . well, it would be easy. But when I said about it; Gran, she seemed positively *scared.* An' then she got mad again. . . ."

Granny Thompson sighed. "Om *tole* yer till om sick of 'earin' it," she said. " '*Oomans* en't wuth a *candle.* There's summat a-gooin' on, my gel, wot you dunt know about. Smart though yer thinks yerself. . . ."

Anita bit her lip. "You're right, Gran," she said worriedly. "I know there is, I can feel it. But she won't tell me. Just sort of sheers off. . . ."

The old lady sniffed. "There's *one* way ter find out," she said. "If yer *wants* to bad enough. . . ."

"I can't *spell* her," said Anita indignantly. "An' I promised no more magic...."

"I ent suggestin' it," said the old lady with some asperity. "Orl om a-sayin', my gel, is that *four* legs is sometimes 'andier than *two*...."

"I don't know," said Anita doubtfully. "I'm a bit out of practice, I haven't done *that* for years...."

"Time yer got yer 'and back in then," snapped the old lady. "Or dunt yer reckon yer kin *manige?* Need a bit of 'elp then, will yer?"

"No thank you, Gran," said Anita frostily. "That won't be necessary...."

The windows of the supermarket glowed cheerfully in the dusk. It was their late night, they wouldn't close till eight; but the large chestnut-brown cat who sat opposite in the doorway of the fishmongers seemed content to wait. It was a handsome animal, long-haired and with a spotless white bib, of which it seemed inordinately proud. Leastways it glanced down at it from time to time in a pleased-looking sort of way and even essayed the odd desultory lick, as if to ensure that its fur remained immaculately arranged. The street was busy; but for the most part it ignored the passers-by. Once, when a pretty girl stooped cooing, it did condescend to wave its tail and *"prip"* obligingly; but its eyes soon returned to the bright-lit frontage of the shop. Inside, Lin sat at the end checkout as busy as ever, lifting items from the endless stream of baskets and trolleys, dropping them onto the little conveyor belt, clicking away at the shiny grey till. The cat yawned, and settled down to wait.

At eight the last shoppers were ushered out and a lad came along shooting the bolts on all the big glass doors. The cat became instantly alert. It trotted to the pavement edge, glanced left and right and streaked across the road like a brown shadow. Beside the supermarket ran what the locals would have called a jitty, a narrow alley leading to the car park at the back. The cat paused by the staff door, staring round. A wall, with an outhouse beyond, offered a vantage point. A quick spring, a scraping of claws; and the animal resumed its vigil.

This time it wasn't for long. The door opened and two girls came out together. One was very pretty, with dark hair that hung nearly to her waist. The other, the blonde, must be Josie; Lin had said a couple of times she was the only nice one there. They turned right, toward the Market Place. The cat followed, keeping its distance discreetly; but neither of the girls looked back.

At first it seemed they were heading for the buses; but opposite the Market Place a small, rather depressed-looking pub proclaimed itself the Green Dragon. They glanced up at the sign and seemed to consider; then they vanished inside.

Cats do not frown; but they can certainly look puzzled. Their follower cast about uncertainly for a time; then it sprang to the nearest of the

16: THE CHECKOUT

pub's lit windows. It crouched on the sill and peered. Inside, men were playing darts, talking animatedly in a haze of smoke. It jumped down, scurried along the pavement. The second window, muslin-curtained, gave onto a little snug. The girls sat at a corner table, glasses of fruit juice in front of them. Josie was talking animatedly; but Lin just looked dejected. She shook her head, and the other girl began again. The cat craned its neck; but the traffic noise from the road, and the chatter of the other customers, masked the voices.

It also masked the approach of a small, seedy-looking man in overcoat, muffler and battered cap. Nor did he at first observe the animal on the sill. Then his eyes, which were small, rheumy and set rather close together, lit up at the prospect of sport. *"Whurrup,"* he intoned to the rangy dog that skirmished at his heels; and the lurcher, thus encouraged, flung itself forward with a heart-stopping roar.

Few animals, however adept, can run up plain brick walls. But cats *in extremis* are capable of remarkable feats. The intended victim gained the top of a little dormer window, from which it spat and lashed its tail, glaring at the hunters as they ambled away. In time its nerves stopped jangling. At least it was safe enough here; and it could still see into the street. It blinked a few times, muttered to itself and settled to watch the moon rise over the great spire of the Parish Church.

The clock chimed the hours and quarters; and the "tail" was dozing pleasantly when voices sounded from below. It came round with a start, effected a hasty and spectacular descent. The girls had parted company already; Josie was striding off toward the bus stops but Lin was heading back into the town. The distant chimes struck ten as she turned in beside the supermarket. She didn't stop but headed on, toward the car park.

Her follower, by now, was both puzzled and alarmed. A hasty casting round; and it sprang onto the flat roof of the cold store, where fat ventilators emitted muffled roaring and a gale of warm, meat-flavoured air. It ran to the concrete edge, peered down. It saw the door of the place pop open, the square, foreshortened figure of a man emerge. Keys jangled; and a shadow detached itself from blackness, ran to him. "Oh, James," it said, "It's been so *long*. . . ." The silhouettes blended; a sound like a little gasp, and Lin spoke again. "Please," she said. "Oh, please, let's get in the van."

The cat stayed frozen where it was, struck dumb, it seemed, with shock. Then its neck, which had extended concertina-fashion, contracted with equal suddenness. It blinked and swallowed, as if unable to believe the evidence of its senses. It jumped down, padded forward stiff-legged toward the rusty van parked by the supermarket wall. Scrapings sounded from inside, a muffled bump. The springs creaked faintly, then Lin's voice came once more. "At last," she whispered. "Oh, at *last*. . . ."

The miles are nothing to a fleeing cat. London Road, the Park, passed like things in a dream; Kettering was lost over the horizon before it paused. It pounced then, in a wild red rage, on a fieldmouse that in another life had been its friend. It ate it, snarling, all but paws and tail. Later, it was very sick indeed.

Once, when Linette talked, the old fields of Northamptonshire had come alive. She knew everything about the Middle Ages; sowing grain and building churches, Dancing Manias and the Black Death, the Plague Stones where they threw the coins in vinegar. But that was over now, over for good. "It *isn't* what you're doing," shouted Anita. "It's *not*, it's *not*. It's the sordidness. Doing it in a grotty old *van!*"

Lin faced her, truculent and tearstained. "Things *are* sordid," she shouted back. "Everything's sordid, sordid and hateful. Life's sordid, haven't you found that out yet? Don't you know anything at all?"

"But he's *years* older than you. Years and *years! That's* why your father gets mad! I suppose that's why you didn't go to College!"

"Yes," screamed Linette. "Because he had me when I was *fifteen* and he's been having me ever since and I don't *care!* And it's nothing to do with you and I hate you, I always did, I shall never speak to you again. You're just like all the rest. You think you're something special, but you're *just like all the rest....*"

"But I'm *not*, Gran," said Anita desperately. "She said the most awful things, that I was . . . jealous, an' selfish, an' I only ever thought about myself, never her. . . . An' it isn't *true.* . . ."

Granny Thompson sighed, and laid her crochet work down. "Gel," she said to the air, "the times om *warned* yer. But it ent fer them, it ent ever bin fer them. It's fer *you.* . . ."

Silence. The old lady cocked her head. "Anita?" she said. "Gel?"

The air of the sitting room swirled, almost made a shape. There was a sob. "I *loved* her," said Anita. "She was my *sister.* . . ."

"An' then yer found it wadn't like that at *orl,*" said the old woman gently. "An' yer didn't want no *sharin'*. Gel, I *knows* yer, yer done it orl afore. Gel, that's 'oomans fer yer. Choppin' an' changin' they are, orl on 'em, kent sit still a *minit*. 'Ere terday an' gorn termorrer. Though I esspect yer kent 'ardly blame 'em fer that. . . ."

In the corner of the little room, a vase of new green beech leaves trembled violently. "You're right of course," said Anita sorrowfully. "I know that really, deep down. I've been a beast. . . ." The twigs shook again; and suddenly there was power. Granny's hair crackled; a small, slumbering Familiar woke and fled squawking. "Satan spare us," groaned the old lady. "Weer's the gel orf to *now.* . . ."

Anita's voice shrilled, distant in her mind. "I'm going to *see* her, Gran," she said. "I've got to put it right. This very minute. . . ."

Linette sat up in bed with the covers pulled to her chin. Her eyes

16: THE CHECKOUT

were large and her face was still a little pale. "Well at least," she said, "I know you're . . . not an ordinary person now. But what on earth's *wrong?* It must be the middle of the night. . . ."

"It is," said Anita shortly. She scotched on the bed. "Look, Lin, I've been absolutely rotten to you. Skulking about like that an' following you, an' then the things I said. . . ." She swallowed. "It was all true," she said. "What you told me. Every word. Will you . . . forgive me? Please? I really want to help. . . ."

The other girl set her lips. "You *can't* help," she said. "Nobody can. There's nothing to be done at all. . . ."

"But there is, I'm sure there is. There must be something. But I have to know . . . all about it first. Lin, won't you *trust* me?"

Linette shot an alarmed glance at the door. "I *can't,* we shall wake my Dad up. He's ever such a light sleeper. . . ."

Anita grinned. "Not tonight he isn't," she said. "Lin, *tell me.* . . ."

Lin gulped in turn. Then it all came out with a rush. How you see somebody in the street and it doesn't matter at all at first except you can't quite get them out of your mind. And then you meet and talk and after that you just can't keep away, it's like a magnet pulling. And you try to stop it but you can't, it grows and grows and there's nothing you can do; and everybody tells you, your parents tell you and all your friends, and you're throwing your life away but it doesn't matter any more, nothing matters except that you're with the person and when you're not you're aching right inside, all day and all night too. Till you get an awful job, an awful terrible job, and knowing they're close sometimes helps a bit even if you can't see them. And you nearly come to hate them too but by then it's just too late, it's like a sort of drug, you've got to have them all the time, be with them. "Like on the films," said Lin with bitterness. "It happens on all the films, it's supposed to be nice then. Well, it happens sometimes in real life too. Just sometimes. Only then I suppose it's more a sort of disease. . . ."

"Don't say that," said Anita, appalled. "Don't ever say a thing like that again. . . . Lin, why can't you just go off? You know, do a bunk?"

"Where to?" asked Linette, starting to cry a little. "We haven't got any money, either of us. We couldn't go abroad; so wherever we went *she'd* find us. James's wife. He married her in London, when he was living there; and he didn't want her then, he told me so. She got him with an awful beastly trick, kept telling him she was pregnant. Now she wears *curling papers.* And she's been foul to him, she found out all about us early on, somebody saw us in a pub one night, you know what Kettering's like. And he doesn't like the supermarket either, he only stays there 'cos of us. He's an under-manager you see, there aren't all that many jobs. He had his own firm once, he was working with his Dad, only they went bankrupt, that's why he came down here, he said if you can't break it up you've got to join it. . . ." She smiled, wanly.

"Amazing," she said, "the works of a modern supermarket. I think they call them Human Interest Stories. . . ."

Anita frowned. "There's only just one thing," she said. "I'm sure of *you,* I've never really had any doubt. But are you sure of him? I mean, it would be terrible. If . . ." She let her voice trail away.

Lin looked serene. "I could *show* you," she said, "only it's getting late. . . ."

"As a matter of fact, it isn't," said Anita airily. "I stopped Time for you, that's why your Dad can't hear us. . . ." And so the board came up, the floorboard under which Linette had stored her treasures, the silver dog-brooch that showed he was a faithful Knight and the *triskele* that hadn't brought much luck and all the rest, the silly things that matter most of all, the skipping rope made from Real Jute and the blue clockwork penguin who could swim in a bowl of water and the furry toys she couldn't have on the dresser, and the vibrator he had given her for when it got really bad, which Anita dropped when its purpose was explained as if it had suddenly got hot. But Lin just laughed. "It's the eighties now," she said, "you have to learn to live with things like that. They'll blow us all up soon; then we won't have to worry about anything, will we?" She opened a little album. "Look," she said, "that's me at the seaside. We actually went away for a whole weekend once; I said I was staying with a friend from school, and James was on a Course. And that's us playing tennis, and that's us on the Links. . . ."

Anita frowned at a colour Polaroid. "Lin," she said, "what's this?"

Linette peered. "Oh, that was a party we went to years ago. Everybody was in fancy dress."

"So *that's* James," said Anita. She was excited now. "He's got a super face. . . ." He had too; not handsome but sort of *broad,* with long-tailed greeny eyes. "It *suits* him," she said, hardly believing. "It's just right, he's a Mediæval man. . . ." A huge idea had dawned. "Linette," she said, "I *can* send you away. Both of you. Somewhere nobody would ever find you again. . . ."

"But there *isn't* anywhere. I *told* you. . . ."

"There *is,*" said Anita, breathing quickly. "There *is.* And it isn't very far away at all. . . ."

Lin looked uncertain. "Would I be able to . . . see you?"

Anita set her mouth. "No. But that doesn't matter. You'll *always* be my sister, nothing can change that now. . . ."

Linette put her face in her hands. "I wish I could split myself in two. So one of me could stay. . . . Anita, you're the b-best friend I ever had. . . ."

"Nonsense," said Anita briskly. Then it got to her as well and she took Linette in her arms. "You'll have to be ready," she said. "James too. I want you to come to a party. A *fancy-dress party.* . . ."

Linette jumped back. "I couldn't, I just couldn't. I'd s-spoil it for

everybody else. . . . ."
"You *wouldn't*," said Anita fiercely. "Lin, it's the only *way*. . . . "

"The Great Charm," whispered Anita. "Please Gran, just this once. You and Aggie could do it, I *know* you could. . . ."

The old lady looked uncertain. "Well, I dunno, gel," she said. "Kent do *that* without a Clearance, that's fer sure. An' they wunt *give* it. 'Elpin' 'oomans, wotever next. . . ."

"But Gran, don't you see? We'd be helping them to *sin*. Damning their immortal souls, an' all that rot. They couldn't *refuse*. . . ."

Her Granny looked up sharply. "Gel," she said, "I never *thort* on it like that. I reckon it'd work. . . ."

Party invitations are always exciting to get. But when they're brought by a seal-point Siamese with a collar of tinkling bells, they're things of wonder. Lin gripped James's hand the tighter, feeling her own heart thud. Winijou was still ahead of them somewhere, he'd met them at the road. Only now he seemed to have vanished. She ducked under low branches. Despite the times she'd been, she was still not sure of Foxhanger after dark. It was all right though, because there was another cat. Large and stertorous this time; and though the moonlight made it hard to tell, it seemed a very odd colour indeed. It arched its back and spat; but it too waved them on. And there was light at last, two twinkling spots of fire. Gateposts had been set up in front of the cottage; on top of each sat a portly little dragon, who sparked up if he thought you needed it. James drew back; but Linette laughed, feeling excitement go to her head like wine. "It's all *right*," she said. "Oh, do come on. . . ."

She'd given her dress an awful lot of thought. Great ladies wore veils and hennins in those days, and girdles at their hips and lovely gowns; but she was no great lady, she was a checkout girl. So she'd come barefoot, in russet. There were flowers in her hair though; and James looked good as well in his jerkin and leggings and funny nightcap hat.

Anita met them at the door. She never had been able to pass up a chance, the things she'd done with ermine were beyond belief. Lin swallowed, and dropped low. *"Mi levdi,"* she whispered, right in her part already; but Anita pulled her up, laughing. "Come *on*," she said. "Everybody's here, I want you to meet them *all*. . . ."

Surely, thought Lin, she must be dreaming already; because the cottage wasn't a cottage any more, not once you got inside. An ox was roasting in the Great Hall, the spit turned by some highly improbable Things; and candles, hundreds of them, were making a mist of light and musicians were playing high up on a gallery, strange instruments that wailed and bonked above the roar of talk. "These are my friends the Carpenters," shouted Anita. "This is Charles and this is Sir John, he's really very famous. John, that tabard's *great*, it's really *you*. . . .

An' these are my cousins from Northampton, an' this is Mr. MacGregor, he's a really super vet, an' this is Ella Mae, she's flown from America specially. I mean Long Strand, where all the Indians are. . . . An' this is Mr. Strong, he's come all the way from Dorset. . . ." And on and on; Lin had lost track before she was halfway through.

"Gran said to say hello," yelled Anita, even louder than before. "Only she can't come for a mo', she's busy with the spell. . . ." And certainly from a side room were coming rumblings and concussions, interspersed with irate shouts. "Aggie, kent you even *count* . . . ? Well yer'll *atter*, I kent find me *glasses*. . . ."

There were goblets of wine, great tankards of mead and beer. Lin's head was spinning before they danced *La Volta*. Then the figures swirled into fresh and stately patterns; because Time was getting older all the while, and it was a *pavane*. "For a dead princess," gulped Anita, the wine making her light-headed. Her hand touched Lin's, the last time ever; and suddenly there was nothing. Just the two of them, and a funny sort of mist.

Lin dropped to her knees. She said, "Where's *James*. . . ." and Anita laughed. "It's all right," she said. "He's here. . . ."

Lin stared round her, at the silence. "What's happened?" she asked dazedly. "Where's the *spell?*"

Anita laughed again. She said, "You're right *inside* it," but the other shook her head. "It was just a party," she said. "It was lovely; but they always end the same."

"Not this one," said Anita. Her eyes were glowing strangely. "Come outside. . . ."

They followed her, stood staring. The woods looked different somehow, in the early light. The bushes were coppiced, as they used to be; great mounds of leaves made homes for creeping things. And it was quiet, so quiet; not a sound, in the whole breathing world.

Lin's voice was very small. "Anita . . . where are we?"

Anita smiled. "Near home," she said, and pointed. "There's a big hill over there. One day they'll build a town on it called Kettering. It'll have supermarkets. All sorts of funny things. . . ."

It was a tiny whisper. *"When* are we then?"

Anita swallowed. "They'll fight Agincourt tomorrow," she said. She turned to James. "You'll be one of the Gentlemen Abed. But I don't suppose you'll mind that at all, will you? I wouldn't. . . ."

She pushed her hair back. "You don't *have* to go," she said. "You're still being *shown*. . . ." She hesitated. "It wasn't . . . all maypoles an' dancing, you know. People . . . didn't live that very long. . . ."

She'd already seen the look in his eye though. He rubbed his face, and spoke for the first time that whole night. "But how we'll live, girl," he said huskily. "How we'll *live*. . . ."

Anita touched the great quiver of arrows on his shoulder. "You're not James any more then," she said to him. "You're Jack the Fletcher, an' this is your lawful Wife. Her name is Linet. . . ." She couldn't stand any more then, so she ran away. Because that's how it has to be when you really have a friend. You love them as hard as you can; and then you let them go.

When she looked back they were already running down the slope. Linet turned once, she thought she saw her wave; then the morning mist had swallowed them both.

"Checked out," whispered Anita. She sat a long time with her head down; but when she straightened up her face was calm. The cottage was making itself again behind her, like a pale blue picture of a house; and Kettering forming, far off on its hill.